JAILBAIT
ZOMBIE

JAILBAIT ZOMBIE

Mario Acevedo

An Imprint of HarperCollins*Publishers*

This book is a work of fiction. The characters, incidents, and dialogue are drawn from the author's imagination and are not to be construed as real. Any resemblance to actual events or persons, living or dead, is entirely coincidental.

HarperCollins books may be purchased for educational, business, or sales promotional use. For information please write: Special Markets Department, HarperCollins Publishers, 10 East 53rd Street, New York, NY 10022.

FIRST EDITION

Eos is a federally registered trademark of HarperCollins Publishers.

Library of Congress Cataloging-in-Publication Data has been applied for.

ISBN 978-0-06-156714-8

09 10 11 12 13 OV/RRD 10 9 8 7 6 5 4 3 2 1

To the memory of author Jerry Rodriguez and artist John Berkey

ACKNOWLEDGMENTS

Much thanks to HarperCollins, specifically my publisher at Eos, Lisa Gallagher; my editor, Diana Gill; her assistant, Emily Krump; online marketing manager Michael Barrs; marketing manager Christine Casaccio; and publicist Jack Womack. Also great thanks to my agent, Scott Hoffman, and the staff at Folio Literary Management, LLC. I have to mention my critique group: Jeanne Stein, Sandy Maren, Jeff Shelby, Tamra Monahan, Warren Hammond, and Margie and Tom Lawson. Several other groups have kept me going: Lighthouse Writers Workshop, Mystery Writers of America, El Centro Su Teatro, and the Chicano Humanities and Arts Council. To Stevon Lucero for his wonderful discussion on metaphysics. To Dr. Ricardo Cantú, of California State University–Los Angeles, for his enthusiastic support. Erika Paterson, Manuel Ramos, Jennifer Mosquera, and Eric Matelski: thanks for the props. Big hugs to my sons, Alex and Emil, and family, especially my sister, Sylvia.

JAILBAIT
ZOMBIE

CHAPTER 1

"Felix, drop your pants."

The last time I heard those words, they were from a topless stripper.

Tonight was different, but the wound on my leg hurt too much for me to protest Mel's words.

Mel was the acting head of the local *nidus*, Latin for "nest," in this case the community of Denver vampires. Tendrils of anxiety writhed from his orange aura, a bright contrast against the gloom of an autumn night. With a greasy gray mane combed back to his shoulders and scraggly white muttonchops, Mel projected none of the glamour associated with Hollywood vampires.

We were on a deserted construction site in Aurora, a suburb east of Denver. Though Aurora's the second-largest city in Colorado, it's the Fresno of the Front Range: square mile after square mile of strip malls and cheap rents that run together to create an asphalt grid of nothing.

I rested against the foreman's trailer, unbuckled my trousers, and slid them to my knees. Smoke and blood trickled from the teeth marks on the inside of my left thigh.

"Smoke?" Mel asked, astonished. "That damn zombie must have left silver fillings when he bit you."

Silver. No wonder this hurt so much.

Mel's right index fingernail extended into a talon. "Hold still."

I gripped the muscle around the wound to distend the punctures. Mel crouched and slid the razor-sharp nail into an opening where the smoke puffed out. A fresh jolt of pain coursed up my spine and out my arms. He flicked his wrist and a tiny piece of smoking goo spun to the dirt.

He spit into his palm and pressed it over the wound. "This is as close to a hand job as you'll get from me. Doesn't mean we're in love or anything. In fact, please don't call me in the morning."

I massaged the injured muscle. "How about a card on Valentine's?" The vampire enzymes in his saliva dulled the pain and accelerated my supernatural healing. By this time tomorrow, all I'd have is another battle scar to add to my collection.

I put weight on the leg and it finally felt like I wouldn't collapse from the pain. I fastened my trousers and limped to the edge of a hole excavated for the basement of a large building. Concrete slabs formed two sides of the hole but the rest was still packed dirt.

The zombie shambled within the hole where we'd chased it. He—obviously once a man—cradled his head under one arm and used his other to grope along the concrete. His mottled, waxy complexion and the clumps of trash stuck to his grimy clothes made it look like he'd been rotting in a shallow grave for a week.

I had removed the special contacts that masked my *tapetum*

lucidum, the mirror-like retinas at the back of my eyes. The contacts were part of my cover to hide from humans, but wearing them kept me from using night vision or seeing psychic auras.

I didn't know if zombies had night vision; I had no idea about any of their powers other than they were supposed to be hard as hell to destroy. Tonight I had discovered an important fact: they had no auras, which made them a bitch to track in the dark.

The zombie clawed the dirt wall, climbing up a foot before stumbling backward. He dropped his head. It plopped against the dirt and rolled like a lopsided melon. The animated corpse sank to its knees and crawled along the ground, one arm searching in a wide arc.

The head worked its mouth and turned onto its face, where it used its nose and chin to inch toward the body. I was more disgusted than fascinated. Yes, zombies are undead, as we vampires are. But comparing them to us was like comparing turds to eagles.

The Araneum, the worldwide network of vampires, has one standing order: *Destroy all zombies.*

The reason?

We must ruthlessly protect the Great Secret—the existence of the supernatural world—from humans. Their disbelief in the supernatural was what kept us vampires safe.

We've seen what humans have done to one another.

War.

Genocide.

Walmart.

Against their growing technical prowess and corporate savagery, what chance did we the undead have? Our best hope for survival was to remain cloaked by superstition and fable.

Zombies have no regard for keeping the Great Secret. They materialize (from where? I don't know) and begin their rampage for mortal flesh, literally mindless of the consequences. Vampires have been able to disguise zombie attacks as examples of deranged cannibals—Jeffrey Dahmer copycats. But eventually the zombies would make one attack too obvious to hide, and then humans would be on to all of us supernatural creatures. After that, we could only expect the methodical obliteration of the undead.

Therefore, all zombies must be exterminated.

Protecting the Great Secret is what I do for the Araneum. My day job is private detective. My real job is the pro bono work I do as a vampire enforcer.

"This your first zombie?" Mel asked.

"Yeah."

"How'd he get the drop on you?"

"I was stupid," I replied. "After I laid him out with a shovel, I was going through his pockets."

"Why didn't you decapitate him?"

"I did. Right after that he shot from the ground, head in hands, and clamped onto me. Don't let that walking corpse routine fool you, he's got moves."

The zombie found his head, picked it up, and stood. Strands of muddy drool hung from the lips and the neck stump. The dull eyes swiveled left and right and fixed upon a wooden surveyor's stake pounded into the dirt. The zombie approached the stake and yanked it free. He worked the square end of the stake into the raw meat of the neck opening in his torso. Using both hands, he fit his head over the sharp end of the stake. He gave himself a rap on the top of his skull and the head squished tight into the collar of his shirt.

Looking at this repugnant creature was like watching an abscess ooze pus.

Where did the zombie come from?

Who made it?

And why?

Mel propped himself against a length of pipe that he'd used to club the zombie. He handed me a wallet. "Your zombie dropped this."

The wallet looked—and smelled—as if it had been recovered from a Bourbon Street gutter. I opened the wallet and sorted through a Colorado driver's license, supermarket cards, and a debit card. The money bills and business cards were scraps of wet, dirty pulp.

I read aloud, "Name on the driver's license is Barrett Chambers. From Morada." That was in the San Luis Valley, over two hundred miles away. How did he get here?

I slid the wallet and cards into my coat pocket. I brushed my hands across my trousers to wipe away the slime.

The zombie made noises like he was gargling sludge. The smell hit us. Make that sewer sludge.

"This guy doesn't seem much for conversation," Mel said. "Wouldn't do any good to question him."

A young vampire named Dagger appeared from behind an excavator and walked to the edge of the hole. Mel had brought Dagger because the newbie bloodsucker wanted to prove himself as an undead terror.

Trouble was, Dagger was a high school dropout and a punk. Once undead, he had changed his name from Bartholomew, said it lacked vampiric panache. Must've taken him all day to find that word in the dictionary.

Dagger carried a metal garden sprayer. He set the sprayer between his feet. "I filled this with super unleaded. It's gonna make one hell of a flamethrower." He waved the sprayer nozzle at the zombie. "Hey, smelly boy, feeling cold dressed in those rags? Let me warm you up."

The zombie turned toward Dagger. He stopped at the bottom of the wall, raised his arms, and emitted a guttural moan.

Dagger laughed, kicked dirt into the zombie's face, and aimed the nozzle. Gasoline splattered on the zombie's head and soaked his clothes. He waved his arms to block the spray.

Dagger took a cigarette from his shirt pocket and set the butt between his lips. He dug a plastic lighter from his pocket and held it to the cigarette.

"I wouldn't do that," I warned.

Dagger dismissed me with a fanged sneer. "Hey, I got it, Pops. Anything happens, I got my vampire reflexes." He bobbed side to side.

I wanted to find the vampire who had turned Dagger and slap her. She hadn't done our bloodsucking tribe any favors by converting this arrogant dumb ass.

Dagger thumbed the lighter. It sparked and the gas fumes went *whoosh*. His clothes on fire, Dagger screamed and tripped over the sprayer, tumbling him and the sprayer on top of the zombie. They tangled together, their flailing bodies sandwiching the sprayer. Flames jetted from the pile, followed by a roaring fireball that mushroomed into a column of black smoke.

The heat slapped Mel and me and we were surrounded by the stink of burning compost. We stepped back. Mel covered his sideburns and said, "Awesome. I would've paid good money to see this."

The charred bodies settled in a burning heap.

We experienced vampires have a mandate to protect the newly turned, to protect them against everything except their own stupidity.

"That Dagger," Mel said, "what a dumbass."

"At least he took one with him."

Mel ambled toward the excavator and climbed over the treads to get into the cab. "Gotta make sure the zombie is history." He fumbled in the cab and tossed a padlock to the ground. A minute later the diesel engine grunted to life. The excavator boom lurched up and jerked left and right.

I hobbled out of the way.

The bucket on the end of the boom swiveled outward until its claws pointed down. The boom dropped and the bucket cleaved the bodies. Mel raised the boom and the bodies fell apart in halves. Smoking embers of flesh and clothes fluttered to the ground. He lifted and dropped the boom again and again, hacking the bodies into smoldering pieces. He yelled out the cab: "Hey, I oughta get a job at Benihana."

After Mel had chopped Dagger and the zombie into hash, he pulled the boom up and away. He climbed down from the excavator and stood beside me.

The pile of dirt looked like a lumpy mass of rancid bread dough. "Good job, Mel, but we can't leave evidence."

"No problem. I'll make some calls."

This wasn't all we had to worry about. "There's a more pressing issue, I'm afraid."

"What's that?" Mel asked.

"Where did this zombie come from?"

CHAPTER 2

I recognized the smells. Ditch water. Smoke. The stink from under my uniform and body armor.

I was back where my private hell had begun.

Iraq.

Four shadows moved cautiously through the evening gloom. They lurked toward me along the bank of the canal. Only I knew they approached annihilation.

I was certain they were insurgents sneaking to attack my soldiers and me. Only later would I discover the gruesome truth. They weren't insurgents: they were civilians.

A man, two women, and a little girl.

The family I helped slaughter years ago.

I didn't want to see this again. Once in a lifetime, even an immortal lifetime, was more than enough.

My *kundalini noir*—that black serpent of energy that animates my form instead of a beating heart—wrestled and beat against my ribs like it wanted to escape.

The Iraqis took timid steps, moving like hunted deer.

I tried to shout a warning but my mouth was dry and breathless.

I tried to jerk my hands up but my arms were cinched down as if in a straitjacket.

I tried to close my eyes and turn away but could not. My eyes were pinned open and my head locked in place, forcing me to watch the despicable horror.

Automatic gunfire burst loud as thunder. Red tracer bullets crisscrossed the air in a red net of death. The Iraqis started to fall even as grenades exploding at their feet made them dance like grotesque marionettes.

Gun sights materialized before me and centered on the smallest of the figures, the little girl.

Bang.

The recoil of an invisible carbine pushed against my shoulder.

Silence.

The huge eyes of the little girl bloomed with pain, the irises forever ringed with terror, dark as the night I last saw her alive.

The little girl fell onto her back.

In that moment, the joy and hope was sucked out of my life. Shame bore upon me like the weight of a mountain.

My legs weakened and I collapsed to my knees into a pool of blood spreading from the little girl.

A woman whispered my name and it echoed in the darkness.

Felix . . . ix . . . ix.

Then became louder.

Felix . . . ix . . . ix.

A plume of vapor wafted from the little girl. The plume rose and twisted, creating her ghostly twin. A filmy gown clung to her youthful form. When I first saw her years ago on that terrible night in Iraq, she might have been twelve at most. Now as she hovered in the air, she grew through adolescence, becoming taller, her face longer, her figure ripening from little girl to young woman.

My name echoed even louder. It echoed again and again until the sound reverberated in my skull like the deafening crash of a drum.

My *kundalini noir* convulsed and dissolved into a thousand spiders that crawled inside my skin as I screamed.

My hands suddenly wrenched free. I clutched my face and balled up into a fetal position.

I sat upright in my coffin. My nerves were raw and electric and my throat hurt. The echo in my head faded as the nightmare receded from my consciousness. I blinked. I was alone in my apartment, surrounded by a smothering quiet.

My *kundalini noir* grew tight as it sought to keep me centered. I rubbed my face and kneaded my hands. I welcomed back my strength and the mass of my physical body.

Homey smells comforted me, a lingering aroma of incense, a trace of yesterday's dinner—rib eye with lots of onions and type A-negative—and the dregs of bourbon and vermouth in the glass on the table beside my coffin.

I swung my legs out of the coffin. I slid off the table and lowered myself to the floor. Once upright, I paused for a moment to get my bearings, then proceeded in a bleary shuffle to the bathroom.

I thought that as a supernatural I'd be immune to nightmares, but apparently not.

I'm the legendary undead monster in human form, yet the ghost of this child tormented me like a fever.

Why the girl? What did it mean that she rose as a young woman like a phoenix from her fallen body?

I thought I had paid my cosmic penance. The girl and her family had forgiven me during a hallucination when I was close to a second death. After their blessing, I was complete as a vampire and felt free to drink human blood.

Maybe this was a new bout of post-traumatic stress. A lot of war veterans never get out from under it.

A headache throbbed behind my forehead. I ran the tap, leaned over the sink, and rinsed my face.

Out of habit, I stared into the mirror, and in my place saw what I always did . . .

Nothing.

I am a soulless immortal with the potential to accumulate wisdom over the centuries. I'm privy to the great mysteries of the universe. So far I'd learned that vampires can be as naïve or as treacherous as humans, and that the corporate vermin who run this planet would sell out their entire race for an extra bump on the bottom line. I've barely held my own in those fights and I've lost one big one. I failed my friend and fellow vampire, Carmen Arellano, and now she's a hostage of alien gangsters somewhere deep in outer space.

If wisdom comes from making stupid mistakes, then someday I'm going to be a genius.

Behind me, morning light filtered through the drawn blinds. I had work to do—even the undead have to make a living—and that meant keeping a human daylight schedule. But this nightmare exhausted me.

Why was the little girl coming back?

What did I have to fear?

Was this simply the memory of that tragedy escaping from a dark place in my subconscious, or was there something else waiting for me?

CHAPTER 3

Mel called. He asked me to meet him in Aurora close to the construction site where we'd found the zombie.

Before I left my apartment, I slathered on plenty of sunblock and applied makeup to protect my vampire skin from the daylight. I drove my Cadillac across Denver to Aurora.

I found Mel with his leg propped on the rear bumper of a rusted and grimy late-eighties Chrysler LeBaron. I parked behind the Chrysler and got out. I didn't need to guess where the putrid odor of decaying flesh came from.

Mel opened the driver's door. "Get a whiff." The odor came out in concentrated form. I had a sudden urge to gag, which embarrassed me, as I am an undead bloodsucker.

Masses of flies, thick as carpet remnants, crawled lazily over the vinyl upholstery. Mel reached to the center console and brought out a translucent storage bowl. Dozens of flies clung to the bowl. He shooed the flies away and opened the lid.

The smell of rancid meat burst out. Lumps of grayish matter, streaks of syrupy blood, and a plastic spoon lay inside the bowl.

Mel put his nose close to the bowl and sniffed. "Brains. Zombie chow." He closed the lid and tossed the bowl back into the Chrysler. He slammed the door. Hundreds of flies thumped against the inside of the windows.

"I don't like what I'm seeing," Mel said. "Looks like the zombie drove himself here."

"I agree," I replied. "I can't imagine that he carpooled with anyone."

"That, and he brought something to munch on. So we got a zombie that's not only commuting but has got the foresight to pack a lunch. Not typical zombie behavior at all." Mel wiped his hands on his denim overalls. "This is not good."

"What do we do about the car?"

Mel stepped away from the Chrysler. "A couple of vampires in the Aurora PD will take of it."

"What do we do now?"

Mel scratched his sideburns and looked around. "Wait for word from the Araneum."

I could already feel myself being pulled into this. Zombies. Yuck. I'd better stock up on bleach and soap.

I sighed. "This damn zombie has already cost me."

"What do you mean?"

"Dagger died owing me money and favors."

"You, too?" Mel's big eyebrows inched up his forehead. "Freeloading bastard didn't leave much except for a motorcycle and an antique strongbox."

"A motorcycle? What kind?"

"Kawasaki 800 Drifter. A real beauty."

I said, "Dibs."

"Fine by me." Mel gave a wily smile. "You should've asked for the strongbox. Dagger wasn't just a mooch but a crook. The strongbox is full of silver and gold coins."

"You didn't tell me that."

"You didn't ask." Mel put his arm around my shoulders. "As a consolation, I'll tow the motorcycle to your place, free of charge."

"Is that the best you can offer?"

"Not really," Mel replied, "but I'll be too busy counting my money."

We left the Chrysler. The reek was a force field that would protect the car until the police vampires came by.

Mel dropped off the motorcycle. He was right. It was a beauty, a Kawasaki Drifter in blood red with black trim. With its retro fenders and wide seat, the Drifter looked like an authentic Indian, plus it had something else the original American machine didn't: Japanese reliability.

I took the Kawasaki on a test cruise, heading west on Highway 72 toward Pinecliff. I didn't take any votes but I was sure I looked way cooler on this machine than Dagger ever had. Riding fast up the twisting mountain road, I glimpsed a black blur zooming from my left. My reflexes triggered into vampire speed but too late.

The object slammed into the side of my head and knocked me off the motorcycle. I saw the wreck unfolding in slow motion, but there was nothing I could do except cartwheel through the air and hope I landed someplace soft.

My motorcycle dropped onto its side, throwing sparks and

shedding parts as it skidded along the highway and onto the gravel shoulder. The bike and I flew off the shoulder, exploded through a scrub pine, and bounced down a steep rocky ravine.

I smashed into a boulder and ricocheted across a pile of rocks. The motorcycle tumbled over me. The bike and I pancaked on gravel and slid down the incline until we slowed to a dusty halt. Dirt and pieces of the Kawasaki showered the area.

CHAPTER 4

I lay on my back, blind with pain. Every bone hollered that it was broken. I tried to wiggle my toes and fingers, and all I got was more pain.

Sledgehammer-to-the-bone pain.

I lay for long moments, not moving, and the pain lessened from sledgehammer to ball-peen hammer.

My vision lightened and became a fuzzy blue that coalesced into a sky with clouds. I still hurt all over but felt grateful as the pain slowly dropped from ball-peen hammer pounding to a drumming by a meat tenderizer. I wiped dust from my face. My sunglasses were gone but my contacts remained in place.

I extended my arms behind me to prop myself up. More pain shot from my right wrist. I lifted that arm and my hand hung at an angle unnatural even for a vampire.

Blood dripped from the cuff of my leather jacket. The blood

clotted and dried instantly, disintegrating into cinnamon-colored flakes.

I sleeved the cuff back. Shards of pale bones, the ulna and the radius, poked through the mangled skin above my wrist. I tried to convince myself that it only looked more painful than it was. With my left hand, I grasped my right hand across the knuckles and gave a firm pull.

Another tsunami of pain pounded through me. My *kundalini noir* thrashed as if it was a snake on a hot skillet.

I worked the fractured bones into place. My vision went black again. All I sensed were my screams echoing from the mountains above. Light gradually came back into my eyes. My screams faded to silence.

I waited a moment to center myself, then surveyed the area. The motorcycle frame and engine lay in a twisted mess like the smashed carcass of a giant insect. I had thought that inheriting this bike from Dagger had been a good deal, but clearly his jinx had followed me. I had nothing to show for what he owed me except bruises, shattered bone, and a long walk home.

I needed something for a splint. I reached for the battered shell of the front fender, sat up, and held the fender upright between my knees. I extended a talon and sawed a length of the fender. I wrapped the strip of metal around my broken wrist and pulled the slack out. Gritting my teeth, I clamped the metal tight. Blood seeped along the edge of the splint. Wasn't pretty, but this time tomorrow I should be okay.

Sunlight heated patches on my face. The crash had smeared the makeup and sunblock I had slathered on to protect my un-dead skin.

I rubbed a sore spot on my skull. What the hell had hit me?

A dirty black shape the size of a grapefruit stirred beside my boots. The shape sprouted a pair of claws and a pointed beak. It rolled to one side and staggered to its feet. Torn feathers drifted from its ruffled flanks.

A crow. Had to be a messenger from the Araneum. This bird was the blur that had collided against me.

The crow swung its little round head and wobbled as if drunk.

I grabbed what was left of my motorcycle's front fender and tossed it at the crow. "I want to talk to your boss, you little shit."

The fender clattered around the bird. It acted unimpressed by my wrath and poked at the ground. The crow jammed its beak into a scramble of weeds and wrestled loose a silver object the size of my little finger.

But the object wasn't silver, it was white gold and platinum; a message capsule the crow wore on its leg. The crash must have knocked the capsule loose.

The crow grasped the capsule in its beak and limped toward me.

I took the capsule and wiped away the dust. I unzipped my leather jacket and leaned forward to create a pocket of shadow. With my left hand I unscrewed the ruby-rimmed cap, keeping the capsule in shadow to protect its contents from direct sunlight. The Araneum sent notes on vampire skin. A touch of sunlight would make the undead parchment burst into flames.

The Araneum must flay the smelliest vampires because when I removed the cap, what shot out was a putrid odor worse than rotting meat wrapped in moldy swim trunks.

I used the point of a talon to snag the parchment rolled inside the capsule. The parchment resembled yellowed onionskin. Keeping the note tucked close to my belly, I fumbled with the note to unfold it with my good hand. The parchment opened to a rectangle the size of a poker card. The message appeared as if it had been written on an old manual typewriter.

Our esteemed Felix Gomez,

Find the creator of the zombies. Destroy him and all the zombies. Immediately.
We expect your usual thoroughness. Report when completed.

Araneum

The crooked letters were typed in the brown color of dried blood. In what aisle of Office Depot would you find such a typewriter ribbon?

I've learned to decipher these messages because the Araneum must pay a thousand dollars for each word, they're so stingy with information.

First clue, creator of the zombies. Meaning the Araneum knows someone is reanimating the dead.

Second clue, zombies. Plural. I've only seen one. The Araneum knows there are more.

Third clue. Him. Gender, male. Although these notes were annoyingly brief, they were precise.

Fourth clue. Immediately. Meaning the threat is big.

Nothing about who and where.

Typical.

The reverse of the note was blank. I reread the front to make sure I didn't miss anything.

I balled up the note and flicked it away. The note arced into the sunlight, flashed and crackled and turned into a puff of smoke.

I had my orders. My Kawasaki lay in sad, broken pieces around me. I had much work to do, beginning with finding a way back to Denver.

I pointed the capsule at the crow. "You're not getting any points for a dramatic entrance. Why couldn't you have come to my office?"

The crow preened and picked at its wings. The dirt was gone and its feathers gleamed shiny and fresh.

The crow marched close to my side and extended one leg. The clip on the capsule was bent so I worked it to cinch tight around the shank.

The crow stamped its foot to test the security of the capsule. A breeze started up the ravine, murmuring through pines and aspens, and stirred the dust. The crow faced the breeze and spread both wings to cup the wind. The crow levitated straight up, claws and the capsule dangling. The crow continued up, up, not moving its wings, riding the wind with an expert grace. The claws retracted and the crow receded into a black speck in the blue sky.

Show-off. I could levitate, though not high or far. Plus it took a lot of work. You don't get anything for free in this world.

I struggled to my feet and dismissed the wreckage of my Kawasaki with a sigh and a shrug. I climbed up the ravine along the trail of scattered motorcycle parts. Every step jarred me like a swat across my back with a burning two-by-four. Once on the shoulder of the narrow highway I dug into my jacket pocket for my cell phone, which fell apart in pieces.

A white minivan came down the mountain and I flagged

it. An enormous dog in the van barked and lunged at the rear windows.

The driver's window lowered. A woman wearing a ball cap and sunglasses studied me and the pieces of metal and glass decorating the skid marks leading off the road. "You okay?" she asked, amazed no doubt that I was upright.

"I'm better than I look," I lied. "Blowout and I hit this." I raked my boot through the gravel on the asphalt. "Any way you could give a ride into town?"

"Where exactly?"

I had to get home. "Near Sloan's Lake."

"No problem," she answered. The cargo door on the opposite side popped open.

I hobbled around the front of the van. The dog's barking grew more fierce. A girl of about ten sat in the passenger's front seat; she eyed me like I was a specimen from Ripley's Believe It or Not.

Remembering the little Iraqi girl reappearing in my dreams, I got a flutter of the heebie-jeebies from this girl's stare. But she was a tiny blonde with a Hannah Montana T-shirt and weighed all of sixty pounds. My paranoia turned into embarrassment. The day I couldn't handle this waif was the day I'd drive a stake through my own sternum.

I slid open the cargo door, and the raucous barking thundered out. A boy—considering the resemblance, the girl's younger brother—moved guardedly across the middle seat to make room for me. The dog in the back—the mongrel offspring of a St. Bernard and a cave bear—flashed yellow teeth and bashed against a wire grid barrier behind the middle seats. The van rocked as the hairy beast lunged from side to side.

The boy put his hand on a latch at the front of the grid. He kept his wary little eyes on me. His arm seemed spring-loaded to throw the latch open.

No wonder this woman wasn't afraid of picking up hitchhikers. Make a wrong move and you're meat scraps.

"Buttercup, easy now," the woman cooed. "Don't be a bad girl."

Buttercup? That prehistoric monster?

I buckled in, keeping as far right as I could to stay out of the line of vision from the interior mirror. Buttercup poked her snarling muzzle through the wire grid and sprayed doggie drool against the back of my neck.

Buttercup had good reason to snarl. I picked up the aroma of young human flesh layered in the strong smell of Buttercup's canine musk. In the ancient bloodsucker days, these kids would've been a banquet for us vampires. But now, it's hands off.

We drove down the winding mountain road into the suburbs of Denver, turning through Golden and reaching Wheat Ridge. The Sloan's Lake area was another five miles away. I caught the girl staring at me through the right outside mirror.

This ride was about to get dramatic.

Her big blue eyes moved in a searching pattern. She unclasped her safety belt and whirled about to stare at me over the side of her seat.

The driver eased up on the gas. "What are you doing?"

The girl's eyebrows pinched together and her eyes became loaded with suspicion. "Mom, why can't I see him in the mirror?"

CHAPTER 5

Time to cover my tracks and find another way home. I bent forward—pain zippered from vertebrae to vertebrae. I flicked the contacts from my eyes and sat up.

Tendrils of alarm lashed from the red auras of the girl, her mom, and the boy. Buttercup picked up on their blossoming panic and the van quaked as the dog jumped and clawed at the wire grid.

I made eye contact with the girl first. Her aura lit up like I'd hooked her little toes to an electrical socket. She sat still, open-mouthed, eyes big as quarters. I eased the girl back into her seat.

The boy trembled as his blood turned ice cold. Terror kept him from doing anything but hold still while I hypnotized him.

When Mom turned to look, I snatched the sunglasses off her face and zapped her. I reached over her shoulder for the steering wheel while telling her how to work the pedals.

All three sat quiet as mannequins, their auras fading to red shimmers. I'd given each an extra powerful dose to keep them under long enough for me to escape. When they came to, they would remember giving me a lift and then me disappearing sometime during the drive down the mountain.

Buttercup howled, rabid with rage, eager to rip me to pieces. Shame that vampire hypnosis didn't work on dogs, especially this volcanic bitch.

I guided the minivan into an alley behind a liquor store, tucked a pair of twenties into the mom's hand, and got out.

How to get home? I didn't want to risk stealing a car. Taxi? A cabbie could recall me. Not too many fares look like they've rolled down a mountain.

I limped two blocks and waited for the bus. Compared with the other people at the bus stop in their eclectic urban attire— chrome army helmet; a cape made of feathers; plastic shopping bags for shoes; the middle-aged man in a denim miniskirt—I appeared normal and easily forgotten.

I took a seat at the rear of the bus and isolated myself behind a moat of pain. My arm hurt too much for me to care about anything but self-medicating and not missing the transfer.

After I got to my apartment, I cleaned up and smothered the pain with aspirin and a whisky sour. I checked voice mail from my landline.

There was a message from Olivia, a favorite chalice: a human who willingly donated her blood. Part of the attraction for chalices was belonging to our supernatural subculture. But once part of our extended family, chalices kept coming—so to speak—for the orgasmic rapture experienced from the fanging.

For us vampires, chalices provided convenient nourishment without the stalking of innocents and the risk that brought.

There's a catch. A chalice was bound to silence about the existence of the supernatural world. Any transgression warranted an immediate and agonizing death. Failure to punish any such chalice meant the vampire master also deserved the final blow from undead to permanent dead.

Olivia's cheery voice sang from the phone. "How's it hanging, Felix? Long and thick, I hope. If you're hungry, call me, baby."

Damn right I was hungry. Plump, horny, and succulent Olivia. Comfort food for a vampire.

I flexed the fingers of my injured hand. My wrist ached. My back ached. Everything ached. Olivia would help me feel much better.

I set the phone aside.

Then, like a curtain falling before me, everything blanked out. An instant later the little girl appeared.

The voice returned, repeating my name.

Just as abruptly, the hallucination disappeared. The voice faded, the echo so faint it was like I had never heard it at all.

I put my hand on the desk to stop the dizziness.

One second I was in my normal world, then *flash* came the little girl, and *flash* again, back to normal.

My *kundalini noir* shrank around a cold ball of fear. My hands trembled from the chill.

I pulled up a chair and sat.

The war was years behind me.

Was I going insane?

CHAPTER 6

I bought a new cell phone. My first call was to Mel and I told him about the visit from the crow.

"What about the bike?" he asked.

"What about me?" I replied. "The damn bird nearly killed me."

"But it didn't. Meanwhile the bike is still fucked up."

"More than that. It's a wreck."

"Man, I don't want to hear that," Mel said. "Where's the bike?"

"Up Coal Creek Canyon. Right where I crashed it."

"I got a friend who owns a wrecking yard. He'll retrieve the bike and part it out. Give you a hundred for it."

"Deal." Sucker, I would've given him the title for free.

"What have you learned about the zombie?" Mel asked.

"Nothing yet. Gimme a break, will you? I'm still limping from the wreck."

"That's your problem," Mel said. "Tell you what, I'll send what I got on zombies. Modus operandi. Past history."

"As opposed to future history?"

"Fuck you. You want my help or not?"

"Sure," I said. "Anything would be appreciated."

"It's in the mail." He hung up.

I had better do my homework on Barrett Chambers, aka the now permanently deceased zombie. I keep a hacker on retainer. Every month I mail a few hundred bucks to a P.O. box in Kalamazoo, Michigan. In return I get snapshots into almost every database wired to the Internet. I sent an e-mail to my hacker with info I had on Chambers and a list of my questions.

My next phone call was to Olivia. My wrist hurt more than it should've. I needed her fresh blood to help me heal.

She told me her folks were visiting—I made it a rule not to host at my place—so we met in a hotel. A suite, as I liked plenty of space for our games.

When I fang, I can administer a variety of enzymes. One accelerates healing of the victim's wounds, in this case, the fang punctures. Another promotes amnesia and keeps the victim from remembering my presence. Yet another enzyme gives pleasure. Without it, fanging would burn like being force-fed napalm.

My *kundalini noir* twitched with hunger pangs. Try recuperating after somersaulting from a motorcycle and rolling down a mountain, and see what kind of appetite you'd have.

I gave Olivia plenty of the pleasure enzymes while I guzzled from her throat. As she floated in sexual euphoria, I peeled the metal splint from my wrist and rubbed the torn flesh against the blood seeping from her neck. The warm blood felt as refreshing as a salve. The blood I'd swallowed was enough to help me heal, but I enjoyed adding this ritual to my rehabilitation. Slowly but visibly, the ragged cuts on my arm closed to faint scars.

I made a manhattan and got comfortable in a leather cigar chair. Olivia curled like a Persian cat across the love seat by the bed. I studied her with an artistic eye. She was a work in progress and I thought about what strokes I'd need to finish her off for the evening. When I got down to nothing but ice cubes in my glass, I flexed my wrist and felt it strong enough to put weight on it.

I coaxed Olivia back to consciousness. She offered her neck but I kissed her mouth instead. After a good bout of foreplay and sloppy oral sex (the best kind), I used supernatural strength to hold her in a variety of acrobatic positions while I spanked her chunky bottom with my pelvis. She liked visuals in the mirror, but since I am a vampire, all Olivia got was her image hovering in the air as her breasts and limbs flounced about.

At two in the morning, we ended the festivities with a shower. After we toweled each other off, Olivia blow-dried her long brunette hair. She dressed and fastened a scarf around her neck to hide the healing fang marks.

"I can't spend the night." She pecked my cheek. "My mom insists that I act like a good Catholic girl."

"There's no need to act." I adjusted the crucifix resting at the top of her cleavage. "I can vouch that you are Catholic and very good."

I walked Olivia to her car, then drove home. I climbed into my coffin: tired, satiated, but still sore from yesterday's crash.

The chime from my cell phone awoke me. The ringtone—AC/DC's "Dirty Deeds Done Dirt Cheap"—told me that I had a message forwarded from my work number. I sat up, feeling refreshed, and realized that the Iraqi girl had not visited my dreams. Hopefully that nonsense was over.

I'd answer the call when I got to my office. There's always time for work. I headed into the kitchen and opened the refrigerator. In the ancient days, long before I was around, when a vampire got hungry, he would go to the dungeon and sort through the menu. I stared with regret at the stacks of 450-milliliter bags of chilled human blood. This was progress?

I grabbed a type B-negative and heated the bag in the microwave. Maybe I ought to convert the garage into a dungeon and keep a chalice. Then I'd have to keep another chalice to clean the cage and the litter box. The arrangement would get too complicated.

My office was in the Oriental Theater at the corner of Tennyson and Forty-fourth, on the second floor behind the big neon sign.

The red light on my office phone blinked. Caller ID gave a restricted number. The voice-mail message sounded like a robot learning how to speak English.

"I've found what you wanted on Barrett Chambers. Check your e-mail."

The zombies were on my endangered list.

CHAPTER 7

The replies from my hacker came back in a series of e-mails from various anonymous accounts.

As I sorted through the e-mails, Phyllis called. She represented the Araneum as my minder (that's the closest word I could find to describe our relationship). The arrangement was definitely one-sided; her job was to make sure I understood the implications of my actions . . . and especially of my failures.

"We need to discuss your assignment." Her tone was as inviting as the teeth on a steel trap.

My *kundalini noir* displaced uneasily. This was the first time the Araneum had contacted me like this at the beginning of an assignment. Usually I got my orders via the crow and off I went.

I waited for Phyllis and Mel outside Ojo del Azteca, one of the remaining dives in this part of the Highlands neighbor-hood, also known as the North Side. The dry cleaners next door was replaced by a boutique and the corner space—empty since forever—was an espresso and wine bar. The sky was deceptively bright for such a cold day, a reminder that much in this world wasn't as it should be.

I kept thinking about the reason for our meeting and I formed the impression that the big thumb of the Araneum was about to press down upon me.

Phyllis turned the corner of the sidewalk from Zuni to Thirty-second Street. Besides jeans and a green jacket, she wore a knit cap the color of a maraschino cherry that emphasized her milk chocolate complexion. False advertising—there was nothing sweet about her.

In one hand she pulled a black rollaway carry-on. With her other hand she held the leash of her dog, a freakish golden retriever/blue heeler mix. The mutt had a long, skinny frame and a blue-gray pelt spotted with black markings. Straw-yellow hair sprouted from around its neck and bony legs. The dog looked like God couldn't decide how to finish this mongrel before He gave up.

I said hello. Phyllis responded with a nod. She looped the dog's leash over the metal railing in front of the cantina.

Phyllis removed her sunglasses and put them into a pocket of her jacket. We both wore brown contacts. Her face revealed no hint of her mood. You could read more emotion from a rock.

Phyllis retracted the handle and lifted the carry-on. We entered the bar and proceeded to a table in the back. The owners must have been stingy about paying for electricity because the place was as gloomy as a cavern.

A yuppie Latina in a navy blue power suit—lawyer, I guessed—sat knee to knee with a much younger man. They were tucked in a dark recess where the corner of the bar met the wall. He held her hand. As Phyllis and I passed, the woman lowered her face. The back of his jacket read LARRY'S LANDSCAPING. No question about whose bush he was trimming.

The only other customers—two men who dressed like they raided a Salvation Army donation box for clothes—occupied a table at the opposite corner from us. They fell silent when we entered and stared at their bottles of beer. Both men acted like we'd interrupted a supersecret discussion, probably about the best intersections for panhandling.

Phyllis and I took adjacent chairs facing the front door. She slid the carry-on onto the table, next to my backpack.

The front door opened and a wedge of light sliced across the floor. Mel's broad silhouette filled the doorway. He did a quick take of the bar and ambled to us.

Mel carried a battered metal lunch box. He unbuttoned his denim work coat. Both his flannel shirt and his jeans were pockmarked with burn marks.

Mel took a seat. Under his bulk, the chair looked like a milking stool. He placed the lunch box on the floor. He smelled of welding flux and charred flesh. That explained the bandage on his left hand. Mel did a lot of welding but he wasn't good at it.

The bartender left the bar and came toward us. She was a plump woman with a Mayan profile, a Frida Kahlo unibrow, and golden earrings the size of jalapeños. Tattoos peeked around the neckline of her peasant blouse. I ordered a Carta Blanca, Phyllis a Superior, and Mel whatever was cheapest.

When the bartender left, Phyllis glanced at the other customers. They'd forgotten about us and leaned close to one another and whispered.

Ojo del Azteca was a good place to trade secrets.

I looked at the carry-on and wondered what it had to do with our inquiry into the zombie.

Mel fiddled with a zipper pull on the carry-on until Phyllis pushed his hand away.

"It's your meeting," I said to her. "Start with the questions."

Phyllis set her gaze on mine. The heat of her vampiric nature radiated through her contacts. "What have you found out about the zombie?"

I opened my backpack and pulled out copies of the e-mails I'd gotten from my hacker. "Here's what I've got on Chambers. His commercial footprints—use of credit cards, telephone calls, bank activity—stopped six weeks ago, about the time I'm guessing he became a zombie. His last address was in Morada, where I'm headed."

"Any leads?"

"A couple. His landlord. His ex."

Phyllis asked, "What do you expect to find?"

"In Morada? What I'd like to find is a big neon sign saying, ZOMBIE LAIR THIS WAY. But what I expect to find is a trail of flimsy clues. The usual."

Phyllis unzipped the main compartment of the carry-on. "When you get to Morada, you need to consider something else." She said this like she was about to drop a heavy weight on my shoulders.

Phyllis reached inside the carry-on and withdrew an odd contraption. It was a shiny metallic case the size of a large dictionary. A four-sided pyramid sat on top. The pyramid seemed made of glass triangles about six inches along each side. On closer inspection, I saw the sides weren't glass but sheets of thin, transparent quartz. A crystal the size of my thumb stood upright in a cup-sized depression inside the square base of the pyramid. The ornately filigreed case, the use of gemstones as rivet heads, and the gold seams along the corners of the pyramid told me this device had most likely been crafted by the Araneum.

An elongated ruby the size of a pen cap angled from a top corner of the case. Phyllis flicked the ruby like a switch. A faint silvery glow illuminated the crystal.

Mel asked, "Looks pretty, but what the hell is it?"

"A psychotronic diviner," Phyllis answered. "It detects psychic energy."

Psychic energy. The two words boomeranged into my brain. This was another example of how my experiences with the weird and supernatural kept twirling back upon themselves.

What originally brought me to Colorado was an assignment I had contracted with an alien masquerading as a college friend. The alien wanted me to find out what was causing an outbreak of nymphomania at the Rocky Flats Nuclear Weapons Plant. The alien knew all along what the cause was—a bizarre red mercury isotope leaking from a UFO the government was studying at Rocky Flats. What the alien really wanted, and couldn't get because of government security, was a different psychotronic instrument, what he called simply a device, that was stored in the UFO.

I turned my attention to the diviner. "This doesn't look like the device I found in the UFO." That one resembled a box camera with two handgrips. It was a prototype with a more sinister application than merely detecting psychic energy: it was to test psychic control of humans.

After I had retrieved the device from the UFO—at great risk to myself—and learned about its function, I destroyed it. The alien hadn't liked that, but screw him for lying to me.

I studied the diviner, fascinated by the ostentatious decoration. "So this detects psychic energy. What's the big deal? I can take off my contacts and see auras."

Phyllis grew pensive, as if gathering herself to explain something complicated to someone not as smart as she. "Are you familiar with the astral plane?"

"I've heard of it. That's the extent of what I know."

"In our physical world," Phyllis said, "we have three dimensions."

Mel interrupted and said, "Actually four, as you have to include time," proving he's more than his Neanderthal appearance.

"Okay, four," Phyllis relented. "Consider the astral plane as another dimension. One we can access only by using the psychic energy component of our being. You've heard of astral projection?"

"I saw an ad about it in a comic book. Right next to one about X-ray specs."

Phyllis kept her expression arid and inert. "Astral projection is when our psychic selves travel from one place to another across the astral plane. That's one phenomenon involving the astral plane. Others include remote viewing and out-of-body experiences."

I asked, "How does this concern the Araneum?"

"The Araneum is investigating the use of the astral plane."

"For what reasons? Discount travel?"

Phyllis's voice became a little more dry. "Something like that but we shouldn't speculate."

As in, *you don't need to know.*

The bartender interrupted when she brought our drinks. She glanced at the diviner and remained unamused, as if she'd seen stranger things in the bar. She poured the beers into glasses and left.

I tasted my beer. "Where did this diviner come from?"

Phyllis took a collection of papers from the carry-on. They were photocopies of pages from a notebook. The writing on the margins used Cyrillic letters. "In your investigation of Rocky Flats, did you ever come across a Dr. Milan Blavatsky?"

"No."

Phyllis said, "He was a scientist hired to reverse-engineer what the government could of the UFO. These are his private notes."

Workers at Rocky Flats were forbidden from taking classified material. Sometimes the security precautions were concrete solid; other times, they were a sieve.

I studied the small drawings and the cramped lettering. The notes were reduced images of much larger originals. Some of the drawings were simple representations of the case and the pyramid. There was also one sketch of the original psychotronic device. Other drawings were as complex and indecipherable as the electrical schematics of a rocket ship.

Mel traced a big finger along the most complicated of the drawings. His eyes registered admiration.

I went from the plans to the diviner. "I was under the impression the government couldn't deduce much from the UFO. Too advanced."

Phyllis said, "Another lie."

"Figures. Where did you get these notes?"

"After Blavatsky retired"—Phyllis drank from her glass—"he went public with them but didn't get much attention outside of obscure pseudoscience journals."

"Seems the government would've tried to stop him."

"Maybe they did."

"What do you mean?"

"Dr. Blavatsky was obsessed with UFO phenomenon," Phyllis replied. "When he went to a wheat field to investigate a crop circle, he got run over by a combine."

Phyllis waited as if she wanted a chuckle, but to me, the point of her anecdote was that psychic energy studies were not only weird but deadly.

I didn't laugh.

I opened my right hand. "Here's my zombie." I opened my left hand. "Here is the psychotronic diviner." I put my hands together. "What's the connection?"

Phyllis reached back into the carry-on and withdrew a state highway map of Colorado. "The Araneum has triangulated the source of an unusual set of psychic signals." She laid the map flat beside the diviner and noted two thick pencil lines. One started in Boulder. The other came from the southeast, off the map.

"Austin, Texas," Phyllis explained.

The two lines intersected over Morada.

CHAPTER 8

Zombies. Psychic signals. The astral plane. All had something to do with Morada. Even trying to guess made my thoughts loopy, as if my beer had been spiked.

"What's so important about this particular signal?"

Phyllis answered, "The signal is unusually strong."

"What's the source? Supernatural? Human? Alien?"

"We don't know. That's your job to find out."

Mel massaged his temples. "All this mental gymnastics has made me hungry. Anybody up for a snack?"

He set his lunch box on the table. "I've eaten here before. The menu would make a goat puke." He opened the lunch box and doled out three bags of warm blood. "A-negative." He offered straws that we punched into the bags. With plastic bendy straws sticking out the tops, the silvery bags looked like kids' juice containers.

The bartender returned. "No outside food or drink."

Mel waved his bag. "We're on a special diet."

One end of the bartender's unibrow levered upward. Her forehead wrinkled and the makeup cracked like plaster.

I tossed a ten on the table. "Let's pretend we ordered something to eat."

The bartender curled the ten around her long purple fingernails, tucked the money down the front of her blouse between the tattoos of two devils, and walked off.

The blood tasted good but did nothing to improve my understanding of psychic energy or my attitude toward this investigation.

Phyllis pushed the diviner across the table toward me. "You're going to need this to locate the signal."

Given the ambiguities in this assignment, the diviner seemed less like a tool and more like Pandora's box. "So this particular signal comes from Morada. Why is that such a big deal?"

Phyllis hesitated as if parsing in her mind what she could and couldn't tell me. "Usually the use of psychic energy is a passive activity, similar to hearing or observing. But there are some who can focus and direct their psychic energy outward—a psychic energy attack, if you will."

I pulled my chair closer. "For what reason?"

"To enter someone's psyche through their subconscious. Imagine if you could reach someone through their dreams."

Dreams. Were my nightmares and hallucinations the result of psychic manipulation?

I had thought of the Iraqi girl's resurrection as a symptom of my guilt. But maybe it wasn't. Maybe someone had opened up my head and was monkeying around in my subconscious.

I felt as if I was shrinking deep into myself and the world

pulled away from me with a wet, sucking sound. I became queasy from the sense of violation. Everything seemed an illusion—who or what could I trust? I retreated behind my doubts.

I wasn't sure what was going on and I didn't like it.

Mel busied himself draining his bag of blood. He searched with the straw to slurp from the corners of his bag. His eyes turned to me and wrinkled with concern. "Felix, you look like there's a spider crawling in your shorts. What's up?"

All of us wore contacts and we couldn't read one another's aura. I must've really telegraphed my emotions to have them read so easily.

"What about hallucinations?" I asked.

Phyllis had been drinking blood while she studied me with her keen eyes. She put down her bag. "What about them?" Her gaze pulled at me like hooks.

Talking about the hallucinations would stir up my feelings of violation and guilt, but Phyllis might know something that could help.

"The last few nights I've had bad dreams about my turning." I fought to displace my emotions and kept my voice calm as if I were talking about someone else. "I've been getting hallucinations that bring back memories I worked hard to forget. A voice comes to me, repeating my name."

"Whose voice is it? A fanging victim?"

"No."

"Was that it? Just a voice?" Phyllis fired the questions like an interrogator.

"I saw a face."

"Whose?"

"Someone from long ago. Someone dead."

Phyllis played with the straw in her bag of blood. "How do the hallucinations come to you?"

"At first in nightmares. Lately I've been getting them even during the day."

"What triggers them?"

"They just happen."

I remembered the girl. My *kundalini noir* wilted and I felt my shoulders sag with grief.

Buck up, Felix. Don't show weakness. I erased the girl's image from my mind. I straightened up and put a stoic gaze into my eyes.

For the first time since I've known Phyllis, a flicker of regret played across her face.

"What is it?" I asked.

Phyllis hardened her stare. The corners of her eyes twitched. "Are you up for this assignment?"

"You mean finding the zombie creator?"

"And the source of the psychic signals."

I didn't appreciate these jabs she was throwing at me. "Are you doubting my abilities?"

"I have my concerns." Another jab.

"What are you getting at?"

Phyllis shifted uncomfortably as if she were about to say something that would hurt us both. "I'm sending you help."

The comment stung like one of those jabs had connected to my chin.

Mel winced and whispered sympathetically, "Ouch."

Phyllis's meaning lingered in the air, stinking. She'd lost confidence in me as an enforcer.

I asked, "Why?"

"No reason other than my own paranoia."

"I don't like someone from the Araneum describing herself as paranoid," I said. "The rest of us should be paranoid about you."

Phyllis's expression seemed to petrify.

I wanted to break through her calm veneer, so I added, "Unless this business of being paranoid is bullshit."

Phyllis let her face relax. A manipulative gleam sparkled in her eyes. "I wouldn't worry."

"It's my ass. I am worrying."

Her eyes went dim and her mouth flattened, like her mind had clicked off the "show emotions" button. She said, "I'm bringing in Jolie."

The name was a stab where my heart used to be. Jolie was another vampire enforcer from the Araneum. She and I had met through our friendship with Carmen Arellano. We both had been Carmen's lovers. In the days since we lost Carmen, Jolie and I had kept in touch. Our conversations were strained by the mutual understanding that we had unknowingly betrayed Carmen. Because of our mistake, she was now a prisoner of extraterrestrial gangsters.

Jolie and I once commiserated our way to sex. I'm sure both of us were thinking of Carmen as we screwed each other. I know I was. Afterward, we both pretended that the other no longer existed.

"Send for her then," I said. "You don't need my permission."

Phyllis replied, "Jolie's finishing another assignment. You should wait for her."

"I'll get started now. The Araneum said 'immediately.'"

"You should wait. A repeat of what happened to Carmen would be a disaster."

This wasn't another jab, it was an uppercut to my jaw.

I looked away from Phyllis and let my ego absorb the blow.

I slipped a few bills under my glass and collected my backpack. "Phyllis, you don't think I can handle this, bring in anyone you want."

She dropped her empty bag of blood into Mel's lunch box. "Felix, you're the best we have. Unfortunately, even the best can't afford to make mistakes."

CHAPTER 9

The psychotronic diviner sat on the front passenger's seat. A dim white glow shimmered inside the crystal.

I was on the way to Morada. I had borrowed an older Toyota 4Runner from Mel because I didn't want to bang up my Cadillac.

South of Saguache, the highway emptied into the San Luis Valley. Yellow and orange autumn leaves splashed like fire across the evergreens of La Garita Hills. The highway made one last jag before heading straight south along the western boundary of the valley.

I was about to tune the stereo when the girl appeared. Her face and those unforgiving eyes loomed before me.

The voice returned.

Felix . . . ix . . . ix.

Just as suddenly, her face disappeared and I stared at the square grill of a semitruck coming straight at me. Its horn bellowed.

A shock wave of panic and terror ripped through me. I snagged the steering wheel to the right and jammed on the brakes.

The semi roared by, the horn blaring even louder, the driver flipping me off.

The Toyota skidded across the pavement and swerved left. My guts seized in fear that I would flip over. I countersteered. The 4Runner snaked back and forth, losing speed, and came to a halt. The sharp odor of burned rubber came through the vents. The back end of the semitrailer receded in my rearview mirror.

I rested my head against the rim of the steering wheel and let go a long sigh of thanks.

Something shone in my peripheral vision.

The crystal in the diviner burned bright white.

It burned bright white.

The diviner had just detected a psychic signal.

During the hallucination.

This couldn't be a coincidence.

Did this confirm that the hallucinations were psychic energy attacks?

It had to.

The glow in the crystal faded. I put my hands close to the pyramid and my fingers trembled in dread.

If the hallucinations were the result of my guilt, I could find a way to cope. But what defense did I have against a psychic attack?

I imagined a hand groping inside my skull, fingers sifting through my brain. The sense of violation returned.

I felt stripped and humiliated.

Naked.

Unclean.

Why the attack? Why me?

Who was doing this?

A sense of foreboding cut deep into me, as if I were pressed against the edge of a giant knife.

Were the zombies and the psychic attacks related?

What else could the psychic attacks do? Could they only manipulate my thoughts or could they also steal from my mind?

The foreboding cut sharper.

Was the Araneum not telling me something about this assignment?

How much danger waited for me in Morada?

Why was the Araneum sending me out here like this? As bait? Was I that expendable?

I reached behind me for a cooler on the rear seat. A dozen 450-milliliter bags of whole human blood sat in the cooler. I snatched a bag and fanged a hole in an O-neg, inserted a plastic straw, and sipped.

The taste of human blood comforted me. My fear eased and I became filled with a calm and cold determination. I had powerful weapons of my own and my enemies would be foolish to underestimate me.

It was time to get my questions answered. In Morada.

I took my foot off the brake and pressed hard on the accelerator pedal.

The highway crossed a bridge over the Rio Grande, passed a potato co-op, and led to the one stoplight in town. To my left, a giant white letter M decorated the side of a tall rocky hill.

I turned west on Abundance Boulevard. Wasn't much in abundance except for wishful thinking. A sporting goods store with grimy, opaque windows. A big-game meat processor offered family discounts. A couple of antique shoppes sold junk. Faded real estate signs advertised mountain views and country living.

My first stop would be Donald Johansen, Barrett Chambers's landlord. I followed the MapQuest printouts to the address of the apartments on the north side of town.

The street became a washboard dirt road. Small forlorn houses with tarpaper roofs sat behind rickety fences of slack wire. Rusting cars, tractors, and farm machinery rested like broken statues in weed-filled yards.

I got to the address on C Street, a row of five tiny apartments on a scraggy lot. The twisted window screens looked like gray scabs. Half of the windows either had cardboard inserts or were covered on the inside with aluminum foil. Chambers had lived behind door number three.

I parked next to the only car on the lot, a dusty Chevy Lumina, and got out.

MANAGER had been scrawled in black marker on the door closest to the Chevy.

I removed my contacts and checked to see if anyone watched. The only life I saw were a few birds flying overhead and the traffic passing down the street.

I stored my contacts in their case and covered my eyes with sunglasses. I had to be ready to use hypnosis.

I pressed my hand against the manager's door. The texture was rough from the peeling varnish. By feeling for vibrations and using my hearing, I could get a better picture of what was going on inside.

A television commercial sang the praises for yet another breakthrough in toothbrush technology. I heard a gentle rustle, like someone shifting on a chair.

I stood to one side of the door—a habit in case the occupant answered with a shotgun blast—and knocked.

The volume of the TV was turned down.

"Yeah?"

I knocked again. "Hey, Donald, I got the rent money." I emphasized "rent money."

The chair squeaked and approaching steps rattled the door.

"That you, Barrett?" A man's voice. "About goddamn time."

The door jerked open. A guy in his mid-thirties stared out. His flabby face had the dull color of cold cuts that had been forgotten in the fridge. The mood in his eyes went from anticipation to surprise. His dark hair was parted in the middle and hung to his shoulders. He was barefoot and wore sweats and a ratty green T-shirt that said ROCK-N-ROLL FOREVER.

His eyes gave me the quick one, two appraisal, and his expression turned hostile. He kept his hand on the doorknob. "What can I do for you?"

"I'm here about Barrett Chambers."

"Haven't seen him since the beginning of last month. I'm about to evict his deadbeat ass." Johansen squinted at me and grimaced. "Who are you?"

I held out a business card. "A friend of the family."

Johansen's eyes cut to the card and back to me. "What friend? What family?" He started to close the door. "Unless you're here to settle his rent, I'm not talking. You got any problems with Barrett, go to the cops."

I had to search Chambers's apartment, and if Johansen didn't want to cooperate, I had other ways.

I dropped the card into my shirt pocket. I jabbed my hand and the toe of my shoe in between the door and the jamb. Johansen's expression exploded with alarm. One shove using vampiric strength and I was inside. Johansen tripped over a vacuum cleaner and stumbled against the wall. He made a choking noise like a scream for help was stuck in his throat. I kicked the door shut, grabbed his arm, and pulled him upright.

Johansen's eyes fixed on mine, and they said: *Don't hurt me.* I jerked the sunglasses from my face and gave him a blast of hypnosis. His pupils unscrewed into enormous black dots. His aura flashed with a silky red texture.

He went limp in surrender. I wouldn't fang him unless I had to. I asked what he knew about Chambers. Under hypnosis Johansen had to tell the truth, which he readily did. Johansen had no idea what had happened to Chambers or where he had last gone.

To deepen Johansen's hypnosis, I led him to a chair, sat him down, and rubbed the webs of flesh between his thumbs and index fingers. His face and posture relaxed until his head tipped forward in sleep. He should stay under for twenty to thirty minutes.

I left him slumped in front of his TV. A ring of keys hung from a nail on a post by the counter separating the living room from a tiny kitchen. I put on a pair of latex gloves and took the keys.

Outside of unit three, I tried the keys until I found one that worked.

I stood back and pushed the door fully open. The air gushed out in a wave of musty odors and harsh chemical smells. A pile of mail scattered along the threshold.

I entered and closed the door. The interior was dark. His place was one with aluminum foil over the windows.

Propane tanks were stacked along one wall. The tanks had markings of the stores I was certain they were stolen from. Drug labs used the empty tanks to cook meth.

Was Barrett Chambers a tweaker? If he was, didn't mean he was a zombie, just acting like one.

What had happened during his last days as a human? Who reanimated him—step one of the process was killing him—and why?

Shredded cartons of Sudafed—more evidence of meth trafficking—filled a large cardboard box. Stacks of old pizza boxes and empty cans of beer and diet soda littered the floor. Heaps of dirty clothes, car stereos, and all kinds of hand tools lay everywhere.

I opened the fridge and immediately regretted it. The smell was like a cow decomposing. The shelves held lumps of hairy shapes in shades of green and yellow. Even the water pitcher had stuff growing in it.

The bathroom and bedroom weren't in better condition. Interestingly, dry-cleaned trousers still in plastic hung in the closest. That was the extent of any tidy habits.

I searched the drawers and found a large mailer tucked beneath loose underwear and socks, beside the porn. Inside the mailer were letters with postmarks going back seven years with the most recent being from two years ago. Every letter had been sent to a different address. Barrett had flitted from place to place like a plastic bag in the wind.

One letter was from his mom—the return address said MOM—and the rest were from someone named Robbie. Turned out to be his younger brother. Robbie kept sending updates of his progress in school. He asked when Barrett was going to get "right" and come home again. Home was Emporia, Kansas.

I looked at the squalor in the room. Barrett never got right—whatever that was.

I thumbed through the mail piled up by the door. Most were stamped: Past Due.

Barrett Chambers, it seemed, was skidding to the end of the earth and one day fell off the edge.

The problem was that Barrett returned from that edge as a zombie.

How?

I locked up and returned the keys. Johansen would remember hearing me knock and then nothing until he awoke in his chair.

Next stop, Chambers's ex, Adrianna Maestas.

CHAPTER 10

Adrianna lived south of Abundance Boulevard. Here the roads were paved, the lawns neat, the fences straight and in repair. Most of the streets had sidewalks. No cars or tractors sat dismantled in the yards. The contrast between north and south Morada seemed mandated by law.

The address was a tidy cottage in pristine white stucco protected by walls of rectangular hedges. I parked next to a white picket fence. Cottonwood trees flush with gold and copper leaves shaded the porch. Lace curtains were drawn behind the windows.

After using my vampire powers on Johansen I decided to keep a low supernatural profile, so I had put my contacts back on. I figured I could charm anything I needed out of Adrianna.

I rang the doorbell. The door curtains parted briefly. The deadbolt clicked and the door opened a crack, secured by a chain.

A woman with a slender olive-skinned face and black hair

shiny as gloss enamel peered at me. She wore a colored blouse and a neck lanyard with a plastic badge I couldn't read. I got the feeling she was on the way to work. Despite her pleasant looks, her eyes smoldered with distrust.

An older woman inside the house called out in Spanish. "Who is it?"

"Some strange man, Mama," the woman at the door shouted back, also in Spanish.

Strange? I've been called worse.

To my left, the curtains in another window parted and a set of young eyes watched.

"My name is Felix Gomez," I said in Spanish, hoping that by leaning on our common heritage, she would soften and welcome me in. "Are you Adrianna Maestas?"

She gave a guarded nod. I couldn't imagine what such an attractive woman had seen in a loser like Chambers.

I handed her my business card.

She read the card and passed it to someone behind her. Adrianna brought those pretty eyes back to me and remarked in English. "So?"

"I'm looking for Barrett Chambers."

Her face shriveled with disgust like she had milk curdling in her stomach. "Why the hell you asking me?"

I tried to play the sympathy angle. "I'm afraid something bad might have happened to him."

"Oh yeah?" Her voice turned gleefully poisonous. "Well, I hope the worthless bastard drowned in a toilet while rats chewed his balls." She slammed the door with the clank of the deadbolt as an exclamation mark.

Being married to this harpy might have driven Chambers to become a zombie.

I remained outside the door, not sure what to do next. I could break in and use hypnosis to make Adrianna talk. But she wasn't alone. At least two more were in the house. Corralling so many witnesses wouldn't be worth the trouble, especially if Adrianna didn't know much. I'm sure she and Chambers parted ways long before he was recruited into the undead.

The Araneum suspected the reanimator was nearby but where? What new leads could I follow?

I returned to the Toyota. The crystal in the diviner gave a faint glow, on duty and vigilant for more psychic signals.

Faces in the windows of the cottage kept watch until I drove off.

So far, my investigation proceeded as expected. In other words, I had practically zip to show for my efforts. The one break was that I was now certain psychic attacks caused my hallucinations.

To plan my next step I circled back to a café that I had passed on the way to Adrianna's.

This time in the morning, I could use a cup of coffee to stimulate my thinking. The café had a short adobe wall surrounding an outside patio. The picnic tables closest to the café door were busy with customers. I paid for a cup of dark roast and got a table at the far end of the patio. The coffee was good but needed a little blood to round out the taste.

The skies were darkening and a breeze drummed along the café's patio awning. We were due for an autumn rain and I wanted to enjoy a drink in the fresh air before the clouds drenched us.

My cell phone vibrated. The incoming call had a local prefix but I didn't recognize the number.

Who in Morada knew my number? I answered with a simple hello.

The caller—a younger man, I guessed by his voice—asked, "You Felix Gomez?"

"I am."

"You looking for Barrett Chambers?"

The hairs on the back of my hand stood. The breeze had a sudden weight and chill.

"I know something about him," the man said.

CHAPTER 11

One moment this case was a dark closet and the next moment it was like the door had been flung open and the light shone in, intense and scalding with opportunity.

Who was this stranger? "Your name?"

"Gino. Gino Brunatti."

He emphasized his last name like it should mean something. Which it did.

Brunatti. Any Colorado PI worthy of the license knew that name. Along with the Smaldones and Carlinos, the Brunattis were one of the organized-crime families who had moved to Denver from Chicago and the East Coast in the 1920s. They arrived hoping to expand their rackets. Other than adding color to local history and extended stays in the iron-bar hotel, none of the families accomplished much.

Once they were chased out of Denver—too much competition from the other crooks, including the police—the mobsters had moved south. Their descendants set up shop in Pueblo and west into the mountains surrounding the San Luis Valley.

So he was a Brunatti. If he lived in Morada and hung out with a lowlife like Chambers, then Gino wasn't much of a big-time player in the crime world.

Gino said, "That's you at the café."

How did he know? I ducked and swiveled my head, convinced that he was using a sniper rifle to count the hairs on my scalp. Gino might not be a big-time player but he had cojones. Where was he? "How'd you get my number?"

"From Adrianna."

Adrianna? Morada was a smaller town than I thought.

"She gave me your number and a description of your Toyota. I drive down Abundance and here you are. Listen, you can't wipe your butt in this town without everybody knowing how many squares of paper you use."

"Where are you?"

"Look to your right, asshole."

A silver Nissan Titan pickup rumbled into the gravel parking lot and halted alongside my Toyota. The driver snapped a phone closed, and in the same instant, the connection to my phone went dead. Gino.

And he had a passenger.

The Nissan was a large truck. Despite this, when Gino got out, the impression was like watching a giraffe climb out of a wall locker. His long arms and legs unfolded, his lanky torso straightened, and he stood to a height of six foot four at least.

Gino looked to be in his late twenties. Picture a Mediterranean complexion, Roman nose, and thick glossy hair the envy of any man over forty. He wore a leather Broncos jacket in royal blue and vivid orange. I could tell he liked showing off the jacket, and I'd bet he never took it off, even in the middle of summer.

Another man got out from the front passenger's side of the Titan. He appeared older—mid-thirties—swarthy, and tall, with an unzipped nylon jacket hanging around a doughy middle. He made his way to the front of the truck, where he remained facing me.

They wanted to bully me and I wasn't in the mood to play along. I especially wasn't going to let the "asshole" comment slide.

Gino approached the patio and levered his gangly legs over the wall. Jeans sharply pressed. Cowboy boots shiny as oil.

He sat across from me and placed his long-fingered hands on the table. The top of his jacket hung open and showed a wealth of gold chains, each heavy enough to anchor a small boat.

Gino took a napkin from the holder and reached down to wipe the dust from his boots. A bracelet of chunky gold links dangled from one wrist. He tossed the napkin to the ground.

Outwardly, Gino looked every bit the self-assured hustler except for one detail. His eyes. Instead of arrogance, I saw worry.

I thumbed in the direction of his friend. "Why don't you ask him to join us?"

"Vinny's okay where he's at. I got things to say that are none of his business."

I hoped Gino's secrets dovetailed with mine.

"Adrianna told me you're a private investigator."

Gino knew too much about me and I knew next to nothing about him. But he'd come here to talk and this was my chance to listen and learn.

I said, "That's true."

Gino asked, "What's your concern with Barrett?"

"My client hasn't heard from him."

"Who's the client?"

"A client," I answered. "Let's leave it at that."

"I didn't know Barrett had business in Denver."

"So we're even. I didn't know Barrett had business here." I gave Gino a fake smile.

He reciprocated with an equally fake smile.

"If you think I care about any moneymaking arrangements you had with Barrett or with anyone else"—I made an obvious glance at Vinny—"don't worry about it."

"I'm not."

"Barrett was your friend?"

"We've known each other awhile." Gino's eyes keyed on mine. "You said 'was.' Is he all right?"

"I'm sure he's looked better."

"What's that mean? Is he dead?"

Actually undead. "He's not alive."

"You sure?"

"I saw his remains."

Gino whispered, "Fuck." His lips drew back and showed clenched teeth. He acted like he was going to bite his way out of this problem. "What happened to him?"

"I don't know." About the zombie part. "That's why I'm in Morada."

"Doesn't make any sense. He just disappeared."

"I'm acquainted with Barrett's past," I said. "Seems to me that in your line of work, someone disappearing is an occupational hazard."

"Not in this case. I was supposed to meet Barrett to pay him big. The fucker was always scrambling for money. But he never showed up and I haven't seen him since."

"When was this?" I asked.

"Six weeks ago."

This jibed exactly with what I'd found out about Chambers's final days as a human.

"Where did he go?"

A grim mask settled on Gino's face. "That is what's so spooky about this. I don't want Barrett to end up like this guy."

"What guy?"

Gino unzipped his jacket and reached inside.

I tensed. At the first sign of a gun, I would spring over the table, talons and fangs bared to kill.

Gino raised his other hand. "Relax." He pulled out a folded copy of the *Morada Mountain Weekly* and set it before me.

"You wanna see what's got me spooked? This." He set an index finger over an article "Local Man Missing."

The accompanying photograph was of a dumpy-looking middle-aged man in a cowboy hat smiling for the camera. The article said he had vanished. The police were looking into an accidental death. Maybe he fell off his horse and into a ditch. No reason to alarm the family by mentioning the obvious—foul play and murder.

"What's this got to do with Barrett?"

Gino hunched his shoulders and leaned toward me. "I feel like I'm in the opening minutes of a horror movie. You know when all kinds of freaky gruesome shit happens and no one but the audience has a clue what's going on?"

Sounded like a typical day in my life. "How so?"

"I had another friend disappear. Stanley Novick."

That made three. Chambers. The cowboy. Novick. "What freaky shit happened to him?"

Gino's face grew tight like his insides were compressing. Then his hands shot from the table and he gestured wildly. "He's fucking dead."

Gino's conniption caught me by surprise and I got ready to punch him.

"Stanley didn't stay disappeared for long." Gino scissored a hand over his middle. "I found him with his guts gone." Gino chopped across his thighs. His voice got louder. "Plus both legs."

Words spewed from Gino's mouth like blood gushing from a severed artery. "His skull was empty as a coconut. They took his brains." Gino cupped his hands in offering and practically shouted. "His fucking brains. How sick is that?"

A couple of women at another table stared and then averted their eyes. They gathered their cups and plates and slinked to the café door.

Vinny leaned toward us and cocked an ear.

Gino must have sensed this and turned to Vinny. He waved an okay.

Vinny nodded and relaxed.

Gino's nostrils flared and the breath huffed from his nose. His skin turned white as an eggshell and his expression became as brittle. "Who would do this?"

Hungry zombies. The missing brains were the best clue. As for the guts and legs, the zombie reanimator could've been harvesting parts for new victims.

I said, "I don't know."

Gino asked, "Did Barrett have all his stuff? His arms? His legs? His brains?"

Until Mel sliced and diced him with an excavator. "As far as I could tell."

Gino took the newspaper and shoved it back into his jacket.

"What happened to Stan and Barrett gives me the serious willies. Sometimes there's a scuffle over turf—another gang moving in—and if someone gets his, it's usually a drive-by or a simple one right here." Gino touched the back of his head. "I've heard of Colombians and Mexicans doing crazy torture shit, but that's never happened around here."

A gust of cool, moist air whisked dust across the patio. Napkins fluttered off the tables. Gino put a hand over his forehead to keep the wind from mussing his hair.

Vinny called to him and held up a cell phone. "It's Uncle Sal. We gotta go."

Uncle Sal who?

Gino got up from the table. "My cousin told me that if someone came asking about Barrett, that guy would be the one who knew what the score was."

My *kundalini noir* twitched. Was that guy me? I'd come here unannounced to investigate zombies and psychic signals, and yet Gino's cousin anticipated my arrival.

"What cousin? What score?"

"The disappearances." He backed away, shoulders hunched, as if afraid to say more. "We'll talk again." He stepped over the wall and headed for the Titan pickup.

"When?" I got up to follow.

Vinny scowled and hitched the side of his pants to warn he had a gun handy. In other circumstances, I'd take that gun and give him a bullet suppository. But I couldn't risk the gunplay out here in public, with so many bystanders. For now.

Gino and Vinny got into the Titan and drove off.

I couldn't let Gino get away. He had information that I needed and I was going to get it. Even if it came to gunplay.

CHAPTER 12

Hard drops of rain splashed on my face.

I rushed to my Toyota. I'd follow Gino and find a chance to hypnotize him. I'd learn what he meant by: "My cousin told me that if someone came asking about Barrett, that guy would be the one who knew what the score was."

Who in Morada knew I'd be asking about Barrett?

By the time I reached my truck, I was drenched with rain.

I took out my contacts to track Gino by his aura. He'd be easy to spot. Each psychic envelope was as unique as a face.

His aura looked like a dimpled red balloon while Vinny's resembled a dollop of cinnamon-candy-colored syrup. Stubby tendrils of anxious thoughts poked from each aura.

Gino's Nissan turned left and went east, then north on a county road.

Sheets of heavy rain muted the landscape to blurry shades of gray. The sky became dark as dusk. Drivers turned on their headlights, but I kept mine off so that I could stay hidden from Gino.

My wipers beat across the windshield. The windows started to fog because of my wet clothes, not my heavy breathing. I don't breathe. I turned on the defogger.

We crossed over the Rio Grande. The rain-swollen current roiled around the bridge pilings.

I had no idea where Gino was headed, but no matter, once I caught him, I'd know his secrets.

A half mile later, Gino left the county road for an asphalt single lane.

Leafy shrubs pushed close to the road. Branches slapped my windshield. Gino's aura bounced in the squall like the flame of a candle. Even if he swerved into the brush, I'd still be able to spot him.

To my right, a man and a woman darted between the shrubs. At first, I wondered what they were doing out in this storm. Then I realized: neither of them had an aura.

Zombies.

Change in plans. Gino could wait.

I stepped on the brakes and jerked the steering wheel for a fast U-turn.

The Toyota looped across the rain-slick asphalt. I straightened the wheel and pressed the gas pedal. The rear tires clawed at the road and the truck yawed side to side.

What were zombies doing out now? I thought of them as creatures of the night. Well, vampires get around quite a bit in the daytime. Why shouldn't zombies?

Since they showed no auras, their filthy clothes allowed them to blend chameleon-like in the landscape. I searched for their outlines. I caught them up ahead, lumbering in stooped gaits through the woods.

I pulled off the side of the road.

I reached under my seat and pulled out a Heckler & Koch .45 pistol. Normally, if I needed a gun, I packed a .380. Plenty of firepower to discourage even stubborn humans. In case of vampires, I loaded the .380 with silver bullets. Against zombies I needed something with more oomph, like this .45.

I palmed the gun and got out of the Toyota. The pistol felt heavy and reassuring. Nothing like German firepower as backup to my vampire skills.

Rain dribbled down my face. I wiped my eyes and looked for the zombies' trail.

Two sets of prints trampled the grass. I leaned over to study them and got hit with a double dose of wet garbage smell.

One set of prints was of a man's big bare feet. The other prints looked like they came from a small pair of boots.

I advanced with the H&K and moved the square muzzle left and right like the snout of a dog homing in on the scent.

What were the zombies doing out here? Hunting?

For what?

Who sent them?

Perhaps there was an infestation underground and the rain had forced this pair to the surface like a couple of earthworms.

I would drop them both and go through their clothes. With luck I'd find a lead back to the reanimator.

One of the zombies paused beneath a willow. He wore a tattered straw cowboy hat. At the moment I could see him only in outline, but as I got close I noticed that he was looking back at me.

Layers of flabby skin hung around his neck. He stood bowlegged and barefoot, wore a ragged shirt and tight pants with a big metallic buckle. The boxy shape of his face, the thin eyebrows, and the cowboy hat reminded me of someone I'd recently seen.

The missing cowboy. The zombie's face matched the picture in the newspaper.

He hadn't run away or gotten tangled up with criminals. His fate had been worse.

He'd been a victim of the reanimator.

The cowboy zombie lowered his head and scooted away.

I had seen the tracks of two zombies. Where was his companion?

Cowboy zombie disappeared through a gap in the dense shrubs around a stand of scrub oaks. Plenty of cover to hide for an ambush.

My sixth sense tingled my fingertips and ears.

I crept through the shrubs and under the branches of the oaks. Dumpster funk was all around me, but I had lost the zombies.

The tingling of my fingertips amplified into a buzz. The muzzle of the pistol began to tremble.

The damn zombies were close.

I adjusted my grip on the .45 and held it as steady as I could.

I don't breathe.

Zombies don't breathe.

The only sound was the *drip-drip* patter of heavy drops falling through the leaves.

My wet clothes sucked the heat from my body. The chill squeezed my bones. First I'd kill these zombies and then reward myself with a hot soak and an extra-large martini.

Cowboy zombie appeared in the sumacs at the far end of a grassy open patch. His waterlogged hat drooped around his ears. He wiped an elbow across his belt buckle.

My sixth sense screamed *Trap.*

My senses tingled so hard I couldn't keep the pistol steady and I gripped the H&K with both hands.

I stayed beneath an oak tree and scanned the brush around me. Nothing lurked.

Cowboy zombie was at least fifty feet from me, too far for an accurate shot. But after meeting Barrett, I had learned to keep my distance from these smelly tricksters.

I raised the pistol and centered the sights on his chest.

Pow.

The bullet ripped through his shirt and tore into his sternum in a splat of rotted meat. The impact knocked the hat off his head. The zombie shook and flopped to his back. His heels pawed troughs in the mud and his hands clutched at the wet grass.

Incredibly, he rolled to his knees and retrieved his hat. How unstoppable was he? This H&K could kill a bear.

Exposed ribs flopped hatch-like from his chest. A lump of pulp dropped from the hole. He grabbed the lump and came to his feet. He shoved the lump into the chest cavity and tamped the ribs back into place.

I leveled the sights on his nose. The next shot would blow his head apart like a melon.

The zombie screwed the hat on his head. Mud plopped from the wilted brim. He wiped his belt buckle and shuffled closer as if daring me to shoot again. No problem, I had plenty of bullets for both zombies.

Both zombies?

Where was the other zombie?

This was a diversion.

Stars exploded in my head.

Pain rattled my skull and spine.

My knees buckled.

I rallied and straightened my legs. I pivoted to the left and my gun hunted for the other zombie.

She swung in a blur of arms and legs from an overhead branch. Her boot heels came straight at my face.

I raised my pistol and squeezed off shots in a panicked spasm of self-survival.

More pain thudded across my forehead.

The strength drained from my hips and knees. My legs became jelly. Sharp branches ripped at me while I tumbled.

Tumbled.

Tumbled.

CHAPTER 13

What woke me was the sensation of having a hot iron pressed against my face.

Even with my mind fogged up with pain, I instantly knew what this was.

The morning sun.

My *kundalini noir* shrank and corkscrewed in terror.

I slapped my hands over my face and curled into a ball. Hot rays prickled my skin. I squinted through my fingers.

The gray light of a rainy dawn broke to the east. A semicircle of yellow light hovered over the horizon, marking the place where the sun would rise.

The morning sun, the great devourer of vampires, was an instant away from roasting me into ash.

I lay in a rocky puddle at the bottom of a shallow ravine. I was surrounded by trash, weeds, and trees. My wet clothes were matted with mud and garbage.

My head swam in pain, but unless I moved . . . NOW . . . the next sensation would be cooking alive.

I drew the collar of my coat over my head. I sat up and crawled to the nearest well of shadow.

Sunlight lashed at me. The air burned with microwave intensity.

I splashed through the syrupy mud like a wounded, desperate dog and dove headfirst through the bramble.

I burrowed into a layer of wet dirty leaves. I scooped them over me until I was covered in a paste of leaves and mud. I lay still in the protective coolness while the ravaging sunlight stalked the open ground.

Worms and beetles crawled out from the fetid mud and kept me company by climbing over my face. I cinched my fingers over my nose and kept my eyes clenched tight to keep the visitors out.

A headache banged against the inside of my skull.

I stole a look at my wristwatch. My vision was blurry and I had to study the watch face to read the time. Almost eight. The morning after. The blow to my head had knocked me out all night.

Rain plopped through the leaves overhead. Then more rain. The downpour smothered the sunlight. The worms and beetles vanished as if they'd melted into the mud.

Rain channeled through the tree and came out in a spout from a fork in the trunk. I knelt under the spout to wash away the filth. I relished the cleansing and the reprieve from death. The water poured over me like a baptism.

Why hadn't the zombies finished me off?

Couldn't they find me?

I peered into the ravine. Flattened grass and dislodged rocks marked my path down the slope. Soggy cardboard and paper trash littered the rocky puddle I'd fallen into. No, I had been lying in plain sight.

Maybe the zombies thought they had killed me.

Or maybe they had a more pressing task.

As the rain beat down, I picked my way out of the ravine. I looked for my pistol, which I found in a patch of dandelions. A quick check of the magazine showed I had three rounds left. The muzzle bore was clear but gritty mud remained in the recesses of the pistol. Letting a gun get this dirty—for any reason—was as bad as stealing from your mother.

I scrambled up the ravine and kneeled at the edge. I parted the brush with the barrel of my .45.

No zombies.

Spent cartridge casings glittered in the mud under the oak. Some fight I had put up. I went down making a lot of noise but that was it.

Carefully, I made my way back to my Toyota.

The doors were open and my belongings were scattered over mud torn up by footprints.

If my *kundalini noir* had a mouth, it would've groaned.

My clothes lay in soaked lumps. The cooler sat empty with the lid open and gaping at the rain. The bags of blood looked like silver hamsters where they rested in the mud.

Had the zombies taken anything?

They had.

Now I understood why the zombies had left me alone.

They had found a prize too valuable to waste time killing me.

The psychotronic diviner.

CHAPTER 14

When the Araneum learned that I had lost the diviner, they were going to skin me for sure. My head throbbed harder. My *kundalini noir* sank to the pit of my belly.

Why did the zombies take the diviner? Were they attracted to shiny pretty objects?

Or did they recognize the diviner for what it was? In that case, what did the zombies and their reanimator know about psychic energy and the astral plane? Was he responsible for the psychic attacks? And my hallucinations?

Not all my clothes and belongings had been gone through—my overnight bag and backpack remained unopened. When the zombies found the diviner, they must have lost interest in everything else and hurried away.

The rain let up but the clouds remained low and threatening. Much like my recent bad fortune.

I felt clammy in my wet clothes and had to change. I was

miserable enough on the inside. Might as well be comfortable on the outside.

I gathered my belongings, drove back to town, and found a Laundromat next to a truck stop. My first priority was to wash up and change. With customers wandering in and out of the men's room, for privacy I locked myself in a utility closest. I gave myself a sponge bath, shaved in the mop sink, applied makeup, and put on clean dry clothes.

While my dirty clothes churned in a washing machine, I sat in my Toyota, cleaned my H&K, and inserted a fresh magazine.

This pistol was one of the most powerful in the world but wouldn't do much good if I walked around with my head up my ass.

I'd made one huge mistake as a human—when I'd accidentally killed the Iraqi girl and her family—and that has led me to the path of the undead.

Later I'd made one huge mistake as a vampire—I had let Carmen get kidnapped by the aliens.

The stakes in this investigation were too high for more screwups. The Araneum depended on me. The zombies were a big enough threat in the physical world. What would happen if they got into the astral plane?

But that was speculation about the future. I had to focus on what I could control, the here and now.

I checked my cell phone for messages. Only one. From Gino. The time stamp showed that he had called yesterday evening. About the time I was taking a snooze in a mud puddle courtesy of the zombies.

Gino wanted to meet again, at a restaurant called Humphreys. He gave directions and emphasized the time, noon sharp.

I called back. His voice mail answered. I didn't leave a message.

I clipped a holster to the inside of my waistband. I racked the slide of the H&K to chamber one of the fat .45 rounds.

I reviewed my plan. Question Gino. Under hypnosis. Interrogate Vinny and their uncle Sal. They might know enough to add another piece to the puzzle. Find the creator of the zombies and destroy him and every one of his creatures. Get to the bottom of the psychic energy signals and the hallucinations. Retrieve the psychotronic diviner.

I holstered the pistol.

I was ready for anything.

I had to be.

CHAPTER 15

Humphrey's Kountry Kitchen was on the west end of town, past a Shell station minimart. There were two vehicles in the restaurant parking lot, a Buick LeSabre and a Ford pickup hauling a trailer with a pair of camouflaged quad bikes. I didn't see Gino's silver Nissan Titan.

I was deliberately ten minutes late. Where was he?

I went down a block and turned around. I parked on the shoulder where I could check out the restaurant and the neighborhood.

The rain started again. I looked through the arcs my wipers swished across the windshield. People wandered around the Shell station across the street, moving about the cars and gas pumps, or in or out of the minimart. I studied the dark windows of the buildings facing me, a real estate office and a honey wholesaler.

Maybe Gino had been dropped off at Humphrey's. Either the Buick or the Ford could be his wheels. I flipped open my cell phone and punched his number. His voice mail picked up again.

Where the hell was Gino? He might be sleeping off a hangover, playing errand boy to Uncle Sal, drilling some tail . . . or had the zombies gotten him?

Frustrated and more than a little paranoid, I snapped the phone closed and dropped it into my coat pocket.

Without Gino, I'd be playing Whac-A-Mole looking for clues.

Then again, Gino might be in Humphrey's waiting for me.

I drove to the restaurant and parked beside the Ford pickup. I got out of my Toyota and stepped into a muddy puddle. Goddamn weather. I pulled the collar of my barn coat tight around my neck. Fighting zombies was trouble enough without the misery of getting soaked and cold. This was too much like being back in the army.

A For Sale sign sat in the front window of the restaurant. Guess even mountain views and country living get old.

I started through the front door of the restaurant when the hallucination of the girl came to me, the apparition so real I could almost feel the heat of her body.

If this was a psychic attack, I wouldn't give in.

I planted my feet and stood strong. I imagined swatting the image out of my head. But the hallucination tore into my thoughts.

She called my name. Her voice filled my head, drowning out all other sounds. Its echo bounced inside my skull, gathering volume until her voice became a deafening shriek as loud as a fire alarm.

The top of my spine buzzed. I pressed one hand across the back of my neck to dampen the sensation. The vibration continued down my psychic column and my spine shook.

Panic and fear gouged me to the bone. I stumbled into the restaurant and collapsed on the wooden bench in the foyer.

The shriek halted like someone had turned off a spigot of noise. My head held the fading echo. As my helplessness and panic subsided, my strength returned—and my anger.

Psychic energy attacks. Zombies. Gino's mysterious cousin. The loose ends in this mystery tangled around me.

A woman appeared in the doorway to the dining room. She wore an apron and had a pen stuck in her mop of henna-colored hair. Her eyes and forehead crinkled in worry. "I saw you keel over like you had a seizure or something. You okay?"

"Yeah." On the outside. Inside I was a mess.

"You waiting for somebody?"

Gino, but it wasn't her business. "Sorta."

"Sorta yes or sorta no?" Her tone went from concern to a hard scold. "Either get in or get out. No loitering."

Feisty shrew needed a kick in the butt to learn about customer service. I followed her inside to see if Gino was here.

A pair of elderly couples sat at a square table in the middle of the room. The old women unsnapped clear plastic bonnets they had cinched over their blue hair. The four geezers complained that they couldn't remember when it had been this cold and rainy. Try last year.

Two beefy guys wearing down vests over camouflage hoodies—hunters, I was sure—occupied a booth at the far corner.

No Gino.

The waitress fanned a laminated menu toward the empty booths along the wall. "Your pick."

I took a seat facing the front window and ordered coffee. I sneaked the bag of type O-negative from my coat and squirted the remaining blood into my cup. I stashed the empty bag back into my pocket. I sipped the warm brew and it comforted me like a hug from a chubby hooker.

What now? Where was Gino? Where were the zombies?

My ears tingled, then my fingertips.

Danger.

I set the cup down.

My *kundalini noir* coiled, like a viper ready to strike. I curled my fingers to hide my extending talons.

The hairs on the nape of my neck stood up. A shadow glided across the fogged restaurant window. My fangs pushed down from my gums and threatened to poke out from under my lip.

The front door opened. A figure entered the foyer and stood behind the window separating the foyer from the dining room.

The figure wore a blue hooded slicker. The feminine outline suggested a woman.

It was her.

I could feel it.

The girl in the psychic attacks.

How was this possible?

A prickly sensation trickled from my head to my fingertips and toes.

Her rain-shellacked slicker glistened in the fluorescent light from the foyer ceiling. The brim of the slicker's hood cast a shadow across her forehead to the middle of her face, masking her eyes. Moist strands of brunette hair curled from under the hood.

She clasped the hood in both hands and pushed it up and back as if lifting the visor of a helmet. As she did this, the anticipation turned my stomach into mush.

Her face was on the mature side of adolescence, a woman yet

still retaining the soft lines of a girl's features. The elegant sweep of her nose matched the trace of an elongated face and a delicate chin. Her nose and cheeks were rosy from the outside chill.

This was her.

The girl.

The adolescent girl from my hallucinations. That phoenix who had risen from the ghost of the little Iraqi girl.

The prickly sensation became centipedes digging at my skin. I'm an undead bloodsucker; this creeped-out feeling was not supposed to happen to me.

Her right eye twitched. She rubbed the heel of her hand against the eye. When she brought her hand down, the right eye remained open and still.

Her two dark eyes rested on me, as if I was the only object in the world. The gleam in those eyes bore deep—probing, knowing, menacing.

My *kundalini noir* twisted like it wanted to find a hole and hide.

For a moment, all I could see were her eyes.

The eyes that had haunted me across the oceans and years since I first saw them in Iraq. Deep as wells, dark as the night I'd last seen them.

My fear became cold, heavy, and paralyzing, like I'd been trapped under a giant block of ice.

Her right eye twitched again.

I am vampire—a seasoned warrior, a supernatural killer—and this woman, this ingenue, *this girl with a nervous facial tic,* made me shrink in terror.

CHAPTER 16

My body screamed: *Danger, get away.* This . . . girl . . . woman
. . . whatever . . . was poison. My legs tensed to catapult me
through the roof.

I forced myself to stay put. Since when did I run away?

Relax. Look tough but nonchalant.

Who the hell was she? Why was she here?

She had been only the stuff of hallucinations, but now she was
standing in the doorway.

The girl walked through the foyer into the dining room and
stopped by the counter. Water dripped from the hem of her
slicker and soaked her green sweatpants.

Everyone else in the restaurant seemed to have vanished and
it was only her and me.

My hands trembled.

Control yourself, Felix. Don't let her see you panic.

She had no weapon that I could see. In any other circumstance, a quick bite to her tender neck was the most I'd need to keep her in place. If that didn't work, I'd use the .45. The advantage was mine.

Her right eye twitched again. She blotted her eye. When she lowered her hand, those eyes were no longer threatening but uncertain and vulnerable.

Her spell on me dissolved, slowly.

I looped a hand around my coffee cup to feel the warmth. The others in the restaurant came back into focus: the two hunters at a booth, the four geriatrics at their table, the bitchy waitress marching by with a carafe.

The girl took a halting step. She looked afraid.

Good. She needed to be afraid of me.

Keep looking tough.

I had to see what this woman was. Human? Supernatural? If so, what kind? What did she want? My hands flinched upward to remove my contacts but I hesitated. Too many witnesses.

The girl leaned from one foot to the other as if debating whether to leave or to approach me.

She crossed the floor. Her gaze became fragile. A wrong move on my part and she'd be out the door.

I didn't dare so much as blink.

She stopped beside my booth. Her eyes were a rich honey brown and shiny with fear. This close, I could see fresh pimples on her chin and in the crease along her left nostril.

A teenager. I'd been terrorized by a teenage girl with bad skin.

She reached for the top of her slicker. Was she going for a weapon?

I crossed my arms and set my elbows on the table. I curled my hands and readied my talons.

Without a word, she unzipped her slicker and took a seat on the opposite side of my booth. Her green sweat top said Morada Panthers in yellow script. Water seeped from the folds of her jacket and puddled around her elbows. Her fingers were red and her knuckles white from the outside cold.

She acted scared of me, yet she had come this close.

What did she want?

She took a deep breath and clenched her fists as if steeling herself for a dangerous jump. Her right eyelid blinked repeatedly, semaphoring her anxiety. She put her hand on her upper cheek to keep the eye still.

I smiled to try and put her at ease. After all, I wasn't exactly bad company. At least not in public.

The girl said, "Felix Gomez."

It was the voice that echoed through my hallucinations. It was like a spike had been hammered into my head.

She added, "I know what you are."

The girl had said *what*, not *who*.

The fear returned and my fangs throbbed against the inside of my upper lip.

Her eyes widened as she continued. "You are a vampire."

CHAPTER 17

The girl's words lanced through me.

My brain sputtered in bewilderment, my thoughts misfiring, my body shocked into paralysis.

Slowly, my mind found its track and raced toward one thought.

Kill her.

No human except for a chalice could live with the knowledge of the undead.

I readied my arms for a swipe of my talons across her throat. How far out the door could I get before her blood gushed across the table?

I had murder on my face and the girl saw it. Fear spread into her eyes. The color left her face. She recoiled, and when scooting out of the booth, she noticed my talons.

Her eyes turned back to mine and seemed to pulse.

My name echoed in my head.

Felix . . . ix . . . ix.

The echo amped up to a rush of noise.

I clutched the table to ground myself.

Not again. Not now. Not here.

The echo increased to a ringing shriek. A thousand needles vibrated against the inside of my skull. My vision went blurry and turned the world into a grainy fog.

Everything from my jaw to my balls trembled. My *kundalini noir* quivered like a stick in an earthquake.

Nausea snaked up my throat. Bile pushed over my tongue, bitter and foul.

I started to heave. My arms and legs jerked in spasms. I had the sensation of falling.

My head and shoulder smacked into something hard.

Warm liquid dribbled on my face and chest.

The vibrations stopped. The needles disappeared. The shriek trailed to nothing.

But there was no silence. Someone yelled, a fresh voice that bounced inside my skull. A woman.

"Hey, I asked if you were okay."

My eyes quit shaking and I focused to get my bearings.

I lay at the bottom of the booth and looked up at the underside of the table. Pastel clumps of gum clung to the wood. The liquid dripping on me was coffee.

The waitress crouched beside the booth. She yapped like an angry terrier. "You told me you were okay. Now I find you on the floor about to toss your cookies. You on drugs?"

The bile seeped back down my throat.

"You hear me? Are you on drugs?"

I felt dizzy and sick. "No, I'm not on drugs."

"Then quit acting like you are."

I pushed from the floor and crawled onto the bench. Puddles of coffee rolled across the vinyl upholstery and wet my trousers.

The girl remained at the edge of the booth, frozen, her eyes huge.

She showed no fear that I was a vampire. Some, upon meeting us, turn away and shriek in terror. Others are drawn as if a vampire was what they'd been waiting for all their lives. Still others, like this girl, accepted us vampires with guarded fascination.

Why was she the same girl from my hallucinations? Did she project the psychic signals? Or was she misdirection about the true source?

I sat upright, slowly, to let my head clear.

The waitress picked my coffee cup from the floor. She walked off, grumbling. "If you're sick, the county hospital is up the road. I'm not cleaning up any vomit."

One of the hunters paused in the act of devouring a monster burrito. Red chile sauce dribbled from the mouth in his pumpkin-like head. "Yeah, that was disgusting. I about lost my appetite." He went back to devouring.

I patted my face and hands with a paper napkin to blot the coffee. Carefully, so I wouldn't smear my makeup.

The girl slid into the booth. She tilted her head in amazement as if she'd made a great discovery. The line of her mouth became an amused grin as if I was the butt of a joke.

I was drenched inside out with embarrassment. I'd come to Morada strutting my bad vampire stuff and first the zombies smacked me down, then this girl.

Our waitress came back with a towel. "Tell you what, mister, you take your business elsewhere. Don't worry about the bill."

What could I say? I couldn't make a bigger ass of myself. I tossed a couple of dollars and got up.

The girl stood from the booth and zipped her jacket in a quick, impatient motion. The waitress leaned across the table and wiped as she complained about the meager tip.

The girl and I retreated for the door. We were quiet but hardly inconspicuous.

The four geezers watched in astonished curiosity, the liver spots on their withered skin darkening, their rheumy eyes swimming behind enormous spectacles.

Getting kicked out of the restaurant worked to my favor. With no witnesses, I could act against the girl.

She pulled the hood of her slicker over her head. We stepped into the cold rain.

I needed to learn what she knew about psychic energy and zombies. But more important, was she responsible for my hallucinations?

"Who are you?"

She turned to face me. "Phaedra Nardoni."

So I had a name. That was a start.

Phaedra continued to the 4Runner. She waited by the front passenger door, her shoulders hunched against the rain. Vapor puffed from her mouth.

How did she know this was my vehicle? How much did she know about me? My talons inched from my fingertips.

Her gaze shot to my talons, then my face. The gleam in her eyes pulsed once in warning, like the hammer of a gun cocked back.

That gleam was enough to make my *kundalini noir* catch like it was about to feel a stake. She *was* responsible for the hallucinations. In the restaurant, when I climbed off the floor, the girl acted as if she was as surprised by what happened as I was. If she didn't know it then, she knew it now. This power—a psychic attack—was her weapon.

At the moment, I had no defense. She could get inside my brain at will. The violation I had known before returned.

I felt myself falling inward again in search for what I could trust, what I could believe, what I could control.

Any hesitation she had when we first met was gone. She stood waiting, defiant with confidence and awareness.

I asked, "You're Gino's cousin?"

"Yeah. He told me about you."

I sorted through my questions. How much did he say? What about the zombies? Did she know about them?

But first, "So where is he?"

"I don't know," she answered. "I came to the restaurant looking for him."

A gust of wind sprayed rain into our faces. I let the water drip. Phaedra wiped her cheeks.

She stamped her feet. "It's cold. Let's get in your truck already."

I needed to remove my contacts and confirm what kind of creature Phaedra was. I've run across humans with supernatural abilities before but none compared with Phaedra's. I had one weapon in reserve. Once alone, in private I would zap her and it would be my turn to mess with her head.

I eased close to unlock her door. A sniff didn't detect the smell of anything undead or unusual.

My nose cataloged the aromas: the wet fabric and plastic of her clothes; the fragrance of moist hair with perfumed shampoo and conditioner; the scent of a flowery deodorant threaded with her perspiration and the rich, intoxicating bouquet of female pheromones.

She wasn't vampire. Or zombie. Despite her psychic powers, Phaedra seemed very human.

We got in and buckled up. Phaedra fumbled with the right pocket of her slicker and drew a pint bottle of water. She pulled at the pour top and chugged a long swallow.

This was the first time I've been this close to a girl her age since I was a boy her age. I wallowed in the forbidden sensuous delight of her tempting adolescence.

"How old are you?" I asked.

"Sixteen."

Sixteen. The number sliced into me like a piece of shrapnel. If the girl in Iraq had been twelve, she'd be Phaedra's age by now. Had she lived.

But Phaedra was not the girl I had killed in Iraq. Why did her face keep showing up in the hallucinations? Did it have to do with the psychic signals tapping the guilt inside of me, the guilt I've been yoked with since I helped kill the Iraqi girl? A guilt that had resurfaced and festered since I've lost Carmen?

Here was Phaedra, another woman careening into my life. We sat alone in my Toyota, the metal and glass cocoon a shelter from casual voyeurs.

She put her hand on mine, her warm touch inviting. There was a tiny quiver in her fingertips, yet she wasn't afraid. Phaedra's large brown eyes remained guarded but inquisitive.

Her fingers clasped my wrist. I could've broken free but remained transfixed, wondering about this mysterious young woman.

"What do you want, Phaedra?"

"It's simple. You have to keep me from dying."

CHAPTER 18

Phaedra was dying? And she needed my help?

I said, "I don't understand."

"You're a vampire, right?"

My fangs sprouted to combat length. My muscles tightened like springs.

Phaedra's eyes locked and loaded. Don't mess with me.

I didn't need another psychic brain scramble. The murderous vampire routine wasn't working, so I bent the rule about having to immediately kill her for knowing about the undead.

I gave a parting flash of my fangs as they retracted. "Yes, I am a vampire." I motioned from her head to my mine. "What about you? Where does that mind power thing come from?"

"I don't know. No one but you believes that I have it."

The Araneum knew about psychic signals. Perhaps the zombies did as well. "Trust me, I believe you." Had she discussed this with someone else? "I'm not the only one you've talked to about this?"

She replied, "That's right. I've been in therapy for my hallucinations."

Therapy? Hallucinations?

Phaedra reached into the left pocket of her slicker and pulled out a couple of small plastic bottles, one white, the other amber. "These are my meds."

Wads of bills tumbled from her pocket. She scrambled to catch them with a clumsy, embarrassed grab.

I scooped the bills that had fallen over the center console. The bills were twenties and a hundred.

She took the money from me and shoved it back into her pocket. "It's my . . . allowance."

Quite a hefty allowance. The hesitation in her voice told me there was more about the money she didn't want to explain.

I took the bottles of meds. The prescription label on the white bottle said: Haloperidol tab .5 mg. The label on the amber bottle: Nortriptyline cap 25 mg.

I returned the bottles. "What is the problem?"

Phaedra dropped the bottles in her pocket and snapped the flap. "The meds are for hallucinations and mood swings. And spasms." She pointed to her twitching right eye. Next she extended both hands and the fingertips showed a slight tremble. "I have Huntington's chorea."

"I left my medical dictionary at home. You better explain."

"Basically, my brain is rotting from the inside out." Phaedra said this with less emotion than I've heard from others complaining about a broken fingernail. "It's hereditary. My mother died of it when she was thirty-two."

"You seem calm about it. If I had this disease, I'd be shitting my pants."

"That's not funny. I lose control sometimes and have shit in my pants. So no more shit jokes, okay?"

Okay. Better that I look sympathetic. "You're sure you have Huntington's?"

"One hundred percent positive. I might live to thirty. Most likely twenty-eight."

Dead at twenty-eight? Wasn't a diagnosis but a death sentence. I'd really be shitting my pants. "With a diagnosis like that, you seem almost cheery."

"Because I have a way out."

"Which is?"

"You."

"Me?"

"Make me a vampire and I won't die."

My *kundalini noir* lunged in attack. I clenched my muscles to keep from showing the reaction.

"In case you're unfamiliar with the concept, we vampires are undead. We exist with one foot in the grave. Sometimes we sleep there. Being a vampire is no picnic."

"Neither is dying of Huntington's."

"We have other problems."

She asked, "Do vampires die of Huntington's?"

"Not that I know of. We're immune to most human diseases. How do you know about vampires? About me?"

"My hallucinations."

"How?"

"I get images in my head."

"Images?"

"Perceptions. I wish I could explain it better but I can't. It's like describing colors to the blind, sounds to the deaf." Phaedra stared at the dashboard. For an instant, her eyes turned vacant. "I send out special 'thoughts' and they wrap around what they find. At first I didn't understand what I was seeing. Over time, I learned to focus my thoughts and I began to create sharper perceptions of *things*."

"What things?"

"Things in a place."

"Place?"

"A gigantic void. Like another world with nothing in it but a way to get from one location to another."

Was Phaedra talking about the astral plane?

She continued, "We have time and space and I've found something more. In this void I can see another side to everything."

Void? She must've read the confusion on my face, and her forehead clenched in frustration. "Sorry, that's not the right word, but I can't think of a better one. Being in this void made me think differently about the world. I began searching. Maybe in this void, this dimension, I'd find it."

"Find what?"

"A chance to not die like my mother. What happened to her was so wrong." Phaedra's eyes glistened. "Day by day, she lost more and more control over her body and mind. The Huntington's took everything. I remember finding her on the floor helpless with a puddle of mess between her legs."

Tears pooled in Phaedra's eyes, the drops fat and heavy with sadness. "I cleaned her up. I could read the awful question in her face. *Why?* I felt so ashamed for her. And I knew that's what waited for me."

How wrenching, but I wasn't much for the emotional wringing needed to drive these heart-to-heart talks, especially since I had no heart. "The Huntington's is responsible for your hallucinations and that in turn has led you to . . ." I didn't want to say astral plane, so I said, "the void."

"Seems that way."

In a cruel twist, nature had compensated Phaedra. What a trade: get psychic power at the expense of your brain turning to mush.

The inside of the windows by Phaedra had fogged up. The windows around me were still clear.

I asked, "You looked for me?"

Phaedra wiped a spot on the passenger window. Rain dribbled along the outside glass. "I didn't know what I was looking for. You are what showed up."

"How did you know it was me?"

"It was like I was walking inside your head."

Phaedra said this casually, but she had been privy to my most buried thoughts. My skull seemed to split open and let a rush of violation flood my brain.

I felt the withdrawal from the world. I clutched at the steering wheel and forced myself to remain engaged in the present.

Phaedra said something.

I was still a little off center. "What?"

"When is it going to happen?"

"It, what?"

"When are you going to turn me into a vampire?"

I tightened into combat mode, taut as the trip wire of an antipersonnel mine. She mentioned vampires and my reaction was to kill her.

What did Phaedra know about this vampiric existence? The lurking on the fringes of civilization. The masquerading as an ordinary human. The fear of discovery. The terror of the morning sun. The long stretch of immortality without the sanctuary of real family and love.

As a soldier I had killed one little girl and that tragedy had since defined my life. I hadn't turned anyone and promised myself that I wouldn't condemn another soul to my fate.

I said, "I won't do it."

"Why? Isn't that what you vampires live for?"

"Not this one."

Phaedra studied me like she hadn't quite figured me out and was looking for the hidden buttons to push.

"There's another reason I'm here," I said. "Barrett Chambers."

I expected Phaedra to recoil in surprise. She didn't.

I asked, "Do you know what happened to Barrett?"

Phaedra nodded. "He became like the others."

CHAPTER 19

Was Phaedra talking about zombies? Now we're making progress. "What do mean 'the others'?"

"I don't know what else to call them. They move through the void but they are not alive. And they're not dead."

I wanted to fill in the blanks by mentioning that Barrett had been a zombie, but the less Phaedra—a human—knew about the supernatural world, the better to protect the Great Secret.

Zombie behavior was new to me. So were psychic signals and Phaedra's use of the astral plane. Maybe the geniuses of the Araneum could figure it out. For now, what mattered was that Phaedra was in the middle of this supernatural whodunit.

I had part of my mystery solved. I knew the cause of the psychic signals and who was responsible. "How long have you been going into this void?"

"Years. Most of the time I didn't know what I was doing. Whenever I mentioned it, the docs would up my meds. See this"—she pointed to the zits in her face—"side effect of the haloperidol. Plus dry mouth." She swigged from her bottle. "The images didn't stop, I only quit talking about them. I kept sending signals and seeing what I could learn."

"What about what you did to me today at the restaurant? What kind of a signal was that?"

"Don't blame me," she replied. "That was a reaction to you. When you showed your claws and I saw the look on your face, my thoughts lashed out."

"I promise to behave myself," I said, knowing this was one promise I would always have trouble keeping. "You said your mother has passed on. Where's your dad?"

Phaedra gave a chuckle that said, *Him? Like he matters in my life.* "My father's doing life in Trenton, New Jersey. For murder. He doesn't speak to me, and I don't speak to him. I'm sure he preferred being locked up to dealing with me and my mom. You know, the Huntington's."

"Who are you living with?"

"Right now? My uncle Sal."

"Gino's father?"

"No. Uncle. He's Sal Cavagnolo. For years I was passed among the relatives. Try being the crazy orphan girl going through puberty."

"What's that mean?"

"It means I gave my first blow job when I was eleven. I got laid when I was thirteen."

Eleven? Thirteen? Disturbing to the point of revulsion.

I didn't kiss a girl until I was fifteen. By that age, Phaedra was well acquainted with men and their dirty cocks.

She rattled the pills in her pocket. "Another side effect of these is increased sex drive. Not that I needed an excuse. I was dying anyway, so fucking was a good way to pass the time and make money. What was I waiting for? Usually it was better than watching television. Even with a scumbag like Barrett."

"You slept with him?"

Phaedra gave a devilish laugh. "I never slept with anyone. But if you want to know, I didn't have sex with Barrett. He paid me twenty dollars to look at my titties."

"And that's it?"

"No. I had to watch him jack off." Phaedra put a charge in her voice like she took pleasure shocking me.

Which she didn't. Instead I pitied her. Her story explained the "allowance" money that had fallen out of her pocket. She was dying and traded her youthful innocence for fast, cheap thrills.

"Don't look so sad," she taunted. "I learned lots about sex and even more about the way the world works."

"And your uncle Sal?" I hadn't met the guy but I had already pegged him as a rat. If he abused Phaedra, this was another reason to hang him by his tail.

"Uncle Sal's been good to me. Around him, I can pretend I'm not the family's dirty secret. But my aunt Lorena, Sal's wife, hates me. She sees the effect I have on men. She calls me the *strega*, witch." Phaedra gave a grin that was both ironic and condescending. "I don't know what makes my relatives more uncomfortable. That I'm dying of Huntington's or that I know who among them is a child molester."

"And Gino?"

"He's been okay. Nothing happened between him and me. Besides Uncle Sal, Gino's the only friend I've had in the family."

"Does Gino know about your reputation as a *strega*?"

"He says I'm the nicest of the witches in our family."

"Any idea where I could find him?"

"I know where he lives." Her side of the Toyota was completely fogged up. She adjusted the heater vents to clear the windows.

I drove from the restaurant parking lot. Phaedra gave directions west. "Go half a mile and get ready for a left."

My sixth sense gave an electric pulse, though I suspected it was from my own misgivings rather than from an actual threat. Phaedra knew a lot about me. Too much. The scary part was that she learned it by going straight to my psyche.

I had to learn everything I could about her and confirm how much of the Huntington's was true.

We approached the spur of the mountain where it crowded against the highway.

Phaedra pointed. "Here."

I made the left turn and stopped in front of the county hospital. I fished a street map from between my seat and the center console. The county road went south along Pinos Creek. To the right, the vista remained open farmland; to the left, the ground rose into steep, rocky hills that lead to Horseshoe Mountain. The rainy fog turned the mountain into a jagged gray hump.

I put the map away and continued. We drove past a few houses.

Another county road branched from the right. We kept on the original road, passing a power relay station behind a tall wire fence, and proceeded south on the incline up the narrowing valley. No one but us fools would be out in this rain and gloom. I was sure we'd be alone for a long time.

I pulled onto a wide muddy shoulder and halted.

"What's the matter?" Phaedra scanned the instrument panel.

"I need answers." I removed the contacts from my eyes and looked at her.

Phaedra's aura burned red, a typical human psychic shroud. Not vampire orange. Nor alien yellow. Just plain human red.

The penumbra broke into sharp points like it was covered in finger-sized thorns. I kept my hypnosis power in check, as I wanted to read her raw emotions.

Phaedra's expression held an awed, fearful look like she'd put her face close to an open furnace.

I gave a leer and exposed the long fangs jutting from my upper lip.

Her aura flashed neon-bright with terror.

Good. She wanted a vampire, here I was.

Now for my questions. I blasted her with hypnosis. Her expression softened and her aura took the form of translucent gel.

I focused my gaze deep into the psychic conduit of those brown eyes. "Tell me your story. What do you know about the psychic world and what do you want from me?"

Under the power of my hypnosis, she had no choice but to tell me what I wanted to hear.

The truth.

CHAPTER 20

The tendrils withdrew into the sheath of Phaedra's aura. Her lips parted and her eyes looked into the faraway.

To deepen the hypnosis, I grasped both of her hands and massaged the webs of flesh between the thumbs and index fingers. I could've fanged her but I didn't want my mouth close to her skin. Enough creeps had taken advantage of her and I didn't want to be on that list.

Her hands had smooth, unblemished adolescent skin. Her fingernails were ragged from where she'd been chewing on them.

To verify what Phaedra had told me, I went through the items she'd mentioned. Her name. The Huntington's. The details between Gino and herself. How much she knew of her family's criminal pursuits. What about the source of her psychic powers?

It was all as she'd originally told me.

And the zombies? She had no knowledge of zombies except to call them "the others." Those between the living and the dead.

Like me. But different. Good, I didn't want to be confused with zombies.

It's a crapshoot with hypnosis. When you go deep into the subconscious there's all kinds of junk cluttering the mind. Sometimes you get right to the "truth," like with Phaedra. Other times, sifting for answers was like dredging through mud, and there were the instances where you got a subject who gushed like a broken faucet.

I ordered Phaedra to sleep while I kept kneading her hands. Her head tipped forward and her breathing became heavy.

I let go of her hands and replaced my contacts.

"On three, wake up," I said. "One." I brushed back a wet curl that fell across her face. "Two." I settled into my seat. "Three."

Phaedra's right eye twitched. She blinked and looked around the interior of the 4Runner.

"You okay?" I asked.

Phaedra checked the front of her jacket. Her expression turned cross. "What did you do?"

"Nothing."

"Bullshit."

"You think you know about vampires? Then if you're with a vampire, you gotta expect all kinds of weird shit. But I didn't touch you if that's what you want to know."

Phaedra fumed, angry and perplexed.

I put the shift lever into drive. "Do you want to help me find Gino or should I take you back into town?"

She slugged from her bottle. "I'm no chickenshit. Let's go to Gino's."

I angled from the shoulder and onto the asphalt. "How close are we?"

"Keep going. Past the wooden fences. I'll tell you when."

The mountain pressed against us from the right. To the left, the bottom of the valley widened and narrowed as the stream meandered through aspen thickets. Dense clusters of yellow leaves clumped around the pale, straight trunks. In the flat areas along the stream sat houses, ranging from Airstreams on blocks, to log cabins with porches and garages, to expensive ranchettes with horses and corrals.

White wooden fences bounded the more imposing properties. The white fences became ordinary wood, then simple straight posts holding up wire. After a while, the posts turned crooked and the tangled wire fencing appeared as if it had been scrounged from a salvage yard.

Phaedra sat up and brought her face closer to the windshield. Her breath fogged the glass for an instant before evaporating. "Go past the barn, then take a left at the first dirt road past the fence."

Clouds sank between the mountains like big wet blankets and drenched the air with a steady drizzle.

A red barn loomed out of the mist. Muddy tracks veered off the asphalt. I slowed down.

"Wrong road," Phaedra said. "Keep going past the fence."

I gave the Toyota a little pedal but kept the speed low. I didn't want to lose the fence as scrub bushes hid the posts and thick mist camouflaged the barbed wire.

Phaedra gave a heads-up about the fence line. The strands of barbed wire became slack and disappeared into the weeds.

The ground on the left dropped abruptly and an arrangement of rocks marked the entrance of a dirt road down the incline.

"This is it," Phaedra said. She drew even closer to the windshield to peer over the left fender.

I halted for a moment. The asphalt here was clean, indicating no one had recently come onto the county road. I didn't see any fresh tire tracks in the mud going the other way. No one, it seemed, had been at or left Gino's lately, by car anyway. I put the Toyota into four-wheel drive, just in case the ruts got deep.

Electric lines on tall poles ran parallel to the dirt road. We circled the northern border of the property with the red barn. The road cut through a grove of junipers to a flat stretch of mud and grass. Yellow aspen peeked from behind the dark green junipers.

Phaedra pointed ahead. "That's it."

A long one-story house sat on the right side with Gino's silver Titan pickup parked next to it.

Overlapping siding painted pastel yellow covered the building. A gray satellite dish pointed up from the corner of the roof closest to us. Water dripped over the tops of the rusted gutters. The place reminded me of government housing on an Indian reservation.

I slowed to a crawl and thought about putting Phaedra under again so I could scope the area sans contacts. But if I kept hypnotizing her, she'd wonder about the gaps in her memory and lose trust in me.

The house looked deserted. I halted the Toyota and paused. I put my sixth sense on maximum gain and detected nada.

Phaedra chewed on a fingernail. "Gino should be here."

"Does he live alone?"

"Yeah, mostly. Sometimes his friends crash and he's got girls spending the night."

"Maybe he's at their houses?"

Phaedra shrugged.

I couldn't be as complacent. This started because of a zombie.

Gino contacted me to investigate the details behind the mutilations and deaths of his riffraff comrades. Now I was here and Gino was missing.

I eased alongside the Titan. Phaedra didn't wait for me to stop before popping the door. As soon as the Toyota quit rolling, she sprang out and circled for the front of the house.

I palmed my H&K .45 and got out. This time, I see a zombie, I'm going to pump him so full of lead he could be used as ballast on a freighter.

I stood for a moment and absorbed the ambience. The fog muffled noise and added a melancholy texture to the afternoon. I sniffed damp earth and the faint scent of a cedar fire from a distant chimney. I focused my sixth sense like a ray and scanned the building, the road, the surrounding tree line, the open grassy area to my right, the wall of mountain behind us. Everything seemed normal.

Phaedra cupped her hands against the front window and peered inside. Her breath fogged the glass. She wiped the spot clean and peered again. She backed away and shook her head. *No Gino.*

I tried the aluminum screen door at the entrance. Locked. I gave the knob an extra twist and broke the deadbolt. The main door was also locked.

Phaedra dragged a plastic milk crate under the window. She stood on the crate and jimmied open the sliding glass window. Moving quick as a squirrel, she levered one leg over the windowsill and tumbled inside.

Me and my vampire superpowers remained outside, still screwing with the door.

Phaedra screamed.

Chapter 21

I charged the door and kicked it off the hinges.

The odor of human gore filled my nose. Dried blood, lots of it.

I entered the room, pistol held at the ready, fangs extended, my nerves tingling. My *kundalini noir* tightened into a protective coil.

Phaedra was doubled over against the wall, between a couch and an upright lamp. She gasped in the effort to speak.

I made a shush motion.

Phaedra covered her mouth and withered, sliding down the wall to the baseboard.

The front room had an ugly plaid couch, coffee table and end tables covered in vinyl woodprint, and mismatched lamps. A bong, a lighter, and a bag of pot sat on the coffee table.

Blood on the carpet trailed from the hall on my left and to the kitchen in front of us.

The kitchen table was on its side, two legs broken off, and the chairs scattered like they'd been thrown aside.

I crept along the wall, my eyes peering down the sights of my .45, and turned the corner into the bedroom.

Blood-soaked bedcovers lay twisted from the mattress and across the floor to the hall. A heap of clothes covered a chair in the corner. The butt of a pistol stuck out from under the only pillow along the headboard. A cell phone was plugged into a charger on the nightstand.

Tough guy Gino must have been asleep, taken by surprise, and dragged out. I didn't see evidence—women's clothing, for example—that indicated he hadn't been alone.

Congealed drops of blood clung to the headboard. If he had been clubbed on the head, there would be a fine spray of blood spatter across the headboard and walls. From the looks of the blood pattern, I guessed that he had been stabbed and the drops on the headboard were what had flown off the blade.

Phaedra appeared in the doorway. One hand still covered her mouth and she looked liked she was about to throw up.

I backtracked from the bedroom and examined a ruffled trail on the carpet nap. Phaedra put her free hand on my shoulder and stayed close.

Our boots left dirty tread marks. There was a series of faint shoe prints across the middle of the carpet; one had heels like a men's shoe, the other a continuous sole like the bottom of a cross-trainer. Not much mud in these prints. The zombie attack happened before today's rain had started.

Another detail. These prints didn't match those of yesterday's zombies. Meaning, at least two more zombies for a total of four.

When I stopped for a closer look, Phaedra bumped against me and recoiled, startled.

A wide shallow mark showed where a heavy object had been dragged, probably Gino's body. Considering all the blood spilled in the bedroom, there were only scattered drops on the hall carpet. Whoever took Gino must've wrapped him in a blanket or bedsheet. Either that or he didn't have much blood left when they carried him out.

The table and chairs in the kitchen had been pushed aside to clear a path to the back door. Cornflakes littered the floor. Maybe I'd luck out and find a bloody handprint on the door. No, the doorknob and frame were clean.

The back door was shut but didn't look right. I adjusted my grip on the pistol. I hooked the edge of the door with my shoe toe and pulled. The door swung open. The knob clattered to the floor. The back screen door lay twisted in a puddle of rainwater on a concrete patio slab.

I paused at the threshold. A weedy yard gave way to junipers and Ponderosa pines climbing up the hill behind the house. A metal tube snaked to a white propane tank in the yard. I studied the muddy ground beside the tank and saw no tracks or evidence that someone hid behind it. Convinced that no surprises waited, I stepped out and examined the patio slab.

Rain splashed into a line of pink puddles between the door and the far end of the slab. They had carried Gino this way. I crossed the slab and looked for prints in the mud or a path broken through the weeds. The few remaining footprints had been obscured by the rain.

The weeds and grass were bowed in two trails leading east, toward the creek. They had left several hours ago. I didn't see any point in following. The rain would've obliterated their prints and I couldn't leave Phaedra behind.

They had gone east. What was there?

Gino was a big guy, how had they trucked him off? In a litter carry, or was he chopped into convenient, easy-to-carry pieces?

Back inside, I found Phaedra leaning against the refrigerator, hugging herself and trembling. She mumbled, "At least they didn't cut him to pieces like they did Stanley."

I wouldn't be too sure. "You mean Stanley Novick?"

"Yeah."

"How'd you know him?"

"Through Gino. He told me what happened."

Why had they taken Gino instead of leaving his mutilated corpse?

Phaedra's right eye blinked so fast I thought her eyelids would spring loose. She pressed it with the palm of her hand.

We had broken into Gino's house and tracked mud and left our marks over everything. I wasn't interested in preserving the crime scene. This wasn't *CSI*, I was after zombies.

I took her free hand. She wouldn't move.

"Come on," I said, "there's no point in staying."

I led her out the front door. She followed in a faltering shuffle.

We got back to the 4Runner. Phaedra opened the door and reached for her water bottle. She dug the meds from her slicker. Her trembling hands rattled the bottles. She took a tiny blue pill and a red-and-yellow capsule and downed them with a gulp of water. Her right eye kept blinking and she pressed her hand over it.

"You better?" I asked.

Phaedra lowered her hand. Her eyes became hard as marbles with a look that accused me of causing her troubles.

The echo began.

I covered my ears and locked my legs to keep from stumbling. "Goddamn it," I yelled, "stop that."

The echo crashed like it rang from enormous bronze bells. The vibration shot from my brain and down my spine. My hips gave out and I sank to my knees. "What do you want from me?" I screamed.

The echo quit. I blinked, grateful that my head was quiet and clear. The front of my trousers were soaked from kneeling in the mud.

Phaedra looked down at me. Rain dripped from her slicker. "Don't ever patronize me. Don't take me for granted."

"I haven't. I won't. What gave you that idea?"

Phaedra propped the Toyota's front door open, sat inside, and waited. "So we understand each other, okay?"

Yeah, we understood each other. I had my duty to perform. I straightened upright. "Okay. Sure." My wet trousers pressed against my knees.

"You know who the others are, don't you?" Phaedra asked.

"I do."

Phaedra pulled a handkerchief from her pocket and cleaned her nose. "This is all a big secret, isn't it? You as a vampire. The others."

"It is."

"Why?"

"There's a world parallel to the human one. You've discovered a way into it." Mud had splashed on the slide of the pistol. I used my cuff to buff away the smudges. "This world is full of vampires and other supernatural creatures."

"Why is it a secret?"

"Because we can't trust humans."

"Why?" she asked.

"Humans are the most treacherous and cruel of all creatures." Add to that equation Phaedra with her mental mojo. "They wouldn't hesitate to destroy us."

"How can humans be worse than the ones who killed Gino?"

"I'm not going to debate that right now." I racked the slide and caught an ejected cartridge in the palm of my left hand. The gun should fire, no problem. "What's important is that we have a strict rule about revealing the existence of the supernatural world."

"What's the rule?" Phaedra asked.

"If a human finds out about the existence of vampires"—I pointed the pistol at her—"I'm supposed to kill them. Like I have to kill you."

CHAPTER 22

If the echo started, *blam*, Phaedra would eat a .45 slug.

No echo. Only her eyes looking back at me. Red and puffy like a pair of bruised welts. They said: *Go ahead.*

I already had enough guilt over killing one girl. I didn't need more from killing another.

Where would I go from here? Now that I've confirmed the zombie attacks, I was sure I could find them on my own. I no longer needed Phaedra.

The Araneum had ordered me to find the source of the psychic signals. I hadn't been told what to do next.

But Phaedra knew too much about vampires and the supernatural world. Then again, every human she had shared this information with—her doctors, therapists, family—all thought she was nuts. No one would believe these stories.

I'd use this as wiggle room around the rule.

I lowered the pistol.

Phaedra's lips crooked in triumph. "Every rule has an exception, right?"

"Always." I slipped the .45 into its holster.

"I thought so." Phaedra slammed her door closed.

The rule had only one exception that allowed humans to live with the knowledge of vampires. Those humans must be chalices, sworn to never reveal the Great Secret or else get killed.

Phaedra wasn't a chalice. I couldn't bring myself to drink her blood.

The other way would be to turn her into a vampire, a request she'd already made. But she was only sixteen and I'd already decided not to fang her. I haven't turned anyone yet and I had no plans to, especially a young woman like her.

Every time I dwelled on Phaedra, my thoughts curved back to the memory of the Iraqi girl. In my mind, Phaedra and the Iraqi girl were practically conjoined. I had already killed one, I wouldn't harm the survivor.

I got in the driver's seat and started the engine.

Phaedra asked, "Who are the others? What kind of monsters are they?"

"You gotta make a promise." I drove from Gino's house. "You have to keep this a secret."

"And if I don't?"

I stepped on the brake. "It's not my rule, okay? You violate this rule, we both die. It's that simple."

She gave a petulant sneer.

My talons extended, quick as wasp stingers. My arms were about to snap at her and I fought to keep them close to my side, my hands quaking from the effort.

Terror sparked in Phaedra's eyes. For a moment she made no

motion other than to let out a nervous exhale. Her right eye started that nervous tic. She gulped and said, "Hurt me if that's what makes you feel better. I won't stop you." Her expression hardened in contempt. "You might even like it."

The words sounded practiced. Evil. I had the image of sadistic uncles and cousins whipping her naked back and ass with belts to punish her for their sins.

I wasn't one of them, but Phaedra had to know the consequences to both of us.

My talons withdrew and I slowly and carefully put my hand on her knee. "You talk, we die. For me, I know it won't be pleasant. Understand?"

Phaedra's eyes said: *so what?*

"You don't understand." I let go of her knee and settled into the driver's seat. "I'm scared of what could happen. Me. A vampire. Think about that."

"Scared of what?"

"Other vampires. The ones in charge of keeping us a secret."

"What would they do?"

"Skin me alive. To a human? Something worse."

"How many vampires?" she asked.

"Thousands at least."

She folded her hands on her lap, not in surrender but to bide time. "All right. I'll do as you tell me."

Good. I smoothed my coat. I drove the Toyota toward the county road. I felt relieved for two reasons. First, Phaedra understood what was at stake. Second, I'd gotten the point across that her psychic powers couldn't always protect her.

She put a hand to her blinking eye to keep it still. "You were going to explain about the others."

Might as well tell her. I was miles past the line I was never supposed to cross. "Zombies."

Her eyes moved in a searching pattern. She gave a tiny chuckle. "This is all crazy."

She shut her eyes tight, so tight that her eyelids seemed glued together. "Maybe this is a hallucination."

"Phaedra," I said, "open your eyes and deal with this. You wanted to know. Here it is. Gino's dead. So is Stanley. Zombies killed them. And you wouldn't have recognized Barrett. None of this is a hallucination. You could be next."

Phaedra kept silent and stared out the windshield.

We trekked north, down the canyon.

"What are they like?" she asked. "The zombies?"

"Disgusting. Revolting."

"How are you better than them?"

I laughed. "Don't put me in the same category. They're walking bags of septic waste. Besides, Gino asked me for help, right? I'm the good guy in this story, aren't I?"

"Are you?"

"For your sake, you better hope I am."

"And your job is to wipe them out?" she asked.

"As extinct as possible."

"Does the government know about them?"

"Our government knows a lot of stuff." The feds certainly knew about aliens and UFOs. "But zombies? I don't think so."

I better be right. Otherwise our government had their greedy, scheming hands on the supernatural. We'd be enslaved and destroyed.

The rain lifted. The clouds parted and sunbeams bore down from the sky. Where they touched, they illuminated the ground with a searing brilliance. The autumn colors—the yellow aspens, the red cottonwoods, the orange gooseberries and currants—made the landscape as brilliant and lively as a fresh oil painting. My eyes stung from the intense light and I put on my sunglasses.

The clouds dissolved, and when the road turned level and the land flattened into planted fields, the sky was an azure blue.

Phaedra turned off the heater and unzipped her slicker. She squirmed in her seat. Her breasts, round as apples, filled the front of her sweat top. The shoulder belt lay snug between her breasts and emphasized the swell of each firm boob. B-cups for sure. Maybe Cs. The yellow stripe on her sweatpants followed the curve of a shapely thigh. She looked as fertile as the moist farmland.

Her scents—from the damp hair, shampoo, soap, her perspiration—made Phaedra a smorgasbord of temptation.

Bloodsucking pussy hound that I am, I had scruples. Regarding sex, I don't go where I'm not invited. In Phaedra's case, I wouldn't consider an invitation.

"You're quiet," she said, not pulling her eyes from the road.

"There's a lot on my mind."

"About Gino?" She arched her back and those fine titties pushed against the sweat top. "Or something else?"

That "something else" hovered in the air for longer than I should've let it. Minutes ago, Phaedra was buried in sorrow. Now she teased. Was this hot-cold emotional routine a family trait? Maybe growing up around career criminals had taught her how to flip between feelings as easily as turning a page in a book.

I had to change the subject. "How much do you know about your family business?"

"Is that important?"

I let my foot off the gas. "Here's another rule. I ask a question, you give a straight and complete answer. If I ask, consider it important."

She put those brown eyes on me and they were stormy with resentment. "I'm not supposed to talk about what I know or don't know. In our family business, silence is golden. Anything less than golden is . . ." Phaedra pantomimed putting a gun to her head. "Even for me."

I pressed the gas. The Toyota lurched forward and we rocked against our seats.

"Your family and the business have new priorities. You saw what happened to Gino. Unless I stop the zombies, keeping the family secrets is going to be easy because all of you will be dead."

Phaedra's face softened, then hardened, her eyes moving left and right as thoughts jumbled in her head.

I could use hypnosis but I wanted Phaedra to make the decision to trust me. "What do you know about the family business? Is it drugs?"

"Mostly. What they don't handle directly, they collect a tax from anyone smuggling through this area."

"Tax? Protection money?"

Phaedra's eyes said: *Of course. Don't play stupid.*

"Anyone who?" I asked.

"Mules. Mexicans. Some Russians. Mostly people from out of state going east–west, north and south. Oklahoma. Nebraska. Wyoming. Illinois. Of course California and Texas." She paused to breathe. "But I wasn't really paying attention when the subject came up."

"Some of them might object to paying this 'tax'?"

"Probably."

"Who then?" I asked.

"I just gave you a list. Take your pick."

"What kind of drugs?"

"Pretty much everything that's illegal or stolen from a pharmacy."

"Anything else?" I asked.

"Running hijacked merchandise. Farm machinery. Lot of cars."

"So you know more than you let on?"

"I got ears."

"And the family talks around you?"

"I'm invisible except when the men get all horny and want to take off my pants." Phaedra said this too casually.

I remembered the bills that had fallen from her pocket. "Is that where the money comes from?"

Her face reddened like I'd squeezed her neck with giant pliers. "Is that what you think I am? A whore?"

"A few minutes ago you were all but bragging."

Her right eye fluttered like the wings of a wounded moth. "Quit staring at my eye."

She covered both her eyes. "Quit staring at me. Stop it. I've done nothing wrong. I've done nothing wrong."

The shame washed from her to me. I put my arm on her shoulder. She rubbed her nose across the cuff of my coat. I slid my arm free and opened the center console. I took out a tissue and gave it to her.

She wiped her nose. "Let's pretend we didn't talk about that."

"Sure."

My fingertips and ears itched with a warning.

I checked the rearview. A red pickup truck gained on us. I looked to the front. On the right, a black pickup shot from behind the fence along the power relay station.

I didn't need Phaedra to tell me who these trucks were after.

CHAPTER 23

As a vampire I have supernatural powers. The Toyota doesn't. The two vehicles ahead were closing the trap. If I whipped around, at this speed the Toyota would flip over. I'd survive, but I couldn't risk injuring Phaedra.

I reached for the H&K.

Phaedra grabbed my arm. "Stay cool. Stay cool."

The black pickup bore at us suicide-bomber style. I couldn't swerve out of the way and slammed the brakes to keep from colliding. My Toyota skidded on the wet asphalt, the tires screeching when they burned through to dry pavement.

The front end of the red pickup following me dipped as the driver rode his brakes.

The two pickups boxed me in.

Each of the pickups had a driver and passenger. I didn't need a program to know they intended to knock me around. Four of them, one of me. Even without the H&K, the odds were in my favor—if I fought as a vampire. Phaedra's presence complicated the situation. If I revealed myself as a vampire to these goons, no problem, as I would kill them. But Phaedra, what if she was caught in the cross fire?

As soon as the vehicles stopped, we were all out in a flurry of opening doors and starting the showdown. The black mouths of three shotguns and a pistol gaped at me.

I fixed each shooter in my mind. I could snatch my pistol and drop each one with bullets to spare. Those I didn't kill outright I would finish off with my fangs.

Phaedra bolted from her seat in the Toyota. She moved so fast I didn't realize what she was doing. Phaedra grasped a wiper arm on the Toyota, set a boot against the front tire, and hoisted herself on the hood.

Phaedra stood erect between the guns and me. She balled her fists and screamed hysterically. "Stop it. Stop it."

The men drew back and lowered their guns, acting unexpectedly concerned about shooting her. Vinny, Gino's friend who I met yesterday, waited by the door of the red pickup.

One man didn't lower his pistol. The driver of the black pickup. His eyes burned with venom. Like me, his Mexican roots were obvious in his *indio* face. He had the lean hungry physique of a Tijuana alleycat. His neck appeared withered like his body had been drained of everything good and decent. Go to a crowd of a thousand people, look for the psychopath, and this was the man you'd pick.

A third vehicle—a blue Chevy Blazer—came straight at us from the direction of the hospital. The Blazer fishtailed and straddled the road, its front tires rolling into the weeds along the shoulder. A kid with a ponytail hopped from the Blazer and shielded himself behind the opened driver's door. He drew a bead on me with his pistol.

A man with a thick face like the front end of a battering ram came out the front passenger's side. Loose striped shirttails flapped from under the bottom of his jacket.

"Phaedra," he shouted. His big chest heaved from exertion. He hustled between my Toyota and the black pickup. He carried himself like the man in charge. Two of the men clustered around him, psycho at his left.

"Uncle Sal," she yelled.

Sal? Had to be Sal Cavagnolo.

He waved his hands in a downward motion. Pistols disappeared under jackets. Shotguns fell across car seats.

Everyone relaxed a bit except for the psycho, who kept a snarl in his eyes.

Phaedra climbed down over the front bumper of the 4Runner. She kept repeating, "Gino's dead."

"How do you know?"

"We were at his place. There was blood everywhere."

Cavagnolo glared at me like I was responsible for the bad news. "What were you doing there?"

She raised an arm in my direction. "We were looking . . ."

"I was talking to him." He turned up the heat in his glare, thinking—wrongly, of course—that I'd wilt. "What's your business here?"

"That's between Gino and me."

Cavagnolo's eyes simmered with insult. He approached me. His men reached for their guns.

"Was he there?"

"No. Like Phaedra said . . ."

Cavagnolo cut me off. "I only asked if he was there. Otherwise keep your mouth shut."

My fists balled up, ready to bash Cavagnolo's meaty face.

"Uncle Sal"—Phaedra moved between him and me—"don't be stupid."

His lips screwed together in a way that told me she was one of the few—maybe the only one—who could speak to him like this.

"So you couldn't find Gino. That doesn't mean anything," Cavagnolo said.

"Maybe he's in Saguache visiting what's her name," Vinny chimed. "That chick Dirty Tina."

I stepped from the 4Runner toward Cavagnolo. I kept my hands open and above my waist. Phaedra moved to stay in front of me.

Cavagnolo's expression turned acid. "My nephew Gino had shit for brains for talking to you. Your name is Felix Gomez, right?"

"You got it." Hearing my name coming out of his mouth made me feel unwashed.

"It's a pretty name." Cavagnolo paused to let the other men chuckle. "Goes with a sissy asshole who hides behind a girl."

I was going to lance Cavagnolo's head like a boil. I tried to nudge Phaedra aside, but she clamped onto my arm and stayed close.

"Gino's truck is still at his place." I pulled up beside Phaedra. "Lot of blood on his bed. Looks like someone cut him bad and hauled him off."

The men tried to remain stone-faced but they shuffled like they felt razor blades under their feet.

Cavagnolo's gaze focused to a point on the horizon. He kept

quiet and his mouth curled into the makings of a scowl. His expression abruptly relaxed as if he'd made a decision. "That's my problem. I'll deal with it." He motioned to Phaedra. "You, get home."

She gave a rebellious shake of her head.

Cavagnolo cocked a thumb to the Blazer. "Now, darling."

Phaedra looked at me over her shoulder. *What should I do?*

I gave her a gentle push toward the Blazer.

Cavagnolo said, "Cleto, help her out."

The psycho clasped her arm with his bony, paw-like hand. For a second, the hatred in Cleto's eyes morphed to pleasure. She jerked her arm loose and continued between him and her uncle.

Cavagnolo whispered as she passed. Phaedra turned subdued and humbled. He gave her a tender pat on the shoulder.

The kid with the ponytail came forward and helped her get in the front passenger's seat of the Blazer.

Cavagnolo closed within arm's distance to me.

Behind him, the Blazer pulled away and headed north.

"You and me"—he held up two fingers and pressed them together—"let's go back into town and talk."

"We can talk here."

Cavagnolo didn't reply. He walked to the black pickup and climbed in. Cleto drove. A guy in a light green jacket got into the backseat of the cab.

I remained standing.

Cleto gunned the engine of the black pickup. Cavagnolo lowered his window, hooked a thick arm out, and thumped the door. "You got tampons in your ears, pussy face? That wasn't an invitation, it was an order."

CHAPTER 24

Our parade convoyed back into Morada, the black pickup leading, me next, the red pickup close behind.

Up ahead, Cavagnolo started yakking on a cell phone. A quick look in my mirror and I could see Vinny in the truck behind me get his phone. He and Cavagnolo weren't exchanging recipes. I reached under my seat for the spare pistol magazines and slid them into my pocket.

I was certain of Cavagnolo's agenda. Break my legs. Ask me questions. Kill me. Dump my body into a deep hole.

I liked my agenda better. Whack all of his men if I had to. Ask him questions. Find out what I could about the zombies. Maybe I'd let Cavagnolo live if he behaved himself.

Cavagnolo turned left off Abundance Boulevard into the northern half of Morada. A block down the street the pavement ended and we drove over a dirt road.

The black pickup pulled into the setback of a large wooden shed painted white. Elkhorn Tools and Machinery was printed in crude letters above a bay door, partly open. Cleto parked in front of an office door to the left of the bay. A deer rack hung over the office entrance. I halted next to the black pickup.

The red pickup pulled ahead and stopped on the shoulder of the road. Vinny dismounted and went to the office.

Cavagnolo and Cleto got out of the black pickup. I followed.

Vinny held the office door open. Heated air gushed from inside. I wiped my feet on the jute doormat. The dingy room looked like every garage office I'd ever stepped into. Last year's tool calendar hung from the wall. Piles of forms, receipts, and open binders surrounded a CRT monitor on a battered shop desk. Rusted transmission gears served as paperweights.

Cavagnolo continued through another door in the back of the office.

My sixth sense ticked the alarm. Out the corner of my eye, I saw the guy in the green jacket dart through the bay door. He bootlegged a baseball bat against his thigh.

Vinny stayed in the office.

The back door opened into a darkened storage room. A space heater with orange coils was fixed to a floor-to-ceiling post. The room smelled of oil, gasoline, and musty blankets.

Cavagnolo and Cleto stood beside the heater, their expressions calm and fixed on me.

I paused at the door, only long enough for my senses to sweep the room. Clothes rustled to the right on the inside of the door. If I had my contacts out, I could zap them all in turn and take my time culling their thoughts.

But not yet. They waited in ambush and I would turn the tables in less than a second.

I brought my reflexes to vampire speed. My senses magnified every detail. Dust motes floated like tiny gemstones in the glow of the space heater. The thick smells separated into layers that I could now taste. The metallic notes in the used grease. The difference in the tang between unleaded gasoline and two-stroke fuel. Horse sweat and dog musk on the blankets. The slick aroma of fresh gun oil. Human perspiration carrying the spicy scents of adrenaline, prosciutto, oregano, and garlic.

Cavagnolo and Cleto kept their eyes on me, betraying nothing.

The drumming heartbeats from those hoodlums told me what their faces weren't saying.

Murder.

To my immediate right, around the corner of the doorway, human smells wafted strong. Lots of sweat and garlic. The goon with the baseball bat must be waiting there.

Nylon fabric rustled. Calloused fingers adjusted their grip. Nostril hairs trembled as breath rushed past them. A tongue rasped across dry lips.

I stepped over the threshold and snapped my arms to the right. A baseball bat swatted toward me.

I seized the goon's hands where they held the bat and swung him around, using his momentum to yank him off his feet. I put my hips into it, jerked him around in a circle, and flung him into the shelves next to Cavagnolo.

The goon landed on his back, smashing through the wooden shelves. Dust, machine parts, and tools exploded though the air.

I brought my hand to my waist and snagged the .45 from its holster. Cleto tilted to his left and started to bring a sawed-off shotgun from behind his leg. By the time his shoulders turned square to me, I had already aligned the sights and aimed the pistol at his chest.

CHAPTER 25

Cleto froze. The sawed-off shotgun remained close to his leg. His eyes registered that I was an instant from drilling him with a volley of .45 slugs. One twitch of my finger and his sternum would be hamburger.

Cavagnolo blinked. His mouth gave no expression but astonishment showed in his eyes. Cavagnolo put his hand on Cleto's arm and gave a quick pat.

Cleto bent his knees and let the shotgun settle on the floor. He stood straight and the hate in his eyes was hot enough to light a match.

"Wise decision." I stepped to the side. "Tell Vinny to get in here. I don't like anyone watching my back who's not on my team."

Cavagnolo called to Vinny. He hustled to the door, pockets jingling, pistol in hand. His blanched expression said: holy shit.

I motioned with my H&K for Vinny to get inside. He looked at Cavagnolo, who gave a quick nod and waved him in.

"Tell your man outside to stay cool," I ordered. "We had a little accident, that's all. A workplace injury."

Cavagnolo told Vinny to use his phone.

I stared at Cavagnolo. "You do it."

With an angry huff, he pulled a cell phone from his pocket and in a brief exchange told whoever was outside to sit tight. "It's all okay." Cavagnolo lifted the cell phone in my direction. "Anyone else you want me to call? Maybe send for pizza?"

"You can call the local morgue and make reservations if you'd like," I said. "Might save some time later."

Cavagnolo's eyes could've spit poison darts. He dropped the phone into his pocket.

I pointed to a spot by the space heater. "Grab a chair and sit there." I motioned to the guy I'd thrown into the shelves. He moaned softly, and as he moved his legs, the broken shelves rained more parts on him. "The rest of you, help him."

Cavagnolo dragged a folding chair from the wall. He opened the chair and swiped a hand across the seat to clean the dust.

I pushed a plastic chair into a corner opposite him. I picked up a clean shop towel and draped it across my chair. I sat and rested the .45 on my lap.

Cavagnolo took a seat, his knees bending slowly as if he were waiting for a signal to jump. His eyes remained on mine. This guy was king of the stare-downs but an amateur compared to me.

Vinny and Cleto helped the third guy to his feet. He gave another moan and staggered along.

"He needs a doc, Uncle Sal."

"You know where to take him." Cavagnolo said this out the corner of his mouth as he kept his stare on me.

I raised the muzzle of the pistol. "Keep this among us."

Cavagnolo's eyes didn't waver. Guess he was used to being on the wrong end of a gun. Pretty big-city attitude for someone out here in the boonies. "Don't worry," he said. "This is no sewing circle."

Vinny and Cleto put the other guy's arms across their shoulders and carried him out. I gave them a minute. "Let's swap places."

"What for?"

"In case your boys try something funny, I want the joke to be on you." I got up and stood in the pocket of warm air by the space heater.

Cavagnolo sat in the other chair, moving carefully like he expected a bad surprise.

"I don't care how you pay your bills," I said. "The only reason I'm here is because of Gino." And the zombies.

I would get to hypnosis but I wanted Cavagnolo to tell me things on his own.

He took a long breath and leaned back in the chair, the extended pause telling me that he had a lot of angles to figure out.

"What's happened to Gino?" he asked.

"I don't know."

"Is he dead?"

"I'd be surprised if he wasn't."

"Why's that?" Cavagnolo asked.

I told him about the blood and finished by saying that I didn't have a clue how Gino had been hauled away. "The trail went out the back door and I lost it. I can't imagine how anyone could've carried a big guy like him for much distance."

Unless Gino's attackers—the zombies—had hacked him into take-out portions.

"Remember what happened to Stanley Novick?"

I expected Cavagnolo's face to break apart in anguish. Instead he gave a smug grin. "Yeah, I remember. So what about him?"

"Maybe there's a connection?"

"Or maybe not."

A dead nephew and this was Cavagnolo's response? Was he always this callous or was he hiding something?

Cavagnolo said, "What's your beef in all this? Why do you care?"

Because of my orders from the Araneum. "I was hired to find out what happened to Barrett Chambers."

"That stupid asshole? Good luck." Cavagnolo smirked. "I'll tell you what happened. That bum beat feet. He owes money from Cheyenne to goddamn Phoenix."

"How much does he owe you?"

Cavagnolo chuckled. "Not one dime. I know his type. He'll make more promises than a politician, but after you lend him money, he's as hard to catch as a fly."

"What if I told you he was dead?"

The mirth slid off Cavagnolo's face. He held on to the glumness for a short moment, then went back to smiling. "Then I'd tell you the dumb ass ran out of luck."

"Help me understand something," I said. "Barrett is dead. As is your nephew, Gino. And there's the late Stanley Novick. You don't seem to be too concerned that these people are getting picked off like gophers."

Cavagnolo let his eyes dart to my gun. "I am concerned." He added, "There's a lot about the business my nephew didn't know."

"Gino mentioned the possibility Stanley was murdered in a fight over turf. But he didn't buy it."

Cavagnolo asked, "Is there something about the way Gino was snatched from his house that completely rules that out?"

No.

"Any reason you don't want my help?" I asked.

"Starting with the fact I don't know you and you come across as a creepy-ass fuck, plenty."

Cavagnolo's cell phone chimed. He raised one eyebrow. *May I?*

"Go ahead."

He dug the phone out of his pocket and answered. "Yeah. Yeah. Things are still cool. I'll let you know when we're done." Cavagnolo closed the phone and kept it in his hand. "How much longer we chatting?"

"Until I hear what I need to know."

Cavagnolo pasted that fuck-you stare back on his face.

We'd done enough regular talking. Time for vampire hypnosis.

We were alone. I thought of a way to cover the spell of amnesia.

I walked to him and pressed the pistol muzzle against his forehead. His only reaction was a quick grimace as if what bothered him was the feel of cold metal instead of the likelihood that a .45 slug was about to blow his skull apart.

"Close your eyes."

"What for?"

I tapped the muzzle of the .45 against the front of his skull. "Do it."

His expression stayed fierce even as his eyes closed.

I lowered the pistol. I flicked the contacts from my eyes into the palm of my free hand. Cavagnolo's aura glowed with a calm shimmer. I had sent one of his men to the doctor and now poked a gun into his mug. This man must have antifreeze for blood.

"Now open your eyes."

CHAPTER 26

My hypnosis hit him like the lash of an electric whip.

His irises popped open to the diameter of my pistol's bore. His aura gave a thousand-watt flare and dimmed to a steady red glow.

If I fanged him, I'd get into his subconscious that much quicker and deeper. This time of the afternoon, I could do with a blood refresher. All that testosterone fueling his Italian machismo would give me a nice buzz, better than triple espresso juiced with whiskey. But if Cavagnolo's goons returned, finding me deep in the bliss of noshing on his neck, they'd get the drop on me. Supernatural or not, letting their bullets turn my torso into a sieve was not the way I wanted to end this case.

I opted to massage his hands between the thumbs and forefingers. His hands were big and hard as mallets. Scars crinkled his knuckles. Cavagnolo took care of business with a personal touch.

His eyes fell into the black trance. His breathing lapsed to an even, unhurried rhythm. In this state, I could order Cavagnolo to tie a noose around his neck and he would.

"Sal." I waited for my use of his first name to draw him out. His eyes sparkled with a glimmer of recognition. I asked, "What do you know about the disappearances?"

Stems of anxiety grew from his aura. His breathing skipped to a faster cadence.

I massaged his hands again and repeated the question.

His aura and breathing calmed.

"It's freaky as hell," he whispered in a dreamy voice. "Stanley. Gino. Barrett. Gone."

"Who's responsible?"

"Don't know."

"Why are you keeping it quiet?"

"No choice. They can't find out."

"Who can't find out?" I asked.

"My crew."

"Find out about what?"

Anxiety blistered across his aura. "The work I do."

"What work?"

"For the Feeb."

FBI? Cavagnolo padded his wallet by ratting on his buddies? "You're an informer?"

"Yes." A storm of tendrils whipped from his aura. Even under this deep hypnosis, Cavagnolo knew what would happen if the word got out he was a fink. His men would treat him to a steel pipe massage followed by a dive into a wood chipper.

"What's in it for you?"

"Plenty. I get to keep my ass out of prison. I get the cops to put muscle on my rivals. I get a government check regular as clockwork. Plus I get to pocket what I earn."

Sweet deal if you discounted the getting discovered and murdered part.

"Let's talk about Stanley and Barrett. What's with them?"

"Somebody's trying to scare us."

"You scared?"

Despite the hypnosis, Cavagnolo managed a grin. "No."

"Why not?"

"It's the business. Drop your guard and you get filleted. We'd do the same thing."

"Could it be another gang?"

"Maybe. Maybe it's one of us gone psycho."

I hadn't thought of that angle. "Who?"

"Don't know."

Were the murders an inside job? Maybe in cahoots with the zombie maker? As usual, the more I learned, the further I found myself from the answer.

I didn't want to ask the zombie question directly, not yet. The question would stay in Cavagnolo's mind, and if someone else used supernatural hypnosis on him, he'd have no choice but to tell. I didn't know what or who I was up against. The best strategy was to keep my undead tracks covered as much as possible.

I could plant subliminal commands but they wouldn't last long. A couple of minutes for complicated orders. A simple instruction like wake up at a specific hour might remain until the next morning.

I let go of his hands and replaced my contacts. "On three, you'll wake up." I went straight to three and punched him across the face.

Cavagnolo fell from the chair and hit the concrete floor where he lay spread-eagle. He lifted his head from the floor and blinked. He turned onto his haunches and sat, looking groggy and confused. He rubbed his cheek and realized that I'd hit him. "You son of a bitch."

"Quit jerking my chain, Sal," I said, "or you'll get more of that."

"What the hell you talking about?" His eyes turned from me to the chair, clearly wondering how one moment he and I were playing cat-and-mouse chitchat, and the next, I had knocked his guinea ass to the ground.

He wouldn't wonder about the lost time.

Cavagnolo acted like his knees were stiff and he couldn't get up. I pushed his chair close.

"You want revenge for what happened to Gino? Let me handle it and stay out of my way," I said.

Cavagnolo sneered. "Go screw yourself."

"No, screw you."

If zombies were involved, I had to destroy the infestation without human intervention.

Cavagnolo brushed dirt from his shirt and the back of his pants. He acted like we'd merely gone through a minor spat, but in his heart, I knew he wanted my dismembered corpse in a trash compactor.

I beckoned for Cavagnolo to accompany me through the office and out the door.

Vinny was gone, probably taking his buddy to the doc. The black pickup had moved to the other side of the street. Cleto eyed me from behind the steering wheel; his passenger watched through the open front window.

"Sal, some of your boys might decide to take me out on spec. Bad idea. Make sure we all stay friends. If I have to shoot, believe me I'll use you for target practice." I poked him in the side to emphasize my point.

Cavagnolo's face went steam red with humiliation, but unless he wanted to die like a fool, what choice did he have?

We circled the Toyota and I checked for footprints in case somebody planted a little explosive souvenir under the chassis. Looked clean.

I stopped by the driver's door of the Toyota. "Remember, make sure your men stay cool. You don't want to start trouble in public like this. Might affect your cozy arrangement with the feds."

Cavagnolo's eyes could've burned holes though me.

I waved to his goons and drove off.

I checked my rearview mirror. Cavagnolo hustled across the road, oblivious to the mud. He got his cell phone and gestured in my direction.

This wasn't over.

CHAPTER 27

I needed something with more detail of the area than I could get from my Colorado road map. I drove east toward Alamosa, the *big* city of the San Luis Valley, to find better maps.

A Chevy Blazer appeared behind me. Sunlight reflecting off the windshield kept me from seeing the driver.

The Blazer tailed me for a minute, then zoomed close to smack my rear bumper. My Toyota shimmied. The moron driver was trying to ram me off the road.

Had to be one of Cavagnolo's men. I didn't have time to waste with this bullshit. I'd better take care of this loser quick.

I eased to the shoulder. The Blazer pulled behind me.

The driver got out. He wore sunglasses. Because of his ponytail I recognized him as Cavagnolo's driver from a couple of hours ago. Apparently he'd dropped Phaedra off and had orders to bring me back to Uncle Sal. Or shoot me.

Sorry, you little punk. Not today. Not tonight. Not tomorrow.

His aura was an undulating bubble of confidence. He stood as tall as his five-foot-plus frame would allow. After making an obvious adjustment of the drape of his jacket over what had to be a pistol, he started for me in a tough guy swagger. Cavagnolo's errand boy was as intimidating as a shih tzu wearing a spiked collar.

I took out my contacts and put my sunglasses on.

I waited with my window down.

The punk halted two paces from my door. "I got a message from Sal."

My biggest complication would be getting his sunglasses out of the way. I acted like I didn't hear him.

"What?"

He took off his sunglasses to demonstrate his seriousness and hooked them into a jacket pocket. His eyes showed no fear. Either this kid was high or merely stupid. I'd vote for both.

He reached to pull his jacket off his hip.

I gave a grin that belonged on the Joker. "Hold on." I removed my sunglasses and gave a super-duper jolt of hypnosis.

His eyes dilated wide like everything in his mind wanted to spill out through them. His aura burned red hot. He slouched, mouth open like he wanted to catch bugs, and his head sagged toward me.

"Good boy," I said. "Come here. Give me your right hand."

He advanced and placed his hand on the windowsill. I took his hand in mine and caressed the web of flesh between the thumb and forefinger. His aura dimmed.

I could send the kid away or hurt him. Too easy. He was on Cavagnolo's payroll and would have to learn the price of taking his money.

"Now go back to your Blazer, take off all your clothes, and lock them inside. Then stand with your back to traffic, bend over, and grab your ankles." I patted his hand and sent him off.

He turned about and walked robotically to the Blazer. Since he was giving oncoming traffic the full moon treatment, I should've told him to stick a flower in his butt.

I wanted to wait until the cops came by. Better not push it. I put my contacts back in, signaled left, and accelerated onto the highway.

I reached Alamosa in ten minutes. With a population of eight thousand people, it was small town, but compared to Morada, Alamosa was a megapolis.

I found a sporting goods store and bought a compass and a topographical map of the Morada area. I gassed up, hit an ATM for more cash, and headed back to Morada.

I thought about what Cavagnolo had said. *Maybe it's an inside job.* Who? For what reason? Was the insider working for the reanimator? If so, why?

I passed the spot where I'd left the punk kid in all his glory. He was gone and a tow truck was snagging his Blazer. I think the cops got him.

Back in Morada, I cruised the streets. The county buildings sat on F Street, on the tidy south side of town. The rectangular lines of the courthouse reminded me of a humorless, square-hipped chaperone. The jail was around the corner. I saw a state trooper's patrol car and a van with sheriff's marking but not Cavagnolo's punk kid.

I stopped by the county museum in my hunt for clues. What I was searching for might be as obvious as an old framed letter, if I knew where to look. But there was no mention of zombies or walking dead among the artifacts belonging to the pioneers or Utes. I read a display of "sightings," meaning UFOs, in the valley. A shiver ran through my *kundalini noir*. I've had enough of extraterrestrials for a decade.

The sun dropped close to the ragged horizon on the west. Long shadows slanted across Morada. I needed a drink, something to eat, and a place to stay—in that order.

The prudent course of action would be to head east to Monte Vista or Alamosa. Get away from Cavagnolo's convenient reach. But if he wanted more trouble, I'd make it easy for him to get another lesson.

The closest tavern was My Final Bender. I'd turned by this place earlier when I followed Cavagnolo on the way to the Elkhorn garage. I parked under a linden tree next to a Ford Escort that should've been junked ten thousand miles ago. Smoke curled from under the hood, which was held in place with a knotted length of garden hose.

The wooden door to the tavern had more gouges in it than a workbench in middle-school shop class. Two pillars of smoke swirled above the mounds of cigarette butts flanking the door. Inside, I expected country, but hip-hop belted from cheap loudspeakers hanging from nails in the dingy plaster walls.

Yellowed masking tape held a faded menu to the wall. Bold underlined letters scrawled with black marker announced: No Foood!

The yeasty smell of forgotten beer replaced the reek of tobacco smoke. Two guys at the bar nursed drinks and gummed unlit cigarettes.

A sign covered the center of a spiderweb of cracks in the mirror behind the bar. The sign read: NO SMOKING. STATE LAW YOU FUCKERS.

The only way this joint could've been more of a dive was if it was located in an Alabama swamp. If the other patrons had no quarrel with the trailer park ghetto decor, then I doubt any of them would've noticed that I cast no reflection in the mirror.

A short Latino wearing an aloha shirt as long as a muumuu worked the billiard table. The dress code for the day must have been thrift store special.

I picked a seat midway down the bar and took care not to rest my arms on the sticky places.

Mr. Munchkin in the aloha shirt sidled next to me. Gleaming white cross-trainers gave him Mickey Mouse feet. "Whaddaya want?" Matching rings protruded from his lower lip, right nostril, left eyebrow, and around both ears. He must have been deathly afraid of magnets.

"Manhattan." In a clean glass, please.

The music became especially loud. Something about a homie's true love for his 12-gauge. Other than the beat, sounded perfectly country western to me.

Mr. Munchkin shouted: "We got beer. And we got beer."

I was so overwhelmed by the ambience I missed noticing that all the liquor bottles on display were empty.

"Beer then."

"Then what?" Mr. Munchkin asked. "We got Bud Light. Miller Lite. Corona Light."

"Only light beer?"

"We're a healthy bunch. Gotta watch the calories." He flashed teeth capped with yellow gold.

"A Corona."

"Bottle or glass?"

One of the guys at the other end of the bar hacked and coughed into his armpit. He wiped his mouth with the back of his hand and returned to his Bud Light.

"Bottle," I said.

"Wise choice," replied Mr. Munchkin, "'cause we ain't got no glasses."

I debated whether I should chance drinking anything, much less staying. The grime in this place was a bigger threat to my well-being than Cavagnolo.

The front door opened. A big-haired frosted blonde entered. She had the hard look of a has-been party girl taking the express lane from thirty to senior citizen. She stopped beside me and laid her pink sequined purse on the bar counter.

The blonde peeled off a denim jacket with pile lining and revealed a tangerine tube top squeezing a pair of leathered breasts. Shiny earrings hefty as horseshoes drooped from her earlobes. Her blue eyes were the color of faded ink.

She parked her narrow jeans on the adjacent stool. Her perfume would've made a skunk cry for a gas mask.

The woman raised one painted eyebrow in a come-hither look as subtle as a tire iron smacking my nose. "Buy a lady a drink?"

Lady, what lady?

I glanced around the bar to gauge the others' reactions. This was a place where livers came to die, not for tourists to hook up with the locals.

Mr. Munchkin arrived with a Corona Light for me and a Bud Light for her. He didn't ask her, the usual? Nor did he ask if I was buying.

She picked the bottle by the neck and raised it in a toast. "Appreciate it."

I'd lost my thirst and let beads of sweat collect around my bottle. "What gives . . ."

She completed the question like she had practice. "Shawna." She propped an elbow on the edge of the bar, leaned on that arm, and gave a pensive look like she was trying to figure out how much money I had in my pocket. "And you?"

"You didn't let me finish my question. I was going to say, what gives with you being here?"

"Thought you might like some company." She took a pull on the Bud and left a smudge of lipstick.

Shawna had popped into the bar the minute I sat down and had singled me out. Maybe she's a hooker—in Morada?—and that's why the regulars took no notice.

Or something else was going on.

"How about a real drink?" I asked.

Shawna put the beer down and reached for her jacket and purse. "That's what I'm talking about. Lead the way, cowboy."

CHAPTER 28

We got into my Toyota and headed east a block on Abundance Boulevard. There wasn't much in Morada, but fortunately, the town had a liquor store, they weren't that backward. I stopped on the curb outside the store and gave Shawna a twenty and a ten.

"Any good vodka." I had to qualify that. "Make sure it doesn't look like lighter fluid."

Shawna flashed teeth the color of buffed porcelain and went inside. I took out my contacts and did a sweep of the street and traffic. Nothing suspicious. I put my contacts in.

Shawna came back carrying a paper bag. "I got Grey Goose. A bottle of tonic. A lemon. Some ginger ale."

"Where to?"

She aimed a long fingernail down the street. We passed the traffic light when she told me to slow down. "It's on the left."

A lighted plastic sign outlined with flickering bulbs announced

DeLuxe Restaurant Motel. Shawna said to park behind the restaurant.

The DeLuxe was an old motor court with a ground-in smell of cooking oil and wet garbage. Small rooms faced the compact asphalt square of a parking lot. Floodlights at the corners of the eaves didn't do much except make the shadows appear that much darker. Pickups with rifle racks in the cabs were nestled in the carports between rooms. Every bumper had an NRA sticker.

Shawna directed me to an empty spot at the right corner. It didn't surprise me that when Shawna got out, she already had a plastic key tag in her hand. It also wouldn't surprise me if she knew my name as well.

"You always this prepared?" I asked.

"Oh, honey," she replied, "me and the owners go way back."

Shawna set the bag with the liquor and goodies on the door-mat next to a Folgers coffee can containing kitty litter and ciga-rette butts. After unlocking the doorknob, she twisted the key into the deadbolt and grabbed the doorknob. She jiggled the key and thumped her shoulder against the door until it opened.

She flicked on the room lights.

I opened my coat and waited by my Toyota, convinced this was a setup. But I detected nothing. Even my sixth sense drew a blank.

I grabbed my backpack and entered the room. The place smelled like the bottom layer of a neglected laundry basket. Shawna put the Grey Goose, tonic, and ginger ale next to plas-tic disposable cups on the dresser. I nudged the door shut with my foot.

I set my backpack on a card table covered with green contact paper. A placard on the wall above the table admonished:

ABSOLUTELY NO COOKING OF ANY KIND IN THE ROOM.
NO HOT PLATES. NO CAMPING STOVES. NO STERNO.
NO SMOKING. NO CANDLES. NO INCENSE.
NO DRESSING OF GAME IN THE BATHTUB.
PLEEZ UNLOAD GUNS BEFORE CLEANING.

Bullet holes punctuated the last warning.

Shawna grabbed a small plastic tub from the dresser and offered it to me. "We need ice. Go to the back door of the kitchen and ask for some."

I walked past her to check the bathroom. "You get it."

Shawna shrugged, took the bucket, and left.

No one waited behind the bathtub curtain. The bathroom window faced a cinderblock wall on the other side of a narrow alley. Steel bars covered the window.

The bed was a couple of twins pushed together. Duct tape held the legs tight. Underneath I found a roach clip, a knee-high stocking, a couple of .270 rifle cartridges, and a copy of the *Alamosa Valley Courier*. The paper was from two days ago. The headline of a front-page article read: "Local Business Owner Missing."

Someone else had disappeared?

A quick glance told me that the business owner was the latest of area residents who had vanished. The article mentioned a loving wife and family and, only as an aside, introduced a gambling problem and debts.

Yet another zombie recruit?

I left the newspaper under the bed. I stuck my pistol in a pocket of my barn coat and laid the coat over the back of an unraveling wicker chair. I took off my boots and socks. I stood barefoot on the carpet, closed my eyes, and calmed my senses, making myself aware of all sensations, from the texture of the carpet against the bottom of my feet to the drum of air inside my ears. My mind was a smooth pool of water and every disturbance rippled across its surface.

There was the rumble of traffic on the boulevard. I heard television programs from the adjacent rooms. A radio tuned to a sports call-in show. The creak of a rusty hinge. Phone calls.

Steps approached the door. The quick steps belonging to a woman.

I pulled myself from the trance just as Shawna shoved the door open. The cascade of outside air chilled my feet.

She came in and put the bucket and ice on the dresser. She moved her shoulders and hips to a tune only she could hear. "Let's start the party."

I locked the front door behind her.

Shawna unsnapped her jacket and tossed it over the foot of the bed. "You never told me your name."

Details. As if she didn't know.

"Felix Gomez." I dropped ice into cups.

"Nice name, Felix. Like the cat."

"So I've heard." I made vodka tonics with twists of lemon.

Shawna plopped her skinny ass on the mattress. "What's in your bag of tricks?"

Plenty.

She yanked off her red cowboy boots and scooted them under the bed.

I had a lot of questions for Shawna and I'd get to them in a minute with hypnosis.

She started on her vodka tonic and punched buttons on the clock radio. "We need some goddamn music." The clock kept flashing 12:00 and the speaker belched static. She turned the volume off.

Shawna guzzled half of her drink and handed the cup back to me. "Put some fire in this motherfucker."

"What do you mean?"

"Too much tonic. Don't be stingy with the vodka. If I wanted a sissy drink, I'd follow you to Denver."

Denver? That made a big blip on my stink-o-meter. I never told her I was from Denver. Another question for hypnosis.

Shawna rested against a pile of pillows fluffed across the head-board. Her boobs sagged within the tube top.

I handed her a new drink with maybe one molecule of tonic floating between the ice cubes.

She sipped and gasped in approval.

I asked. "What do you do?"

"What do you mean?"

"For money?"

Shawna gave the most noncommittal of shrugs. Her breasts wobbled like a bowl of watery mashed potatoes. "This and that. Favors, mostly."

"What kind of favors?" I knew that answer already.

She stroked her stockinged feet against the bedcovers. "Let me show you."

I took the cup from her and went to the dresser. I took out my contacts and faced her. "No, let me show you."

CHAPTER 29

Shawna lay on the bed. The penumbra of her aura undulated like the surface on a puddle of red water. Her blue eyes gazed at nothing. A bottle of Windex showed more life.

I knelt beside her and scooped her neck in my hand. My fangs extended and I touched the sharp points with the tip of my tongue. Yes, I'd interrogate her, but first, it was time for dinner.

I removed one of her oversize horseshoe earrings and put my nose into the hollow of her neck behind the left ear. My cheek brushed against hair that was broom-bristle stiff with Aquanet. My fangs found their mark on her throat. Her blood spurted into my mouth. The taste of tramps was a flavor I knew too well.

I sucked deliberately, filling my mouth to capacity, and let the heavy mass of blood swirl over my tongue. Type A-negative I was sure. I swallowed and the luxurious warmth flushed through my body.

I gave Shawna only enough of my pleasure enzymes to keep her aura steady while giving a maximum dose of healing and amnesia enzymes. An hour after my fanging, she'd have no souvenir of my feeding except for a blank spot in her memory.

I climbed on the bed to straddle her hips and cradle her head in my hands.

"Shawna," I whispered. "Talk to me."

Recognition sparkled in her eyes. Her pupils shrank as the focus in them receded to a point deep within her consciousness. Sparkles of psychic energy collected along the aura around her head and made a halo. Probably the only one she'd ever wear.

"Why did you come on to me?" I asked.

Her pupils alternated between dilating and shrinking.

Let me rephrase the question. "Who sent you?"

"Sal."

"Last name?"

"Cavagnolo."

So this rendezvous *was* a setup.

I massaged the back of her scalp. "What for?"

"Didn't say."

I believed her; she had no choice but to tell the truth.

"Cavagnolo told you to approach me at My Final Bender and invite me here?"

"Yes."

Simple enough plan, though so obvious that a blind drunk would've seen it coming. I had told Cavagnolo to stay out of my way and I'd get Gino's killers. But the old man had his pride and the only way to restore face was to take me down. I expected visitors.

Another question for Shawna: "Do you know anything about the mutilations?"

The smooth sheath of her aura turned into an undulating fuzz. A rash of dark spots betraying anxiety broke out across her penumbra.

"Answer me."

Her eyes fixed on a spot miles above. She struggled to obey me while her subconscious fought to keep her pain buried. "I . . . I . . . I've heard."

"Heard what?"

"About Stanley. Barrett. Now Gino."

"What about them?"

The dark spots sprouted tendrils that whipped from her aura. Sweat trickled from her forehead and wet her temples. Her eyes became wide concentric circles of white around the blue middles. "People are scared."

"Why?"

"Because no one knows why folks are disappearing or who's doing the killings."

Shawna shut her eyes and milked tears. Wet mascara filled the wrinkles of her cheeks. She looked terrified and suddenly very old.

I'd hit a wall of emotional distress. It wasn't worth digging through. She'd told me what I wanted to know. I laid her head on the pillow and got off the bed.

Other than confirming that Cavagnolo was still gunning for me, what had I learned? He was more frightened about the killings than he would admit.

But as to who or why? A big goose egg of ignorance hovered over me.

When Shawna came around, she'd want an explanation as to what happened. I dumped the remaining vodka down the bathroom sink. If I told Shawna that she'd passed out from the boozing, I doubt it would be news.

This chase after the zombies was getting murkier by the minute. I had no clue what to do next, so I decided to rest and wait and see if Cavagnolo's men showed up.

I cleaned my pistol, the magazine, and the bullets. I turned the wicker chair toward the TV on the dresser. Like everything else in the room, the TV looked salvaged from a recycling bin. I sat and picked up the remote but the TV wouldn't click. I got up to wiggle the wooden dowel sticking out where the power button should be. The TV buzzed and the screen showed the commercial for a public auction of tractors and manure spreaders.

The goddamn psychic signal started. I jerked upright, alert. The echo remained low, almost a hum. Now that I knew Phaedra was responsible for the signal, the mystery to them was gone.

And just like that, the echo stopped.

What did Phaedra want? What was the purpose of the signal? A warning?

I lowered the volume of the TV and turned off the lights. Let's pretend I'd fallen asleep.

I put my fingers against the door and held still. I collected the faint vibrations from outside, the tiny smells, the whisper-like noises.

Slowly, the hairs on the back of my neck stood on end, like a cold breath had fallen over them. Danger lurked, that was for sure, but in what form?

Footsteps creaked over the gravel in the parking lot. One set. Two sets. Three sets.

I holstered the .45 into the waist of my jeans and put my boots on.

I didn't want a gunfight. Not here. The shots would alert too many people and make my hunt for the zombies much more difficult. I only took the gun to keep the odds in my favor.

I'd attack Cavagnolo's men as a vampire.

CHAPTER 30

I would go out through the bathroom window. The bars on the window were welded to a metal frame that was bolted to the wall of the window opening. I used my talons to saw off the heads of the bolts holding the frame in place. I worked the frame loose and sliced a hole in the screen.

I gave a listen, heard nothing unusual, and peeked out. To the left, the alley dead-ended against a tall cinderblock wall. To the right, toward the street, a metal barrel and a sheet of plywood were arranged into a makeshift barricade at the entrance. The bottom of the alley was full of mud and trash.

I climbed out the window and levitated to the ground. The stink kept me from smelling anything except for rats, raccoons, dead sparrows, and discarded diapers.

I crept close to the metal barrel. Crouching to remain low, I peered through a gap between the plywood and the wall.

Two pickups sat on the other side of the road, the same ones

Cavagnolo's men drove. A red aura bubbling with anxiety surrounded a man pacing between the trucks. The ember of a cigarette lit up his face. He'd been with Cavagnolo earlier but I didn't get his name. A maze of shadows obscured the front of the buildings behind the truck.

The plan must be to catch me in bed with Shawna and then lights out, amigo.

A simple and effective plan. Too bad I was on to it.

When the man guarding the trucks turned away, I leaped over the barrel and plywood. I landed softly on the gravel shoulder and sprinted across the boulevard.

I hid in the shadows and studied the guard. He paused and leaned against the back of one of the trucks while keeping watch over the motel. I stalked close enough to smell that he had steak for dinner. I crouched next to a tire behind him. He tossed the cigarette to the ground.

No need to kill him; I only wanted him out of the way.

He stood with his back to me. I sprung forward and clamped onto the collar of his coat. My momentum slammed him face-first to the ground.

I yanked on his collar and scooted back, gaining speed. I whipped around in a circle until his feet lifted off the ground. I turned in place, spinning completely around and tossed the man against a wall. He hit the bricks and went *uff*. His aura flashed once, then shrank to a dull simmer. He was out for a while.

I went to every truck and clawed the tires. Sharp rubber odors escaped through the ragged holes. I dashed across the street and leaped for the motel roof. This was too easy. I couldn't resist doing a full gainer. Levitating the final distance, I landed with a sound no louder than bunnies screwing.

I trod softly to the edge of the roof overlooking the parking lot. Two men, Cleto and another guy, sneaked along the walls to my room. Each carried a pistol with a silencer. Vinny watched from a position close to a Dumpster.

The two men crept close to my room door. They nodded, once, a second time, and on the third time, Cleto kicked the door to my room. Both men disappeared inside.

I heard them scramble, confused, wondering where I had gone. I followed one man's frantic steps to the bathroom. Cleto stuck his head out the window into the alley and stared right and left. Angry, nervous tendrils snaked from his aura. I should've peed on him.

Cleto withdrew his head. Seconds later he yelled, "Get your ass up, stupid bitch. Where is he?"

There was slapping and the tumble of a body to the floor. Hell of a wake-up call.

After a moment, Cleto and his buddy marched out the door. They muscled Shawna between them, her hair knotted in Cleto's hand. She hobbled along barefoot, with no jacket, and whimpered like a cold, frightened puppy.

Vinny joined the trio and vanished around the corner of the restaurant.

No lights came on in any of the other motel windows. Maybe guests getting roughed up was nothing to lose sleep over.

I jumped from the roof and landed beside my room entrance. The front door remained open. The bed had been overturned.

Within a minute I was back outside, with my contacts in place, fully dressed, and driving my Toyota out of the parking lot. My headlamps swept across Cleto and crew staring at their trucks. The flat tires hung from the chrome wheels like soggy doughnuts. The guy I'd thrown against the wall was up and rubbing his head.

I drove to them. Shawna sat in the backseat of the Chevy's cab.

Vinny's eyes shone like a couple of candied cherries against his ham-like face. He tapped excitedly on the other guy's arm and pointed.

Vinny, Shawna, and this guy eyed me like I'd materialized from the air. I halted with my left front fender beside Cleto and announced, "Hope you guys have AAA."

Cleto spun about. He had such a Holy Shit! expression that it took him a moment to recognize me. His eyes brimmed with surprise and rage. He jerked the pistol toward me.

I tossed Shawna's jacket at him. "If she catches cold, I'm holding you responsible."

Cleto fumbled for the jacket and his pistol clattered to the ground.

I gave the gas pedal a nudge and my front tire crunched over his gun. I rested the muzzle of my H&K on the windowsill of my door. "Who wants to live?"

Vinny and the other guy raised their hands.

Cleto straightened and clutched the jacket in both arms. "Where the fuck were you?" The question came out as a pained groan.

Cavagnolo had sent this wild bunch to do me in, and instead they had nothing to show for their efforts except for a thousand dollars in tire replacements.

"Watching TV. You walked right past me."

"How . . . I didn't see . . . no way." His eyes darted back and forth and he wobbled in a fit of vertigo.

I extended my hand and rubbed my thumb across my finger-tips. "You owe me for the door you busted open."

"The hell you talking about?"

"Cleto, you're forgetting that I'm aiming a gun at your guts. Pay up and I won't air-condition your belly."

Cleto dropped a hand over his stomach.

Vinny dug a roll of bills from a coat pocket. He peeled off a hundred and gave it to me.

I cocked my thumb at Vinny and told Cleto, "Now you owe him."

I eased on the gas and rolled forward. "Tell your boss that I'm not holding what happened tonight against him. *Yet.* Consider it a learning exercise."

Unfortunately, these buffoons were a big distraction in my hunt for the zombies. For his sake, I hoped Cavagnolo would get wise and cooperate before his dismembered corpse wound up in a spare parts bin.

"And Cleto."

His gaze lifted from the pistol I'd run over. "Huh?"

"Take better care of your gun."

CHAPTER 31

I drove west to the town of South Fork. I needed to put time and distance between myself and Cavagnolo. Stupid paranoid bastard wouldn't listen. I'd told him to keep his big nose clear of me and that I would take care of those responsible for the mutilations.

But Cavagnolo interfered, twice. I've made his goons look like drunken clowns. I was positive my name was at the top of his to-do list.

I stopped in an all-night diner. The place had a Lincoln Logs exterior. The motif inside was rustic yellow pine and antlers. A waitress mopped the floor. The few customers were scattered about the counter and booths. Everyone acted like they'd recently come out of hibernation and didn't talk or move much.

The time was 2 A.M. Working both nights and days wore us vampires out. Didn't help that the sun's rays weakened us despite sunblock and makeup. My brain felt like it was full of wet cotton.

A quick snooze in a casket would reset my psychic equilibrium. Maybe I should break into a mortuary.

I took a seat at a booth in the corner farthest from the entrance. I needed space and privacy. The waitress put the mop aside, rinsed her hands in a sink behind the counter, and set a coffee cup and a menu in front of me.

I planned my next moves and wrote my questions on a notepad. Where were the Z? (Shorthand for zombies.) Why had they taken the psychotronic diviner? Could Phaedra use her psychic power to find Z? Why had they attacked Gino? Where had they taken his body? For what purpose? Was the missing man I recently read about also a Z victim?

I unfolded the topographical map and studied the terrain. The reanimator was somewhere in this labyrinth of mountains and valleys.

Or was he? I assumed the zombies remained close in proximity to their creator.

But the first zombie had attacked me in Aurora, hundreds of miles from here.

If the Araneum could find me with a crow, why couldn't they send that bird to look for the zombie farm and leave a trail of poop for me to follow?

My life as a vampire. Do everything the hard way.

The waitress came by with coffee. She glanced over my notes and map. She asked, "You a bounty hunter?"

My eyebrows gave a *huh?* "No," I said, "I'm checking out the real estate."

"Yeah, right." She filled my cup. "With that map and at this time of the morning? Honey, trouble's written all over you."

"Is that a clinical analysis?"

"You like using big words, don't you?" She readied an order pad. "No, it's the opinion of a girl who's had too many boyfriends with lots of different occupations."

So much for being in stealth mode.

I ordered eggs over easy, bacon, and hash browns. Wheat toast. Buttered. After the meal arrived I pretended to smear ketchup over the eggs and potatoes to hide the O-negative I'd brought in. I used the toast to wipe the plate clean of egg yolk and blood.

I kept watch outside. At the moment it wasn't the zombies or Cavagnolo I feared but the sunrise.

The landscape brightened by degrees. Yellow light painted the tops of the surrounding mountains.

Fear wormed through my guts. I could feel the breath of the sun coming to incinerate me.

I retreated to the men's room with my backpack. I locked myself in a stall and waited. I felt like a lobster that had molted and needed to hide until its shell hardened. While in the stall I shaved with an electric razor and applied sunblock and makeup. These mundane details are overlooked in classic vampire literature.

The psychic signal started. I slammed my hands against the sides of the stall to steady myself. The signal echoed once, then shrank to silence.

What was Phaedra doing?

When I stepped out of the men's room, the restaurant seemed normal. Plenty of morning customers. No one acting like they wanted trouble.

The dawn had passed and I was safe from the sunrise. My cell phone chimed to alert me of a text message.

CALL ME
P

Phaedra.

I called her back. On the second ring, she answered.

"Felix, you okay?" she answered, breathless.

"I'm all right."

"Thank goodness. Where are you?"

"In South Fork." This was the first time we'd talked since her uncle took her away. "That was you just now, wasn't it?" I asked.

Phaedra started to answer when in the background of the phone, a woman called out over a loudspeaker. She wanted a price check on enchilada sauce.

"Where are you?" I asked.

"In Del's Budget Grocery."

I remembered Del's as the only supermarket in Morada.

"What are you doing there?"

"Hanging out before school starts."

"You're okay then? About Gino?"

"No, I'm not okay. But I can't bring him back, can I? It's you I'm worried about."

"That's two of us. Let's talk in person. I'll meet you there."

"Better hurry. School starts in a few minutes."

"Play hooky."

"Only for first period. I hate my civics teacher."

We clicked off.

I started back to Morada, concerned that Cavagnolo and friends could've eavesdropped on Phaedra and be waiting in ambush. Maybe I was giving them too much credit because I arrived at Del's Budget Grocery without so much as a bug smacking my windshield.

Huge new pickups and tiny beaters cruised the parking lot in random circles. Whatever the model or make, every vehicle had green and yellow ribbons fluttering from the antennas. Windows were scrawled with Go Panthers!

Kids stood in groups alongside the building. Phaedra remained alone. She wore an off-white ski parka and a backpack, and cradled a paper bag.

She made eye contact and started for me.

A trio of large boys broke from a clique and blocked her. They all had green jackets with Morada High embroidered across the back. Two of the boys wore cowboy hats.

They stood shoulder to shoulder, their hands resting inside their jeans' pockets, each of them assuming a bully's stance.

Phaedra's face pinched with distress.

I had to rescue her but I couldn't afford to tangle with high schoolers. It would cause too much trouble with the authorities. If anything happened, I better handle this sitation quickly and smoothly. I removed my contacts and put my sunglasses back on.

Phaedra glanced from boy to boy. Her right eyelid fluttered in a nervous spasm.

The boys laughed. The shortest of the bunch got close to Phaedra and stretched one leg behind hers. Another boy tipped his hat and moved forward.

Phaedra stepped back and tripped on the leg. She stumbled and dropped the paper bag. Something inside broke and liquid spilled over the asphalt.

My anger turned blade sharp. I got out of the Toyota and

pushed between two of the boys, my vampire strength easily brushing them aside.

Phaedra wouldn't look at me. I reached for her hand and pulled her up. Her face was red with shame. Her right eye was closed tight and the eyelashes trembled.

"This guy your new boyfriend, Blinky?" the shortest of the bullies asked. His jacket had a chenille M decorated with football-shaped medallions.

Blinky? Kids were cruel.

Phaedra kept her head down and wiped tears.

I put my arm around her and we walked toward my Toyota.

Short guy gave me the once-over. "Where'd you find this dinosaur, Blinky?"

He says Blinky one more time and I'll use his tongue to wipe my dipstick. I was a couple of inches taller than him but he outweighed me by forty pounds, easily. Made no difference.

His friends tugged at his arm. "Come on, Jason. Let it go."

Jason gave an arrogant grin, convinced there was little I could to do to him, a minor.

"Who the hell are you, old man? Her Prince Charming? Why bother? She's no princess." He waved a finger to his pals. "She's the school blow-job bitch. Gives good ones too as long as you don't make eye contact with her. You know." Jason blinked his right eye. "Freaks you out. Isn't that right, Blinky?"

At the moment I wanted to use Jason's head as a soccer ball. I let go of Phaedra and pulled my wallet out. I said to Jason. "I'll bet a twenty that in less than a minute, I'll have you singing like a little girl."

Jason chuckled. "A twenty, huh?"

He walked beside me. I turned and put my back to his friends. I lowered my sunglasses.

His eyes came to mine. His irises popped to the size of marbles. His red aura bloomed crimson red and his smirk sagged into a big wide O.

I whispered into his ear. "You know 'I'm a Little Teapot'?"

"I . . . think . . . so."

"Good. On three, start singing. Loud. Add the dancing part."

"O . . . kay."

I put my sunglasses back on and counted.

He set his hands on his hips and bounced on his knees as he sang loud, exactly as I'd told him. His buddies stared. The other students pointed and laughed.

The hypnosis would last about a minute. When it wore off, Jason would have no idea what happened, though his throat would be sore from singing so loud.

I led Phaedra to the Toyota. She watched Jason and barely smiled. I got a sense that she didn't draw much satisfaction from his humiliation.

I did.

Phaedra climbed into the 4Runner like she wanted to leave.

I got in. "I have some questions for you."

She kept her face down and ignored the commotion of everyone else laughing at Jason. She said, "I don't want to talk here."

"Understandable." I started the engine. "Where to?"

Phaedra cinched her safety belt. "The place I go when I want to be alone." She pointed west. "It's my secret place. My hideout."

CHAPTER 32

Phaedra looked strained and shrunken as if she were caught in a giant fist of anxiety and unhappiness. I couldn't pry a word out of her.

She pulled a water bottle from her backpack and sipped. For the next half mile her silence dragged across my mood like an anchor.

I slowed for the county road along Pinos Creek, the way to Gino's. Phaedra motioned to keep going.

She fished a paper napkin from her jacket. She swiped her eyes and her nose. "Do you understand now?"

I wanted to ask, about what? But that would sound like I wasn't paying attention. I kept quiet and waited for her to elaborate.

"Do you see what my life is like?"

"It can be hard."

"This is just one day. They're not going to get any better."

"Sure they will. Soon you'll be out of high school."

And then? I shut up. I could see where Phaedra was going with this. After graduation the worst symptoms of the Huntington's would begin.

Phaedra looked out the side window.

"That was you last night?"

She cocked her head toward me.

"The mind signals," I said.

"Who else could it have been?"

"Just making sure. The world of the supernatural still surprises me."

"What's your point?" she asked.

"Thanks. You saved me last night."

She shrugged. *You're welcome.*

I asked, "How did you know Cleto and the others were coming after me?"

"I overheard my uncle give them orders."

"What orders?"

"You want his exact words?"

"If you remember."

"They were, kill Gomez. Exact enough?"

"Why didn't you call? I don't like you using the mind power on me."

"I couldn't," Phaedra snapped. "It was late and I'd left my phone in the kitchen. I couldn't fetch it. My uncle was up all night and he would've seen me." Her cheeks flushed with anger. "You know what?"

I made eye contact.

She moved to punch my arm. I caught her fist.

She squirmed to pull her hand free. "You don't trust me."

I let go of her hand. "I want to trust you."

"Then start." She rubbed her knuckles. "You can be such a jerk."

Jerk? I'd expected insensitive asshole. Jerk had such an adolescent accuracy that the comment stung.

"Being a jerk comes from being careful."

"Do you trust me or not?" she asked.

Times like now, Phaedra tormented me like an itch I couldn't reach. "Yes, I trust you."

"Was that hard?" She turned in her seat away from me and mumbled, "I thought vampires were cool."

That itch was acting up.

When we passed a gravel road going north, she said, "That's where I live with my uncle."

I slowed for a look. Oaks and lindens created a tunnel over the road, which ran straight to a one-story house with a chain-link fence. "Want to stop?"

"No, keep going."

After another mile she told me to turn south. We took a narrow paved road that curved up an incline into the pine trees. The asphalt ended at a steel gate along a barbed wire fence. A sign on the gate read: NO ACCESS. RIO GRANDE NATIONAL FOREST.

I halted. Phaedra hopped out in an animated rush. She lifted the chain looped over a post at one end of the gate and waved me through. I drove onto a dirt road. She secured the chain behind us and got back in.

Her expression transformed, like she'd changed masks, from sad to happy.

The road turned into a trail that became a wide spot between the trees. We got as far as we could without plowing into the brush.

We both got out. Phaedra slung her backpack over her shoulders. The trees filtered warmth from the sunlight and I felt the chill against my face. Dense mats of pine needles and patches of dry grass spread across the rocky ground.

Phaedra hiked beside me. We started at a brisk pace but she tired and slowed.

She motioned that she wanted to rest and sat against a large boulder mottled with lichen. She guzzled from her water bottle. Up here, the air remained cool enough for the vapor in her breath to show.

"Where's your hideout?" I asked.

She pointed to the trees behind her.

I saw nothing but forest.

Her eyes made a look-again expression.

This time I saw a horizontal line among the Ponderosa pines. It was the roof of an earth-colored shack that blended into the surroundings.

I followed Phaedra toward the shack. As we got closer I could see that the shack was made of adobe daubed with mud. The vigas and rough lumber holding up the roof had bleached to the same soft gray as the dead wood around us.

"Kind of hard to get to," I said.

"It's a hideout. That's the point." Phaedra removed brush that had rolled against the shack and helped camouflage it. The eaves of the pitched roof came to my chest.

I asked, only half joking, "Who made this? Midgets?"

"Penitentes." She went to the south side of the shack.

"Penitentes?" I repeated, analyzing the word as I translated it. "Those who seek penance?"

"They were a lay order of the Franciscans." Phaedra led me to a short door. "They migrated to the San Luis Valley from Santa Fe almost two hundred years ago."

The door was the same bleached color as the rest of the wood. The planks were uneven and held in place with rusted square-faced nails. She swiveled a board on the door and stuck her hand through the gap. After fumbling with a lever arrangement, she pushed the door open. "This is called a *morada*. Means dwelling but it's more like a little chapel. There used to be dozens all up and down these parts. It's what the town was named after."

"So why did they build this place up here?" I asked.

"To hide their secret rituals. Rites of self-flagellation. They used cactus and whips made from yucca." Phaedra said this with an enthusiastic lilt like she would've enjoyed watching.

"What a fun bunch," I said. "I would've come here for drinks and to play cards."

We ducked through the low doorway and stepped down to a dirt floor. Inside, the ceiling was tall enough for me to stand upright. Wire hooks dangled from the joists. Smudges on the wood marked where people had once hung lanterns.

Low benches ran along the eastern and western walls. The benches were constructed in the same manner as the walls, adobe and mud plaster. More of the rough-hewn planks lay on top of the benches.

Phaedra bent over the bench on the western wall. She removed adobe bricks along the edge of the bench. She wedged her fingers under the planks, shifted them back and forth, and worked the planks loose. She lifted the planks and propped them against the wall.

The open bench looked like an adobe sarcophagus. An army duffel bag rested inside.

"What's in the bag?" I asked.

"My camping stuff."

"You sleep up here?"

She nodded. "Told you it was my hideout."

"What are you hiding from?"

"The future me."

The grimness of the comment skewered me. Phaedra meant a future wasting away and dying of Huntington's. If I turned her into a vampire, I'd spare her that hideous fate. But that was the fate God had given her. If I made Phaedra into a vampire, then I'd hold myself responsible for her new destiny as an undead bloodsucker.

Phaedra lifted the duffel bag and dumped out most of the contents: a rolled sleeping bag, granola and candy bars, packets of beef jerky, and a hurricane lamp. She opened the lamp, exposing a candle that she lit with a butane lighter.

The lamp's dim yellow light made our shadows flicker on the walls. She brought the lamp close to one of the bench planks.

"Look." Phaedra turned the board over to reveal an etching of a Star of David and a menorah scorched into the wood. "This is a hiding place within a hiding place. There were Jews among the Penitentes and they snuck here in further secrecy to celebrate their traditions. Did you know many Conquistadors were Jews fleeing the Inquisition?"

I did know. My own past came back to me. Coyote, an ancient vampire I'd met when on assignment in Los Angeles, was a child of the Spanish conquest of America. Half Aztec and half Spanish Jew, perhaps the first true Mexican, Coyote still carried the shameful burden as a survivor of the Inquisition.

"How'd you discover this place?"

"I was hiking by myself about four years ago and found it."
Phaedra sat cross-legged on the floor and rested the lamp in front
of her. She closed her eyes. "You feel it? There's an energy here.
It's a holy place. Aren't you afraid?"

"Unless I'm tied to the floor and somebody's about to stake
me, why should I be afraid?"

"What about things like holy water? Crucifixes?"

"That's movie stuff. I could brush my teeth with holy water.
You want to hurt me with a crucifix? Pawn it and buy a gun."

"Then what's true and what's not about you? As a vampire,
I mean."

I didn't want to explain anything. The more Phaedra pried
about vampires, the worse I felt about neglecting my duty to the
Araneum.

Guilt put its heavy hands on my shoulders. I had no choice
but to kill Phaedra, convert her into a chalice, or turn her into
one of us. But I wouldn't do any of them.

"You look tired," she said. "Aren't you immortal?"

"The trick to staying immortal is that you've got to pace
yourself."

She asked, "What about the zombies? What do you know
about them?"

"Not much."

"Where do they come from?"

"Depends. Several things can cause zombies. A virus. A muta-
tion. In this case, there's a reanimator. He's killing people and
using them for parts to make zombies."

"How do you know that?"

"Other vampires told me."

"How do you pass information? You guys have a newsletter? A website? Blog?"

"Yes. Yes. And yes."

"Will you show me?"

"No."

Phaedra played with the lamp and tried not to appear miffed. "Did a reanimator get ahold of Gino?"

"Most likely. It's what happened to Barrett."

Phaedra blinked. I could tell she was trying to take in the reality of everything that I'd said.

She picked at the laces of her boots. "Who is this reanimator?"

"That's what I have to find out."

"He's the one you have to stop? By stop, I mean kill."

"Yes. I have to kill this reanimator and destroy his zombies."

"Do zombies die of disease?"

"Technically, they're already dead. Make that undead. I'm pretty sure they're immune to colds and pneumonia."

"What about Huntington's?"

"I guess they'd be immune to that, too. In what I've read about zombies, they're not much of a drain on health care."

"Are they immortal?"

"Considering they're undead, I'd say yes. Why the questions?"

"I've spent most of my life thinking about my death." Phaedra twisted a lock of hair from her bangs, the gesture idle, her face blank as if meditating.

She turned to the bench. "I have something else to show you."

She reached into the bench and folded aside a tarp covered with dirt. Whisking away the dust, she lifted an artist's black portfolio from under the tarp. She unzipped the portfolio and opened it to reveal a large drawing tablet.

Phaedra laid the portfolio where the light from the lamp was best. The tablet was full of drawings that had been torn loose and slipped back under the cardboard cover.

"When I looked into the void and found you"—Phaedra showed me the first drawing—"this is what I saw."

It was a charcoal sketch of the little Iraqi girl.

CHAPTER 33

The sketch Phaedra held was a caricature, but the rendering captured mood in a way a camera never could. A round innocent face that had no business being close to war: hair drawn as wild zigzags that got lost in the confused crosshatched texture of the night sky; eyebrows arched in permanent horror; tiny lips twisted in sorrow.

Every scratchy mark directed me to her eyes.

Dark eyes. Frightened eyes. Accusing eyes.

Her eyes were smudges of charcoal, but they projected light from deep within the paper.

I wanted to slap the portfolio closed and push it away. But I was transfixed, both fascinated and frightened that the blackest of my memories was exposed.

Phaedra pulled out another sketch.

Soldiers huddled around the little girl where she lay dying on a poncho. Shadows radiated like spokes from each soldier as if the girl was a hub of blazing light. One soldier knelt by her side and leaned close with a bayonet.

Me. That soldier was me.

I had unsheathed the bayonet to cut away her blood-soaked dress.

Phaedra sorted through the sketches.

A pair of man's hands.

Covered in blood.

My hands.

The emotions burst out of me.

Fear.

Terror.

Despair.

Phaedra held up the drawings like they were exhibits at a trial.

My *kundalini noir* shrank into a tiny ball.

Now I understood. Phaedra had crossed the astral plane to dig into my psyche. She'd uncovered my nightmares and endless shame. Phaedra's psyche had woven into mine and that's why I'd seen her face merge with the Iraqi girl's.

My mind replayed the events of my vampiric life from the death of the Iraqi girl until now. My turning. My service as a vampire enforcer. The loss of Carmen to alien gangsters. The psychic attacks. Phaedra's wish to cheat death.

Were these events randomly strung together or were they a path leading me to this moment?

And this decision?

Turn Phaedra.

I wouldn't do it, but to refuse was to let Phaedra die.

I withdrew from the world, falling, rolling, tumbling—delirious in a miserable confusion.

A mental image of the little Iraqi girl came into focus.

Years ago, I'd been shot by vampire hunters and was close to dying. Wendy Teagarden, a supernatural dryad, gave me her blood and I was taken by a dream. In this dream I met the Iraqi girl and her family. They rose from the dead to confront me. In order for them to enter heaven, they had to let go of their hatred of me. The little Iraqi girl's final words were "We forgive you."

I returned from the dream, strong, complete, hungry.

Why wasn't this memory depicted?

The delirium melted away. Clear-eyed and wary, I stared at Phaedra. "Why are you doing this?"

Her eyes were tiny yellow slits in the candlelight. "I've told you. So you can make me a vampire."

"That will never happen."

"It has to." She jabbed at the drawings. Her fingernails gouged the paper. They left dark shiny smears.

Blood?

She waved her stained fingertips. I smelled the blood. Was this a trick? Had she cut herself on the sly?

The revulsion was too much and I recoiled from her.

Phaedra's hand curled and her bloody index finger clawed at me. "And I selected you."

"Where's my say in this?"

She shook the drawings. "You know what it's like to live with this pain. This humiliation."

I swatted the drawings from her hand. They fluttered to the floor. "Don't talk to me about humiliation. Not after you've been digging around in my head."

"I had to do it." She grasped my wrist. "So you can save me."

I held her at arm's length. "You used the Iraqi girl to manipulate me. I owe you nothing."

Her eyes probed mine, her expression pleading. "Nothing?"

"Not after what you've done."

That pleading expression turned injured. She let go of my hand and lowered her head.

The echo started, faintly. I got ready for a hard blast to my brain. But the echo never rose above a murmur and faded.

Was this the last of Phaedra's psychic tricks? She kept her face down and appeared embarrassed, broken.

She knelt and quietly collected the drawings.

The realization that I had better memories of the Iraqi girl reassured me. The guilt was still there but softened by her forgiveness.

Phaedra had trouble with the zipper on the portfolio. I reached to help her but she brushed my arm aside with her shoulder. After she'd closed the portfolio, she sat with her back to me.

She gave tiny sobs and wiped her face.

I didn't have a solution. Didn't help that she had been dishonest with me from the start. Maybe another vampire would turn her. If he didn't kill her.

I read my watch: 3:11 P.M. We'd been here a while.

The constant anxiety caught up with me. I was tired and wanted to rest. I stared longingly at the open bench. It would be a squeeze to get in but was almost like a crypt in a chapel. This wasn't a polished mahogany casket with a padded silk lining but it had a rustic appeal. A nap now would be too callous, even for me, so I offered an olive branch.

"Don't your relatives worry about you?"

"Fat chance. My aunt dreams of the day she sees my face on a flyer at the police station."

"And Uncle Sal?"

Phaedra pulled the parka's hood over her head. "Like he cares about anything but money."

My eyelids were heavy. I wish I had turned down this assignment. Phaedra was more than I wanted to handle. Now that she had shut up, perhaps I could get some sleep.

Her cell phone chimed. She stood and dug into her jeans. In the glow of the tiny red screen, she squinted with annoyed recognition at the number flashing. She put the phone to her ear. A woman's voice chattered like an angry squirrel.

"Yeah, Aunt Lorena, I'm okay. Yes, I'm sure. Calm down. Why do you ask?" Phaedra's complexion faded. She repeated, "Oh my God." She snapped the phone closed and dropped it into her parka. "We have to go."

I blew the lamp candle out. "What's happened?"

"Uncle Sal's men were attacked."

My *kundalini noir* tensed. "Where? Who?"

"By the river. Cleto is missing."

"How?" I asked.

"Just like Gino."

The zombies were back.

CHAPTER 34

The afternoon sun retreated and cold, dark shadows claimed the forest. Phaedra ran down the slope to my 4Runner. I stayed behind her, in position to catch her in case she slipped on the uneven rocks. When we made it back to the highway, we were again in bright sunlight.

She got on the phone and, after quick frantic conversations, pieced enough together to relate a few details. Cleto was arranging a sale. Of drugs I was sure. Cavagnolo and Vinny had arrived later and found a gruesome mess.

Phaedra opened one of her prescription bottles and shook out two pills. She gulped the pills, chased them with a slug from her water bottle, and leaned against the door. She closed her eyes and grimaced.

I asked, "You okay enough to answer some questions?"

She raised her right hand and made a go-ahead motion.

"When was the last time your uncle spoke with Cleto?"

"A couple of hours ago." She kept her eyes closed. "Why?"

"I'm trying to establish a timeline."

The zombies had attacked recently, in daylight. Why had they become so brazen?

There was another possibility. Maybe Cavagnolo was using the mysterious killings as cover to get rid of Cleto. Maybe Cleto suspected that Cavagnolo was an informant. I couldn't overlook the most obvious of motives.

Phaedra cracked her eyelids and peeked at the highway. She sat up and directed me to a dirt road. We wound through willows and cottonwoods on a course that took us close to the Rio Grande.

Phaedra waved to slow down and pointed to the right, through a trampled opening in the tall weeds. She explained that there were lots of secluded hangouts along the river, and she knew where the meeting had been.

My ears started to buzz. A second buzz began at my fingertips, rushed up my arms, and caused a shiver across my shoulders.

The first vehicle that came into view was Cleto's black Chevy pickup. The second was a white Cadillac Escalade that I hadn't seen before. The vehicles were within a clearing, surrounded by a bowl of dense trees and shrubs. The doors were open on both vehicles. Spatters of blood the size of dinner plates stained the windows and the upholstery.

On the other side of the clearing, Cavagnolo and Vinny stood beside their red pickup. They stared slack-faced at the carnage. Cavagnolo's thumb played nervously over the hammer of his pistol. Vinny remained farther back, looking ready to run away.

Dozens of empty cartridges were strewn across the dirt. The

back hatch of the Cadillac yawned wide. Plastic liter jars spilled white crystals across the ground. Judging by the cat piss smell, it was meth.

Three men lay in heaps so bloody I thought they'd been mulched to death instead of shot. One looked familiar but was so mutilated I couldn't be sure.

Phaedra stepped behind me in slow movements as if worried that at any second the mayhem and bloodletting would begin again.

Cavagnolo saw us and in one quick wipe, his expression went from horror to anger. He scowled, and when he spoke, spit sprayed from his mouth. "Goddammit, why the hell did you bring her here?"

Phaedra brushed beside me. "I had to show Felix how to find this place."

Cavagnolo aimed his pistol at the corpses, not to shoot, but like it was a talisman to ward off evil. The skulls had been pried open and emptied. "What's with taking the brains? Is this some voodoo horseshit?"

More like an afternoon snack for zombies.

I asked, "These your guys?"

Cavagnolo gave a rueful nod.

"Everyone accounted for?"

"Except Cleto." Cavagnolo pawed at the spent cartridges. "He put up a hell of fight." Cavagnolo hesitated. "I can't figure it. We've got no trouble with anybody. So what is this about?"

I said, "Maybe someone's trying to send you a message."

"Who? Why?" Cavagnolo squared his shoulders and leaned toward me.

I didn't give ground. "Back off, Sal. Don't crowd me."

"Then why did you say it?" He tightened his grip on his pistol and gave a look that at any second he was going to drill me through the forehead. "First you arrive. Then we lose Gino."

Cavagnolo better be careful or I'll snap his neck. I didn't want to do that, especially not in front of Phaedra. "What are you getting at, Sal? That I had something to do with this? Get your thinking straight. Stanley Novick was the first to get chopped up like this. That happened days before I got here. And Gino came to me for help, not the other way around."

Cavagnolo relaxed his grip as my words soaked into his head. Heavy breaths bellowed through his nostrils.

I thought this hellish scene would leave Phaedra trembling in terror. Instead, she wandered through the area and inspected the bodies and blood from a distance.

I had to ignore Cavagnolo and think about the zombies. Why did they strike now? Why Cleto? Were they stalking him?

Phaedra called from the edge of the clearing. "Here's something."

A set of bloody prints went south. These prints were deep as if burdened with a heavy load. Cleto?

I didn't need to be Daniel Boone to follow the trail to the river. They had flattened the grass and weeds and left spots of blood and bits of cloth. Zombies for sure.

Phaedra followed me. Cavagnolo stayed behind with Vinny. She stepped gingerly in my footsteps as if afraid the blood and tatters would infect her.

The zombies couldn't have made a more obvious path with a road grader. This sloppiness was the reason the Araneum wanted them exterminated.

Footprints and drag marks continued off the riverbank to the water's edge. The river lapped back and forth and obliterated the tracks in the sand close to the water.

I surveyed the opposite bank. The trees were set back about a hundred feet so the ground was more open. Where did the zombies go?

The river flowed over rocks and the eddies curled around submerged sandbars. Phaedra caught me studying the water.

"You're thinking of crossing?"

"Depends. How deep is the water?"

"That's not a good idea," she said. "The current can be pretty fast and suck you under. You could drown."

No, I couldn't. There was a lot I hadn't told her about vampires.

"Any ideas?"

She used her index finger to note a path across the river. "If you insist, try that line of rocks. The water's knee-deep at the most."

I stepped off the bank. Icy water filled my shoes.

Phaedra held my arm. "Careful."

I've been dunked in the Missouri River and crawled out. Compared to that river, this was a trickle.

I told her I'd be okay and would return shortly. I picked my way along the rocks and across a sandbar. The water lashed about my shins.

Once on the other side, I walked along the water's edge. I searched the sand and river rocks for the trail.

If the zombies carried heavy, awkward loads, the strong current would have worked against them. Sure enough, a hundred feet downstream, I found a confusion of prints. Some of the feet had dug into the sand, like they'd been struggling to haul something from the water. The footprints became an orderly procession away from the riverbank. Broken grass and a string of maroon dots pointed south in the direction the zombies had fled.

To where?

I couldn't imagine zombies, let alone zombies dragging a clumsy mutilated corpse, strolling across the highway during daylight.

The trail continued through the thicket to a hard-packed frontage road. Footprints wouldn't show. The weeds on the opposite side of the road were fresh and undisturbed. The zombie trail stopped here.

I found a circle of water stains close to the shoulder of the road. Whatever leaked was held still for a moment, that's why the spots were in a circle instead of a ragged line.

Held still . . . to be loaded into a vehicle?

What else? That's how the zombies escaped with Cleto.

Then who drove? The reanimator? Zombie motoring skills probably matched their smell, but again, Barrett Chambers had driven himself to Denver.

I returned across the river. Phaedra waited. Water squished from my shoes.

She asked, "What did you find?"

"Not much of anything. The trail vanished."

She whispered, "Zombies?"

I nodded.

"How do they do disappear like that?"

"They have their ways," I replied.

"Should we tell my uncle? That it's zombies?"

I put a flat edge in my voice. "No. Zombies are part of the secrets we have to keep. Besides, would he believe us?"

We backtracked to the ambush place. Cavagnolo and Vinny were on their knees scooping meth crystals back into the plastic jars. They weren't picky about sifting out the grass and dirt.

They stood and each held an armful of plastic jars.

"Phaedra, come here," Cavagnolo said. He handed her his load of jars. "Put these in Vinny's truck. Wait for me there."

She took the jars back to his truck.

Cavagnolo brushed his hands to get rid of the dust and white meth residue. He put his hand on my shoulder and led me out of the clearing. The gesture was a crude attempt to reassure me.

We stood with a curtain of willow branches between us and Phaedra. He suddenly grabbed the sleeve of my coat and yanked the pistol from his waistband.

"I'm going to shut your mouth once for all, you son of a bitch."

The pistol swung toward my face.

My reflexes kicked into vampire speed. I didn't know if Cavagnolo intended to shoot me or only try to scare me. Either way, I had other plans.

I wrenched the pistol from him and shoved him in the chest. I kept myself from punching his face and breaking his skull. I was close to losing myself in anger and the blow might've killed him.

Cavagnolo stumbled backward. His eyes gaped with astonishment. His arms twirled through the willow branches. He tripped and fell onto his back.

I ejected the magazine and racked the slide to clear the chamber. I tossed the magazine into the weeds and threw the pistol at his feet.

"Why are you worried about me keeping my mouth shut? Is this about your deal with the feds?"

The astonishment in Cavagnolo's eyes boiled into rage.

"As long as I'm alive, your secret stays with me. I die and the world will know what a rat fink traitor you are." I lied because I had made no such arrangements.

I reached down and pulled him up by his collar. I brought his face close to mine so he'd get the full brunt of my anger.

Even though I had him by the neck, he growled. "Yeah, I read you. Now you read me. Stay away from Phaedra."

This guy had a brass pair if he was threatening me. "Phaedra wants to talk to me, that's our business. Understand?"

Cavagnolo tried to shake loose.

I said, "Kill me and you're screwed. Two ways. Your secret will get out and your own men will turn on you. And there's what happened to Gino, Cleto, and the rest of that crew. I can stop the ones responsible. If you stay the hell out of my way. Understand?"

He nodded but that didn't hide his rage.

I let Cavagnolo go.

He smoothed his jacket collar in quick motions. "Fuck you. I'm doing you a favor by telling you to stay away from Phaedra. She might be my niece but she's still a fruitcake."

"Phaedra's a troubled girl, that's all."

"Troubled? She's a crazy bitch." Cavagnolo found his pistol and brushed off the dust.

Bitch? That was something Cavagnolo would say about a girl-friend, wife, even his mother, but his niece? How crazy was she?

Cavagnolo shoved the pistol into his waistband. "You're quiet all of a sudden, wise guy." He gave a malicious smirk. "That's because you know I'm right."

CHAPTER 35

Cavagnolo and I stepped from behind the trees and back to the clearing. Flies swarmed around us, perhaps hoping we'd also drop dead and add to the feast.

"What are you going to do about the bodies?" I asked.

"Leave 'em," Cavagnolo answered. "Let them rot. I didn't kill them, so when the cops come asking, I'll tell them the truth. I don't know nothing."

"So that's it?"

"Whaddaya expect? I move them and get caught, then the cops will assume I had something to do with this."

Made sense. I said to Phaedra, "Better go with your uncle."

"What about you?"

"I have things I need to get done."

Vinny held open the rear door in the pickup cab. Cavagnolo nudged Phaedra's arm. She pulled away. Her gaze swept over the corpses and back to me.

There was no horror in her eyes, only a strange disappointment. She stood between an old world and a new reality. What she had dreamed for—a new life reincarnated as an immortal—was possible. I had been her guide for a brief excursion into the world of the supernatural.

Her stare sharpened. My *kundalini noir* cringed as I sensed an echo. But she didn't do it. Instead she turned her back to me and climbed into the pickup.

No good-byes from either of us. There was no reason that I should see her again.

They drove off and left me with a cloud of flies beating around my head.

What would the Araneum tell me to do about Phaedra? For now my priority was the zombies.

I started my 4Runner and drove to a paved road. I stopped beside a gravel quarry and got my map. I noted the places where the zombies had been.

Gino's place. He had been carried from his house toward Pinos Creek. Why not carry him to the road and escape in a vehicle as they had done with Cleto? Why take the creek?

What about this ambush? Was it planned or did the zombies run across Cleto and the others? The zombies had taken him away in a vehicle. Where to?

Next, the ambush on me. That attack happened to the north of here by four miles. I couldn't figure why the zombies were out there.

The attack on Gino occurred at night. The other two during the day.

I thought again about the attack on Gino. The zombies had headed east on foot. They had crossed the ridgeline connecting Horseshoe and Poison Mountains, farther to the south.

Poison? Not a good name.

I marked a line from Gino's house through gaps in the hills. The line wiggled southeast toward San Diego Creek and across the draws and gullies.

I studied the map for clues. Where could the zombies have gone?

Horseshoe Mountain.

Varmint Gulch.

Ghoul Mountain.

Deadman's Gulch.

Ghoul Mountain was next to Deadman's Gulch. If those two places didn't deserve a look, then I might as well give up and head back to Denver.

Something fluttered and landed on the roof of the 4Runner.

A pigeon?

I opened the door and peeked.

A crow stood, waiting. A filigreed message capsule gleamed on its right leg.

I scooped the crow and brought it inside the Toyota. Unless the Araneum was providing an exact address to the reanimator and his zombies, I had no use for their cryptic missives.

I unclipped the capsule and held it low near the floorboards, the darkest place in my 4Runner.

I opened the capsule and let it air out for a moment. I unfolded the swatch of vampire parchment.

It read:

Kill the girl. Continue with your mission.

Araneum

My insides felt hollow. The brown dried-blood letters were bold, the slashing strokes conveying the grimness of the message. Nothing cryptic here.

The crow hopped onto the sill of the open window in my door.

I crumpled the message in my hand.

I wouldn't, couldn't kill Phaedra. The Araneum didn't understand. She was a girl with big problems and had reached out to me, a vampire, for help. She had psychic powers; weren't those important to the Araneum?

Despite the fact that Phaedra knew about vampires, I'd find a way to let her live.

I threw the wadded parchment past the crow. The wad hadn't gone five feet through the sunlit air before turning into a knot of fire and smoke. Gray ash fluttered to the dirt.

The crow lifted one leg and gave a muted squawk to remind me about the capsule.

I screwed the cap back on. "You want it, go fetch." I wound my arm and hurled the capsule into a stand of dense rabbitbrush.

The crow followed my hand and catapulted from the window. It aimed for the tumbling capsule and extended both claws. Midway through the capsule's trajectory, the crow snagged it with a clink of claw on metal.

The crow gave its wings a mighty flap and soared over the brush and the quarry.

Bad form, Felix. The bird was only doing its job. You need to get on with yours.

What I needed was a nap. Fatigue wore me down, and a tired vampire makes mistakes. Those mistakes can mean no more vampire.

I didn't have time to sleep or make mistakes. I had tonight to find the zombies before they picnicked on the rest of town. I headed to Morada and circled south along San Diego Creek.

According to the map, the road climbed and kinked past the local cemetery.

I couldn't sneak around in the Toyota. The approach to Deadman's Gulch was a seven-mile hike over open ground.

I left the 4Runner on the street outside a small apartment building, got my backpack, and followed the road on foot.

I removed my contacts. Dozens of red auras from small animals flitted around me.

The road crested where the cemetery sat on the edge of a plateau. From here, the view looked east across the breadth of the San Luis Valley. Strings of lights followed the perpendicular roads segmenting the flat valley floor. It looked spectacular in a sweeping panoramic sort of way, but I preferred watching moisture bead on the side of a chilled cocktail.

Farther south on the road, isolated houses sprang up on the left and right. A few cars passed on the road. With my contacts out, I could tell from the passengers' auras they weren't interested in me.

Green trash bins and aluminum mailboxes sat on the side of the road. Signs advertised ranches parceled into smaller lots. ACT NOW. FINANCING AVAILABLE.

Ghoul Mountain loomed before me like a gigantic tombstone. On the backside of the mountain, I would find Deadman's Gulch.

Headlamps rocked through the dusty night as a vehicle approached. This far in the distance, they wouldn't see me. I hiked away from the road and crouched behind a natural wall of big rocks. A Subaru station wagon rumbled along, slinging rocks against its chassis.

Now that I'd started my trek, I realized that I'd underestimated the time it would take to reach Deadman's Gulch. I'd have to go cross-country as quickly and stealthily as possible.

Better that I go not in human form but as a wolf. I'd attract less attention if seen by humans. In the darkness they'd assume I was a big dog or coyote. Plus my senses were more acute and I could run faster.

I stripped and put my folded clothes and gun in the backpack, which I hid beneath a pile of rocks.

I cleared a spot on the ground and lay naked in the sand. I summoned the transmutation from human form to lupine. A warmth leached to the center of my chest. My *kundalini noir* coiled into a nervous ball of anticipation.

Shards of pain crackled along my bones as they stretched and twisted into shape. My skull felt as if a grappling hook had snagged the front of my jaws and winched them to a point. Needles pushed out where fur sprouted through naked skin.

Smells flooded my nose and separated into delicate aromas. Tiny sounds echoed in my ears.

I lay still for a moment to let the pain from the transmutation melt away. I turned onto my paws and stood on all four legs.

I crept from behind the wall of rocks and waited beside the road. Dust from road traffic remained in the air and I sneezed.

I remembered the route from the map. I'd head straight to the big mountain. From there I'd go south to the gulch.

The way clear, I loped across the road. My path took me between large dwellings surrounded by dirt and brush.

I caught the scent of horses. Made me hungry.

Horses behind a fence picked up my scent and whinnied in distress.

Dogs barked a warning. *Wolf. Wolf. Wolf.*

I kept my speed at a fast trot. To the left, on the low hills, coyotes stalked mule deer. I crossed the scent trails of rabbits, field mice, and skunks. The stars above grew brighter the farther I got from humans.

I reached the high ground east of the big mountain. To my left, a faint white glow splashed across the shrubs and rocks.

I raised my snout. The air carried the odor of rotting human flesh and a strange pungent smell.

Zombies.

That glow must be from their lair.

I'd creep close and discover their numbers.

I only saw the auras of small creatures: mice, a raccoon, and an owl swooping for a meal.

Zombies had no auras. In this darkness and even with my night vision, they could hide in the rocks and shrubs provided they didn't move. But as long as I could smell them, I knew where they were.

I climbed down from the high ground and went hunting.

Chapter 36

The trail I'd been looking for disappeared into a flat gully. I stayed on the slopes. Should someone surprise me, I didn't want to be channeled into any narrows. I wanted open ground for sprinting at full speed.

Tire prints appeared in the dirt of the gully. The zombies who had taken Cleto must've traveled this way. Large rocks had been placed along the entrance to the gully to make it appear that no vehicle could pass through.

The smell of garbage collected along the bottom of the gully.

How close was I to the zombies?

The gully continued east and I proceeded straight over the rise toward the glow.

Something to my left moved. I slowed and stared at a juniper tree. There was no wind. How did the tree move?

The closer I got to the tree, the stronger the garbage stink. An odor of rotted pork and fruit.

When I got close to the tree, a zombie appeared from between the branches. I growled and bared my fangs.

Strands of filth peeled from the sores on his face and around his open mouth. A torn hat rested on his head. The cowboy zombie.

I picked up speed and circled past him.

He stepped away from the tree and followed. His naked feet crunched through dead cactus. He rubbed the sleeve of his right arm across his belt buckle to keep it shiny.

I slowed to a trot. I didn't want to move so fast that I'd miss something important. If the zombie got too close, I could bound away.

We crossed the slope into the gulch. Another zombie waited. She stank of dead fish that had washed up and lain in the sun. She had hair the color of tumbleweed and pale eyes like the bellies of dead mice. A long blouse fell to the thighs of a pair of strong legs that ended in tall boots.

I recognized those boots. She'd been the one who had swung from the tree and smashed me on the head.

Cowboy zombie and I passed her. She reached into her blouse for her armpit. She flung a gob of hairy pus. I hopped and let it splatter on the rocks beneath me.

The white glow up ahead became brighter. The groan of an engine drifted through the silence.

Zombies gathered behind me, too many to count at a glance. More zombies circled on the high ground and more in the gulch. Where had so many zombies come from?

They moved quietly; the only sound came from the scraping of their feet through the dirt.

I reached the top of the rise. The engine sound got louder. The glow came from the windows of a house. It appeared much like the other human dwellings that I'd passed. It had large windows and a porch in front. The porch opened to a flat wooden platform. Another set of tall windows was under the platform, showing another level to the house. The house was well hidden until I walked right up the gulch. I trotted down the rise for the house.

Strong odors made me wince. More pungent smells stung my nose.

A zombie in a clean white coat appeared on the porch. His hair was neatly trimmed and combed. He walked onto the porch and looked at me. He remained still while more zombies staggered through a door under the platform. He was all too human-like but had no aura so he was definitely undead.

Was he the reanimator?

The Araneum had said *man*. So who was this zombie and why was he different from the others?

I trotted in front of the house. Tire tracks rose from the gulch to a large door on the eastern side of the house. This was where they stored their vehicle.

More zombies loomed in the darkness, appearing from behind the scrub junipers. They moved without speaking or gesturing to one another so I wondered how they knew what to do.

I continued past a large container on tall metal legs that smelled of gasoline.

Along the back, I found the source of the groaning sound. It was a big engine connected to cables leading from the house. I couldn't think of the human word for the machine but I knew it provided electrical power.

This was the zombie farm. The smells of decay and poison. The secret road here. The many zombies.

I knew the location and layout. I'd return with human weapons and leave nothing but ruin.

Zombies stood before me in a half circle. More zombies closed behind me. They moved in loose order as if under someone's command. Whose? I didn't hear a thing.

I turned to my right and started up the slope. Zombies appeared from the brush. I turned right again to backtrack. More zombies.

I was penned against the house. Time to escape.

I chose a wide gap between two zombies. I tore into a sprint. They would never catch me.

The sound of more engines echoed from beyond the rise. A machine with four tires bounded to my right. A similar machine bounded to my left. The zombie riders were the large, well-fed hunters from the restaurant.

I couldn't outrun these two. I spun around to find another way to escape.

A female zombie dove for me. She moved fast and clasped my left hind leg.

I landed on my side, snarling. I snapped at her wrist, severing the hand with one bite. The taste of rotted meat and bitter metals gagged me.

Another hand clutched my fur at the shoulders. Another grabbed my tail.

I scratched and snapped at the zombies. I'd tear apart one hand and another would take its place.

A zombie stabbed me with the stumps of his shredded wrists. He bit my left forepaw and clamped hard.

I ignored the hands clutching me and tore at this zombie's throat. I chewed through his neck. Zombie yuck flowed into my mouth and I let go, shaking my head, hacking and overcome with nausea.

The zombie's head remained locked onto my paw like a giant tick.

Zombies piled on top of me, hands gripping fur, legs, and tail.

I howled in fury. I pushed from the ground to shake the zombies off.

The zombies clinging around my neck suddenly let go. This was my chance to break free.

The female zombie in the long blouse and tall boots stood in front of me. She held the loop of a large metal cable. She lassoed my head and yanked hard. The loop bit into my neck, snagging fur and skin.

Hands clutched my legs and tail and pulled with renewed strength. More zombies joined the female zombie. They grabbed the cable and stretched my neck.

The more I struggled, the harder all the zombies held firm. The bones in my neck began to crack.

I fought the pain but unless I stopped resisting, the zombies were going to pull my head off.

I relaxed and hoped they'd do the same.

The zombies quit pulling but they held on to me.

Everyone knew what happened.

I had surrendered.

CHAPTER 37

The zombies carried me around the house. They climbed the stairs to the platform in front. The female zombie ran the cable through a metal cage on the platform. She dragged me inside.

When they'd pushed me into the cage, the door was shut. The female zombie made the cable loop slack and slipped it free.

Zombies stood around me, their eyes empty of life. I smacked my mouth to clean the foul taste from my tongue. I couldn't believe that these simple, disgusting creatures had captured me.

I studied the wire cage. A real wolf could bend the metal door apart and rip it loose. As a supernatural I should be free without much trouble.

I growled at my captors. However nasty they tasted, I was going to rip the lot of them into pieces.

My neck and legs were stiff and clumsy with pain. Every ache told me how much I was going to enjoy destroying these zombies.

Cowboy zombie poked me with a long, smooth club. I snapped at the club and crunched it to pieces. He staggered from the cage, still grasping the other end of the club.

I flexed my shoulders and stretched my legs to ready myself. I raised my tail in alpha defiance and backed up to lunge.

An electric jolt punched along my spine. I jumped forward, and when my muzzle touched the metal door, another electric jolt snapped though my body.

I backed into the middle of the cage, surprised and worried.

The zombies made a gasping *ghaw, ghaw*—flinging spit from their disgusting mouths—that was as close as they could manage to a laugh.

What had happened? I looked around. A second cable connected the cage to the house. When I had touched the wires, that was when the electricity had gone through me.

The electric shock was too much even for my supernatural powers. One bite on the wires and I'd be flung on the floor, paralyzed from the electricity. How could these stupid creatures be so clever?

I paced in a tight circle within the cage. Barren ground and rocks surrounded the deck down to the gulch. Rabbitbrush and juniper grew around the boulders sticking out from the surrounding hills.

A layer of fresh smells wove through the zombie stink. Animals on the move: mice, hares, doves in flight. And the scent of morning pollen.

Morning.

The skies to the east faded to lighter blue. Yellow light touched the summit of the big mountain.

The dawn was coming.

And I was out here in the open in this cage.

I stared to the eastern horizon. When the sun made its appearance, its rays would burn me to ashes.

I growled in frustration and fear. I barked and howled. I circled left, then right.

The zombies stepped closer, lifting axes and clubs with nails in them.

One by one, the stars twinkled for the last time and disappeared into the gathering light.

The sky to the east flashed green and became yellow. It would be light soon and then the sun, the great destroyer of vampire flesh, would take me.

CHAPTER 38

If I had no way to escape as a wolf, I'd do it as a vampire.

I lay on the plywood and tucked my legs close. The trick during transmutation would be keeping my writhing body from touching the electrified cage.

I cleared my thoughts of fear and let my mind expand into the stillness. The transformation came to me like water filling an empty shell.

A great force pulled from the inside of my skull to flatten my snout. My leg and arm bones felt like they were crushed by enormous stones. My senses were smothered by a storm of pain. Fur receded into skin and my flesh burned with the sensation of being dragged through smoldering brush. My paws molded themselves back into hands and feet in agonizing spasms.

The pain lifted and for an instant my mind was a smooth pool devoid of thought. My senses had turned dull and the complex smells simple. Staring into the landscape, my mind clutched at the names and purposes of the objects. A wire cage that rested on a wooden deck. Juniper. Rocks.

Zombies.

Someone clapped. A man cheered, "Very good."

My muscles throbbed. My joints unfolded like they were breaking through glue.

I drew onto my naked butt and sat on the plywood sheet, careful not to touch the wire grid. I turned toward the clapping.

A red aura surrounded the man who stood between the house and me. His psychic shroud undulated with pleasure and the fuzzy, sparkling penumbra betrayed his curiosity.

He had the broad shoulders of a lumberjack. A fleece sweater covered the top of a white lab coat.

His proud jaw and the cowlick curling over his forehead made him appear like the superhero in a comic book. Only we weren't in any comic book and he was no superhero.

He crouched beside my cage.

I focused my gaze into his. I'd zap him and order him to let me out.

His irises opened like the apertures on a camera lens. Usually the irises pop wide as fast as a bubble bursting. His aura brightened, but it didn't blaze as I expected.

My hypnosis powers were weak.

The man's expression went blank. He staggered from the cage.

Cowboy zombie grasped his arm and pulled him away. Why did the zombie protect this man? Was he their master? The reanimator?

The man gave his head a groggy shake. He rubbed color back into his face. Snakes of malice lashed from his aura. His forehead wadded with deep furrows of anger. He motioned toward cowboy zombie and beckoned for the club.

The man took the club and smacked it across the cage. "What the hell did you do to me?"

The cage rattled. I feared the wires would snap loose and shock me.

I couldn't break free. I couldn't hypnotize him. I was trapped.

The man eased the club through the wire grid. "What the hell are you?"

I was certain he was going to jab me with the club, and when he did, I'd shove it back into his chest.

Instead the man wedged the club in the grid and tipped the cage. I slid across the plywood toward the electrified wires.

I grabbed in panic for the plywood sheet to arrest myself. My fingers touched the wires under the plywood, and the next instant, blasts of mule-kick pain shot up each arm and exploded in my armpits.

My hands tore from the wires and I tumbled backward against the grid.

The sensation was like getting impaled on a red-hot iron bar. Every synapse fired between every cell, and the universe within my head was scorched of everything but pain.

The cage rocked back and settled on its bottom. I curled on the plywood to save myself.

The man levered the cage again, and again I fell against the wire grid.

For the next minute I lived inside a lightning bolt, my being consumed with white pain, every thought obliterated by a tumbling fire that wracked my body.

The pain abated, like the crackling embers of a dying fire. I smelled burnt flesh—my own. My eyes gradually came into focus. Wisps of smoke drifted by my face.

I lay on my side in a clenched fetal position. My *kundalini noir* trembled, exhausted by the ordeal.

The man slapped the club against the cage. "More?"

I couldn't speak. I put my hand against my face—my numb fingers were hard as icicles—and tried to force my mouth to move. My lips were rubbery and cold like those of a dead fish.

He yelled, "You do that hypnosis thing again and I'll fry you like sausage. You understand?"

I pulled from a deep reserve and the effort to speak was like climbing out of a crevasse. "Yes, I understand. No more, please."

"Please?" His aura smoothed. "Don't expect a 'you're welcome.'"

I wanted a sip of warm blood. I wanted a ticket home. I wanted . . . I wanted . . .

The morning light on Ghoul Mountain inched down the summit. The last of the eastern stars disappeared into the cerulean blue.

The dawn approached.

I wanted not to die.

CHAPTER 39

I turned to the man. "Take me inside."

"Why?"

"Please, take me inside."

He tapped the club against the wooden deck. "Tell me why."

The light on Ghoul Mountain broadened and lengthened like a pale tongue. My *kundalini noir* rolled and bucked in apprehension.

The man knew too much as it was. He'd seen me transform from a wolf. I didn't want to tell him I was a vampire. I didn't want to confess my greatest fear and weakness—the rays of the morning sun.

The man scanned the terrain. "What is it? All of a sudden you forgot about my shock therapy. What are you afraid of?"

"I can't . . . can't . . ."

"Can't what? Tell me?" The man swung the club like a baton. "I think we've established that you're going to do whatever the hell I tell you. I got all morning and apparently you don't."

The light on Ghoul Mountain was halfway down its side. My *kundalini noir* coiled in desperation. I couldn't betray the Araneum. "No, please, you don't understand."

"Then make me understand. I'm an intelligent man. Shouldn't be hard."

I could lift the plywood floor and hide behind it. But the electric grid would shock me and I'd thrash around, burning, to the amusement of this demented bastard.

The morning light slanted across Ghoul Mountain.

The dread of annihilation made me feel the flames licking my skin. My mind clawed for ideas to escape but there was only one.

I cried out: "It's the morning light."

The man turned his face toward Ghoul Mountain. His eyes became twin shiny disks, as yellow and menacing as the sun about to destroy me.

He pointed to the east. "The sun?"

"Yes," I yelled.

"The morning light?"

"Yes," I yelled again, the word shooting from my throat.

"What's so dangerous about it?"

Moments ago, electric pain had stripped me of everything but the ferocious touch of its agonizing sting. Now fear, the fear of being roasted into nothingness, the absolute and complete destruction of Felix Gomez, lay waste to every thought but one: *Survival.*

I let cowardice splash over me with a filth that I readily gulped to stay alive. "The morning sun destroys us."

"Us who?"

"Us vampires."

The man looked stunned. "Vampires?"

"Yes. Yes."

"No shit," he replied. "You are a vampire?"

"Yes." My throat hurt from the scream.

Sunlight reached the bottom of Ghoul Mountain and marched into Deadman's Gulch.

The man rapped the club against the deck. He smiled triumphantly. "They said I was crazy for my studies in reanimation."

He *was* the reanimator.

"Look at what I've done." He pointed the club at his mob of zombies and then to me. "I've opened the door to a world beyond death and see what else I've found. A vampire."

"Please, take me inside." I saw myself a pathetic sniveling coward, helpless to do anything but betray my kind. My *kundalini noir* lay in a circle, head to tail, opened its mouth, and began eating itself. My strength emptied out a gash in my psyche.

"Now that I know this, why should I take you inside?" the reanimator asked. "You said us, meaning more vampires. I caught you; I can catch them. I might learn a very interesting lesson by watching what the sun does to you."

The echo started.

Felix . . . ix . . . ix.

Phaedra's face bloomed before me.

The echo ricocheted in my brain and my spine quivered.

What did she want? Was this a warning? Too late, I was already in deep, deep shit.

The echo grew loud. A trembling continued down my spine.

Not now, for God's sake.

I grasped the plywood board and pulled myself into a ball. In a second, that psychic noise would have me thrashing against the inside of the electrified cage.

My psychic column vibrated. My vision blurred. I shut my eyes tight and got ready for the worst.

The vibration suddenly stopped. The echo halted, more abruptly than it ever had. I opened my eyes.

The man set his hands on his knees and stared in amazement. "What the hell is wrong with you?"

At the moment, everything. "Take me inside," I whispered.

The man stood. "Not until you talk."

A zombie brought a camcorder. Unlike the other revenants, his clothes—clean white lab coat, black trousers, and dress shoes—were well-kept and neatly pressed. He was the one I'd seen on the porch last night. Aside from the gummy smears around his lifeless eyes, he looked like a service technician in an ad for Mercedes-Benz.

The reanimator took the camcorder and aimed it at me. The pale triangle of Ghoul Mountain reflected in its lens.

"Smile for YouTube. Time's running out."

I recoiled at the image of the white rays of the sun lapping my skin and the sizzling flesh turning into smoke. "I'll tell you everything."

He lowered the camcorder. "Such as?"

"Everything. Vampires. The world of the supernatural." The dam of self-restraint had broken, and I would jettison every promise and secret in trade for one more day undead.

The reanimator handed the camcorder to lab coat zombie. "Then we'll talk. After all, there will be another sunrise."

CHAPTER 40

Zombies slipped poles through the wire grid of the cage and lifted. They carried me sedan-chair style while lab coat zombie tended the electric power cable attached to the cage.

I swayed on the plywood sheet, vacant eyed, defeated and broken. I, Felix Gomez, combat veteran, vampire detective, had turned yellow to save his hide.

All those stories I've heard of defiant heroes burned through my memory and singed me. They had stared into oblivion and were given a choice. Treachery or death. They had chosen death.

I had chosen treachery. All the heroics in my life meant nothing.

We entered the porch door. Cowboy zombie stumbled at the threshold and the cage tipped. I fell against the wire grid and, as I cried out, scrambled to center myself on the plywood.

Cowboy zombie leered at me over his shoulder. "*Ghaw. Ghaw.*"

This part of the house was at one time the living room. Most of the walls had been knocked out. Thick dirty drapes covered the floor-to-ceiling windows. Cables and tubes snaked across the floor and hung from the ceiling like the vines of a grotesque plant growing out of control. The humid air was thick with the odor of benzene and formaldehyde. It looked like the lab in a straight-to-video horror movie—with me as the starring victim.

Shelves stood along two of the adjacent walls. Bubbles pumped through dozens of glass jars and aquariums on the shelves. Human parts floated inside the cloudy solutions. A blood transfusion machine sat on a narrow table. The machine rocked back and forth, pumping blood from a dismembered torso in a tub and into a plastic bag warming in a Crock-Pot.

The zombies took me to the far end of the room next to a heavy wooden door mounted on a steel pipe frame. The door had been fashioned into a table. Lab coat zombie donned a pair of oven mitts and opened the door to my cage. The reanimator snapped his fingers and the zombies upended the cage.

The terror of what was about to happen made me cringe. I fell across the wire grid, the electricity sparking and burning my skin. I dropped to the floor, jerking about in agony.

A sharp pain like I'd been hit with a nail gun ran through my left hand. The pain reverberated inside me and I could do nothing but squirm in helplessness.

Cowboy zombie pulled away from a red jumper cable clamp that he had pinched to the palm of my hand. Lady tall boots zombie plopped a metal cap on my head and buckled a leather chinstrap. A black jumper cable dangled from the cap.

The reanimator gripped the handle of a large electrical knife switch bolted to a workbench. He closed the switch and . . .

I thought my head exploded. Everything attached to my brain—skull, medulla oblongata, eyeballs—seemed to blast apart. The tornado of pain funneled down my spine, circled my chest, and ran to my left hand. Every nerve ending along that path became a rivet of fire.

The pain receded, like smoke clearing after a bomb blast. The mental noise of anguish rumbled in my brain.

The reanimator came back into focus. He studied me, his hand holding the switch at a half-cocked position.

My *kundalini noir* flattened, limp as a deflated balloon.

I fought to keep my eyes open. "Who are you?"

His expression slipped into pride. "I am Dr. Leopold Hennison. A medical doctor, not some silly academic with a Ph.D." He pointed to a certificate on the wall. "And you are?"

"Felix Gomez."

"Where are you from?"

"Denver."

"A vampire from Denver? I sent one of my zombies to Denver. Barrett Chambers. Would you know what happened to him?"

"Who?"

Hennison closed the switch again. The lightning bolt blasted through me again—the world went white with pain—and when I came around, I wanted to melt to the floor.

"Barrett was the first zombie I made who could drive. You don't know how much his loss inconvenienced me," Hennison said. "Let's try this again." He tapped his fingers on the switch. "What happened to Barrett Chambers?"

I lie and I get more pain. Better to tell the truth. "I destroyed him."

"Why?" Hennison grasped the switch handle.

"Because he was a zombie."

"So?"

"We can't let humans know about the undead. Your zombie could've been discovered and captured."

Hennison loomed close. "What's this worry about humans knowing about the undead? They will soon. About the undead. About zombies. About me."

Hennison backed away. "And they will know soon enough about vampires."

My *kundalini noir* deflated even more. I had betrayed the Great Secret. How could I undo this?

"As for Barrett Chambers," Hennison said, "he was scouting for prospects. Perhaps he wasn't ready to be on his own. Oh well. Science is all about taking risks."

Hennison opened a plastic cooler on the workbench. He took out a Red Bull, popped it open, and guzzled from the can.

Tall boots girl zombie leaned over me and stared at my naked crotch. Yellow drool oozed from her mouth and splattered on my leg.

"We better get you some pants," Hennison said. "Kimberly hasn't lost her oral fixation." He chomped his teeth twice. "Just ask him." Hennison cocked a thumb at cowboy zombie, who covered his crotch with both hands and retreated a step. "Kimberly minds well but let's not tempt her too much."

Lab coat zombie tossed me a pair of filthy sweatpants.

Hennison finished his Red Bull and dropped the empty can into a recycling box. He drummed the handle of the switch. "Remember. Act naughty and it's zap, zap."

I came to my feet. Kimberly's greedy eyes followed the angle of my dangle. I pulled the pants over my legs and wondered if out of sight, out of mind applied to zombies.

I stood, my flesh and bones aching, but I was grateful that my body still worked.

Cowboy zombie tipped the wooden table vertical.

Hennison motioned that I back against it. I hesitated as I studied the metal hoops bolted to where my wrists and ankles would rest.

The doctor started to press the switch handle.

"No, no," I shouted. No more pain. "I'll do it."

Hennison relaxed. Cowboy zombie and Kimberly cinched the metal hoops over my wrists and ankles. I flexed my arms and legs to test the strength of the hoops. I could break free but needed a distraction to keep them from frying me with the electricity.

Hennison tripped a lever on the table. The door pivoted into a horizontal position, stopping suddenly so that the back of my head thumped against the surface.

Hennison unhooked the jumper cable clamp from my hand and removed the steel cap. "Don't get any funny ideas. Now you're wired directly to the generator outside."

"Believe me," I replied, "funny is the furthest thing from my mind."

He chuckled. "Don't get me wrong. We can joke around. A sense of humor makes for good conversation." Hennison waved to his mute zombies. "Trust me that I'm lacking in good conversation."

Hennison was lacking more than conversation but I knew my reward if I said so. He wanted to talk, I needed time to escape, so why not let him gab?

Hennison took off his fleece sweater and smoothed the lab coat underneath. He faced a large mirror fixed to the wall close to the table. He wiped dust from the glass. He watched himself as he turned his face, lifting his chin, his jaw set, as if he was auditioning to be Benito Mussolini.

His reflected gaze swung in my direction. Hennison jerked his head over his shoulder toward me. He turned to the mirror and back to me.

I knew what he saw, or rather didn't see: my reflection.

For a short moment, his brow furrowed in puzzlement. When it smoothed, he smiled. "Let's you and I come to a deal."

"Anything you say. Tell me what you want, we'll shake hands, and I'll be on my way out of here."

"You're being too optimistic," Hennison said. "You and I are going to have a nice, long chat. I ask questions and you tell me the answers."

"I don't want to disappoint you but I'm not very good at this."

"You'll do fine, trust me. Just don't get all macho."

"Let's go back to that deal," I said, convinced that my choices were bad and really bad.

"You decide how comfortable you want to be," Hennison explained. "See, tomorrow I'm going to test your assertion that morning sunlight will destroy you. But until then, we'll chat, and it's up to you whether you want to pass the time in comfort or in extreme pain."

CHAPTER 41

Hennison rattled through a pan of tools on the workbench and selected a scalpel. He propped his elbows on the table and prodded my shoulder with the blade. A sting followed the trace of the scalpel on my skin.

"You're a walking freak show, Mr. Gomez. A Wikipedia of the fantastic. How do you transform from animal to human form?"

"It just happens. You might as well ask a duck how it grows feathers."

"What about not showing a reflection?"

"I'm a vampire." The scalpel bit into my skin. I tried acting like it didn't hurt but I'm sure I winced anyway. "I don't know how any of this works."

Hennison got another Red Bull. "Let's not be so circumspect. Work with me, please. Your translucent skin would be easier to examine after I peeled it from your flesh but I'd rather not do that."

"I second the motion."

"Not that your vote means anything." Hennison sipped from his Red Bull.

"What's this all about?" I lifted my head and motioned with my eyes across the room.

"This"—Hennison swept his arms to take in the breadth of the room—"is my revenge."

"On whom?"

"Everybody."

"Why?"

"Do you know what therapeutic misadventures are, Mr. Gomez?"

"It's when the doctor kills the patient."

"A gold star for you," Hennison said. "I see that you're acquainted with our medical profession. That's what I was accused of. My patients kept dying."

"Must have been hell on the malpractice insurance premiums."

"Not at all. It was a university hospital. The taxpayers paid the bills. What did I care?"

"Your patients died of . . . ?"

"They didn't die. I let them expire. There were no therapeutic misadventures. I was on a voyage of discovery. Would you call a mission into space a misadventure?"

Hennison absently rested his hand on the switch lever.

I gulped. "Of course not."

Hennison pulled his hand from the switch. He paced in a

circle between the switch and me. I hoped that can of Red Bull lasted a long time.

He said, "I was testing my hypothesis to unlock the greatest secret of all, the resurrection of the dead." He waited as if he expected his zombies to cheer him.

They stared at him with empty eyes. Pus seeped from their wounds.

Hennison let out a sigh and puffed his cheeks in dejection. "Genius is a lonely vocation."

Especially when you're surrounded by zombies.

"I take it the medical board didn't see it that way?"

Hennison wagged a finger. "You are so right about that. They acted as if my actions would damage the reputation of the hospital. How many patients died to perfect heart transplants? Were those therapeutic misadventures? I flatline a few patients—in the interest of science, mind you—and suddenly my techniques and procedures are called into question."

If this delusional bastard didn't have an advanced degree, I could see him hosing school buses with an AK-47.

I asked, "Didn't you tell the board what you were doing?"

"You ever hear of something called intellectual property? If I blabbed to the administration about this"—he motioned to his lab—"then every idea would belong to the hospital and its corporate sponsors. I'd be given a plaque and a token honorarium for my efforts." He crushed the can of Red Bull. "Instead they called me a criminal."

"That was when you came to lovely Morada?" I asked.

"Not yet. I tried to interest the Defense Department in my work. I pitched to them, what better weapon against terror than terror itself? We'd free the suspects locked up in Guantánamo after I turned them into zombies. Imagine Osama bin Laden's face when zombies come after him. We'll send their dead martyrs back home and on our side. Brilliant, no?"

"Absolutely," I replied.

Hennison's expression darkened. Shoulders sagging, he turned from me. "Once again, I was cast out. A prophet is never welcome in his own home. The generals thought I was a lunatic. The government would rather waste billions on nuclear weapons, utterly useless toys except to keep their cronies fattened at the public trough."

Kimberly's hand grasped my ankle. Imagine a rotten orange with fingers. She licked her lips and slipped the repulsive hand under the cuff of my sweats.

I raised my head. "Hey, Doc? Little help here."

Hennison stared at the floor and brooded. "Those were trying days. I felt I had nowhere to turn."

Kimberly snaked her arm up my leg.

Cowboy zombie did his undead snicker. "*Ghaw. Ghaw.*"

"Hey, Doc. Help."

"I watched a lot of television." Hennison brightened. "There I found salvation."

"You mean religion?" I raised my voice to get his attention. "A televangelist?"

"Of course not. Not those charlatans. I mean the queen of modern wisdom. Oprah."

"Oprah?"

"An American treasure. She did an entire show called 'Follow Your Dreams.'"

Kimberly's cold fingers crawled up my thigh like a thawing

tarantula. "Dreams." The word came from her mouth like a gargle.

My johnson shriveled. It wanted a pair of feet of its own to run away. "Hey, Dr. Hennison, would you mind?"

Hennison was reaching into the cooler for yet another Red Bull. He did a double take on Kimberly and threw a can. It bounced off her head and sprayed Red Bull. She shuffled backward, giving a disappointed zombie mumble, and withdrew that cold serpent of her arm from inside my pants.

"Thanks," I said. I let sensation return to my crotch. "You were talking about your dreams."

"My dreams." Hennison returned to the mirror. An expression of serenity soothed his face. "Oprah said, don't give up. Every worthy cause is a challenge. The keys to success are faith, persistence, and to ground your efforts on gratitude." Hennison paused to stare at himself. "I did exactly that. I downsized my life to the essentials and invested in my dreams."

"Zombies?"

"It's more than that."

"The revenge thing?"

"Now that I've reanimated the dead, I've only whetted my ambitions. My goals before were laughably modest. Even juvenile. I wanted to even the score on every nuisance, every inconvenience, every parking ticket, every blind date who wouldn't return my phone calls." Hennison marched from the mirror. "Instead, my recent success has fueled my desire for complete mastery of the globe."

"World domination?" I asked.

"For now."

The world wasn't enough? "And then?"

"Think of it, zombies in space."

"I'm thinking. Yes, I see it." I tested the metal hoops on my wrists.

"Do you think that's too ambitious?"

"For you, of course not. Why would you say that?"

"Are you aware of Icarus?"

"I wouldn't worry," I replied. "Compared to you, the guy was a loonie. Come on, making wax wings and flying too close to the sun?"

"I'm glad you say that," Hennison said. "Sometimes I think I'm getting carried away with my plans. It's good to get a fresh opinion."

"You want a fresh opinion? You sir, deserve a fucking Nobel Prize."

Hennison saluted. "Thanks."

I knew the way to his heart, on a wide avenue of flattery and bullshit. Now it was my turn to learn about his world. "Hey, Doc, how come some zombies are more animated than others? Take Lab Coat over there." I motioned with my head.

"You mean Reginald?" Hennison asked. "The sooner to expiration I complete the reanimation process, the more animated—lifelike if you will—the revenant is. But I've discovered another phenomenon. Have you noticed that zombies don't say much but they seem to know what the others are doing? It's as if they have a collective consciousness. The deeper the zombification, the greater awareness they have of one another."

Of course I had noticed how zombies cooperated to capture me. They moved as if they had one mind. They lacked auras so I assumed they had no connection to the psychic world, but I was wrong. What kind of mysterious connection, I didn't know.

Hennison said, "Other than the affordable real estate, the country living, and great mountain views, let me show you why I've come to Morada."

He motioned to Reginald, who went to the shelf and returned with a cardboard box the size of a small valise. He set the box on the workbench and lifted a metal case from inside the box.

The case had a transparent pyramid. This was no doubt a psychotronic diviner.

"Let's talk more," Hennison said. "But before we do, let's look at this."

Reginald brought a second box. From it he removed another psychotronic diviner, the one belonging to the Araneum, the one the zombies had stolen from me.

He placed the diviners side by side. Hennison's had a plain aluminum case fashioned with rivets and welds and cheap switches. This diviner looked like a garage hobby project, especially when compared to the Araneum's ornate version.

Hennison asked, "This is the device taken from your truck." He caressed the filigreed case. "It's beautiful but overdone. I would've spent the money on something else. Who made this?"

"I can't say." That was the truth. The Araneum could've jobbed out its construction.

"Where did you get it?"

"It was a gift."

Hennison grunted in displeasure. "You're playing games. Give me straight answers. You know what this is for?"

"I do."

"And?" Hennison circled his fingers.

Now he was playing games. This was his power trip. I wasn't going to tell him anything he didn't know.

Hennison pulled a wide plastic tube from the shelf where the diviners had rested. He uncapped one end of the tube and shook out large sheets of paper that he unfurled.

He laid the sheets on the table beside me and put heavy bolts on the opposite edges to keep them from curling together.

Hennison grasped my head and tilted it to look at the sheets. They were either copies or the originals of Dr. Blavatsky's notes from the Rocky Flats UFO.

"You've seen these, yes?"

"I have, but all I know is they were used to build those things over there."

"Things?" Hennison straightened as if insulted. "These things are like discovering fire. You know what they're for?"

"Detecting psychic energy?"

"You don't sound impressed."

"I'm not. Look at all the trouble they've gotten me into."

"Why are you in Morada, Mr. Vampire?"

"To find the source of the psychic energy." And zombies.

"Which is why I'm here as well. This device is a keyhole into the astral plane. The trouble is, I can see into the astral plane, but I can't get into it."

He pressed his hand against my forehead and pushed my head to the table. He brought his nose close to mine. I could read every pore and wrinkle in his face.

"If you're here looking for the source, then you vampires also want to enter the astral plane. So it's a race."

Hennison brought his mouth close to my left ear. His breath puffed warmly against my skin. "And guess what? You lost." He straightened up. "Which means I've won." He laughed. He motioned for the zombies to join him.

The room filled with his mad scientist cackle and the *ghaw, ghaw* of the zombies.

Hennison wiped a tear from one eye. "We barely know each other and I am going to miss you, Felix. It's been months since I've had a discussion as stimulating."

"You that lonely out here?"

"I have plenty of contact. I subscribe to e-newsletters and Yahoo Groups. I blog. There's no dearth of communication."

"I meant real conversation."

"Yeah, that's a challenge. Reginald"—Hennison cocked a thumb to Lab Coat—"can about pass for a live human but his brain was too far gone. My fault. See, I conked him a little too hard on the noggin. Reginald, turn around."

Reginald put his back to us. Hennison lifted Reginald's scalp and showed a baseball-sized dent in the skull.

Hennison smoothed the scalp into place. "I didn't mean to kill him. By the time I got him on the table and started the process, too late." He grasped Reginald's chin and gave it an affectionate shake. "Poor guy."

Reginald's eyes had the dull shine of the look from a loyal yet very dead dog.

"I preserved Barrett Chambers's brain enough for him to drive, but you may have noticed that I neglected to keep his body looking April fresh."

"Nothing a little Right Guard couldn't help," I said. "What about talking zombies?"

"Only one. And one too many for now, unfortunately." Hennison yelled toward a stairwell leading to the lower floor. "Sonia."

The zombies in the room fidgeted. What would make them uncomfortable?

Hennison cupped his hands around his mouth and yelled again. "Sonia."

Quick footfalls approached up the stairs, clicking and slapping, the sound of high heels moving in a woman's cadence.

Hennison tapped the workbench impatiently.

A platinum blonde rose onto the landing, hair in a Mary Tyler Moore cut and with puffy pink skin the color of cooked salmon. She wore a white nightgown with a fluffy hem and sleeves and strutted on clear stiletto mule pumps. Her lean bare legs looked impossibly long, like they'd been extruded from a die. Red stitch marks circled her neck, biceps, and the middle of her thighs.

Sonia's gray eyes were shiny as glass and just as inert but the set of her brow and the drag of her lower face expressed seething contempt. "Vhat you vant?"

"Sonia's my mail-order Russian bride." Hennison motioned toward me. "Say hello to our guest."

Her nose wrinkled as if I was the one who reeked of Dumpster cadaver. "Hello, guest."

"Show a little class, will you?" He grasped her wrist and yanked. Sonia stumbled on her heels. Her breasts remained fixed inside the nightgown like a pair of plastic globes.

Hennison laid her hand on my chest. "Feel this." She was cool but not corpse cold.

"I wrap her in an electric blanket, set it on high, and you couldn't tell the difference between her and any horny nurse."

Sonia twisted her hand free. She pulled over a battered wooden chair and sat. "Yes, I have dick privileges, aren't I the lucky one."

Hennison said, "She's pissed because I killed her."

Sonia reached into the top of her nightgown and pulled out

a cigarette. She sorted through tools on the workbench, found a butane torch, and lit it. The nozzle shot a yellow tongue of fire. Her thumb worked the regulator knob and the torch flame shrank to a blue point.

Hennison reached to take her cigarette. "Goddamn it, haven't I told you about the dangers?"

She turned and gave him the shoulder. "Vhat, that it's bad for my health? I'm a zombie, you moron."

"I meant a fire hazard."

Sonia lit the cigarette and took a long defiant puff. "Yes, of course. Heaven forbid that anything happens to this palace." She set her shoe against a metal box and tipped it over. Nuts and bolts, plastic vials, and human hands in Ziploc bags dumped to the floor.

"Don't push me, Sonia. Remember the last time?" Hennison pointed to her neck. "I took off her head and mounted it backward."

Smoke curled from the stitches along Sonia's throat, from inside the cleavage of her nightgown, and from her hair. She crossed her legs and let an expression of boredom sink across her zombie face. "And you turned it back around after you discovered that my blow jobs weren't worth a shit. Big genius you are."

"Women, even undead they're a ball and chain." Hennison shared a brotherly look that we were comrades in the war between the sexes, ignoring that I was bolted to a table and that he had spent a good part of the morning sizzling my vampire ass with high-voltage electricity.

I said, "Necrophilia is a hard sell."

Hennison replied, "Bah. Necrophilia is an outmoded term from an outmoded time. This is the twenty-first century."

"But, Doc," I said, "the stitches. The scars. You have to consider the aesthetics."

"You're right, of course," Hennison said. "What Sonia demonstrates, in her own gracious Slavic way, is that it is possible to create a nearly human zombie. I learned much during her process; the next time the zombie will be flawless. The caveat is that the victim, I mean subject, should be a little younger. Sonia didn't know what I was doing, she thought it was an advanced makeover process . . . which it was." Hennison laughed at his joke.

Sonia ground the cigarette in the palm of her hand. She flicked the dead butt against cowboy zombie.

"Why do they follow your orders?" I asked.

"Because I'm their creator. I take care of them, give them shelter; where else would they go?" Hennison kept quiet for a moment. "Let's try an experiment." He shouted at the zombies. "You're all free to go. Free. Free at last."

Sonia got to her feet.

Hennison grabbed her shoulder and pushed her back into the chair. "Not you."

The other zombies stared at him, to the outside door, then back to him. They picked at their scabs and gave tiny grimaces of confusion.

"I thought so," Hennison said. "I made them. They owe me complete allegiance."

"You're creating an army of zombies."

"More than that. I've tapped into something more profound." Hennison paused, his face flush with imagined glory, as if to cue the trumpets and drums. Maybe in his head.

"Immortality," he breathed dramatically, hesitating again, expecting perhaps that I should cry out, "Not immortality!" but I was too preoccupied pulling at my restraints.

Hennison's face drooped. "You don't seem impressed."

"I am, very. But I'd find it easier to share your enthusiasm if I wasn't bolted to this table."

"Actually, bodies aren't immortal, only the brains."

The zombies drooled and muttered a chorus of "Brains. Brains."

Sonia mouthed the word and licked one corner of her painted lips.

"I've perfected the technique of head transplants. I can swap bodies as easily as you change pants. Let me show you."

Hennison went to the far side of the lab. An upside-down stockpot sat on a pastry cart. He rolled the pastry cart close.

Hennison pulled the key ring on the lanyard attached to his belt. He opened a padlock securing the bottom of the stockpot. "This is a necessary precaution because, well, you'll see." He let go of the keys and they retracted with a *zzziit* back to his belt. He lifted the stockpot.

Cleto's head sat in a steel dish. His face was gray except for the top, which was pale and shaved bald. Tubes ran up his nose and into brass fittings along his temple. A net of wires crossed his scalp and were taped to his skin. His eyes were pressed tight, dark and shriveled as prunes, as if to not see what had happened to him.

On the other hand, Cleto deserved the look.

"Once you understand the biology and chemistry, it's a straight-forward process, a lot like fixing an appliance. The problem is not physical trauma but emotional. One minute you're cruising along on two legs and the next you're as mobile as a casserole."

"Why attack Cleto?"

"Opportunity, mostly. I've been stalking those lowlifes for a while. I couldn't believe my good fortune that I got a fresh head and my zombies got a nice snack."

"What's going to happen to him?"

"I haven't decided. His body was torn up when we captured him. In the meantime I have to keep his head locked up because of the brai . . ."

The zombies leaned into him and their cracked lips pursed to mutter their favorite word.

"You know what I mean." Hennison set the stockpot over Cleto and secured the padlock. "I can keep brai . . . I mean what's in his head, in stasis for an indefinite time."

Hennison came back to the table. "Oh, I can go on and on about zombies. But vampires?" He raised a finger in an inquisitive manner. "I have many, many questions. Are vampires immortal?"

Not if we're decapitated. "We can be killed."

"I figured that from your reaction to the sunrise." Hennison reached for the rheostat knob on the electric knife switch. "I mean, if no harm comes to you, are vampires immortal? You'll live forever and ever?"

That's what immortal means. "Yes."

"How old is the oldest vampire?" Hennison's aura became prickly with hostility. He rotated the rheostat knob. Up or down?

"I don't know," I answered, my muscles tensing as I expected the worse. "Several hundred years."

"A thousand?" The prickles on his aura grew into thorns.

"I'm sure some have been that old."

The thorns on his aura danced like individual flames. "Can this kill you?" He let go of the rheostat knob and grasped the switch.

The electricity bit where the steel hoops held my wrists and ankles. My body tightened in anticipation of the next jolt.

"Yes, this could kill me."

Hennison nodded, pleased with himself. "What about a stake to the heart?"

"Yes." I hoped we weren't checking the list of options.

"Garlic?"

"Poisonous."

"Really?" Hennison stroked his chin and studied the jars and bottles of chemicals along the wall. "An acid bath?"

"Probably."

"Gunshots?"

"Not fatal but very painful."

"How painful?"

He rolled the right leg of my sweatpants to my knee. The thorns on Hennison's aura shrank into a shroud of undulating cilia. Intermittent tentacles whipped out. He couldn't see it, obviously, but I could read his deranged pleasure.

He opened a drawer on the workbench and withdrew a revolver. More tentacles whipped from his aura.

The zombies, even Sonia, leaned close.

Hennison aimed the pistol at the shin of my right leg. He steadied the gun. The bullets shone in the cylinder chambers with their evil promises of pain and destruction.

My *kundalini noir* turned on itself in despair. I steeled myself to be strong. The bullets would tear flesh and shatter bone.

Hennison closed his left eye and focused his right down the sights of the pistol. "Are you afraid?"

"Yes, I am."

"But you said gunshots weren't painful."

"I said gunshots weren't fatal."

"First rule of any guest. Don't correct your host."

Hennison fired.

CHAPTER 42

My mind put everything in vampire speed.

The knuckles on Hennison's index finger turned white as he squeezed the trigger. The hammer cocked and the cylinder rotated. I heard the mechanism click, the spring compress and release. The firing pin struck the back of the cartridge. The primer cap exploded, detonating the propellant in the cartridge and pushing the bullet down the barrel.

The bullet spiraled toward me, my mind so focused on the slug that I could pick out the grooves carved into the brass jacket from the barrel rifling.

Despite that, it happened quick. The trigger pull. The bullet flying out the barrel.

The bullet striking my right leg.

Time reverted back to normal speed. Pain tore up my leg through my spinal column to my head, a thunderbolt of misery that blanked out every other sensation. I couldn't do anything but cry out to relieve the agony.

Blood gushed from the ragged hole, a well of red liquid that turned into a swirl of brown flakes.

Hennison lowered the revolver and admired what he'd done. The zombies went, "*Ghaw. Ghaw.*"

He dropped the gun into a pocket of his lab coat. He went to the workbench and returned with a wooden tongue depressor. He scooped through the dried flakes and they floated light as ash. "Interesting."

I couldn't escape. I accepted the inevitable. The Araneum was sending help—Jolie—and with me captured, that meant the destruction of everything and everyone in this house. Felix Gomez included.

I should've waited for Jolie before starting this assignment.

This was what I was reduced to, wishing for relief by annihilation at the hands of a friend and ex-lover.

Hennison pulled the leg of my sweatpants down to cover the wound. "Don't want you to get an infection."

He told Sonia to go downstairs. He instructed Reginald to put out guards. Kimberly pawed my crotch and gave an abbreviated zombie smile: I'll be back, sweetie.

"I've got another project demanding my time," Hennison said. "Who would've thought that the life of an evil genius would be so busy?" Hennison twisted the foot of my shattered leg.

The pain crushed me to unconsciousness. I came to a moment later.

He said, "I trust you won't insult my hospitality by trying to escape? Tomorrow you've got a date with Mr. Morning Sun."

Hennison turned to cowboy zombie and put the revenant's

hand on the electrical switch. "Watch him. If he tries to escape, close the switch. Shall we give it a test?"

"That's not necessary," I replied.

Hennison hopped up and down. "He's trying to escape."

Cowboy zombie pushed the switch closed.

The hot blast of pain ricocheted inside my body. My muscles locked up and my vision went from blurry to black.

The pain stopped. My arched back rested flat on the table. I tasted charred flesh and belched smoke.

"Excellent." Hennison patted cowboy zombie on the shoulder. "I'm trusting you."

Hennison wagged his finger in my face. "As for you, vampire, play nice."

He walked to the left and turned down the stairs.

The situation couldn't seem more hopeless. The electrical pain was gone but I still felt the throb from my shredded right shin bone. I was locked against a wooden table and wired to a generator.

I relaxed against the table, grateful at least for the respite from Hennison's bestial attentions.

If I lay undisturbed, my leg might heal by morning. Fresh human blood would do wonders for the wound and my attitude. The blood transfusion machine click-clacked at the far side of the room.

The blood sloshed back and forth. I imagined the heavy copper taste warming my tongue. Those thoughts brought relief, like huddling against a candle during an icy blizzard.

Cowboy zombie kept his cold undead eyes fixed on me.

I strained my wrists to test the security of the steel bands. The bands held firm. At the moment I was too weak to rip free, but give me a few hours. How to break loose and not get blasted by electricity?

I lay still and willed my life force to where I needed it most, my shattered leg and my *kundalini noir.* A chill started at my extremities and worked inward through my arms and my left leg. My fingers and the toes of my left foot went numb.

Twin pools of warmth settled in me, one in my body core and the other along my right shin. My *kundalini noir* turned slowly, rotating like an egg incubating under a heat lamp. The pain of my right shin dulled to a cramp as the cells repaired themselves in a growing frenzy.

Thirst rasped my throat. Hunger gnawed at my belly. My chances of escape were thinner than slim. Despair filled my mind like water flooding the hull of a sinking ship.

What buoyed me was the song of hope click-clacking from the transfusion machine.

CHAPTER 43

I don't know what time Dr. Hennison returned. For me, the day was a long stretch of misery.

Hennison bounded up the stairs, grinning pleasantly. He carried a half-gallon-sized Tupperware bowl. The sleeves of his lab coat were rolled to the elbows. Spatters of blood and a greasy black liquid covered his hands, arms, and his apron. He reeked of blood and meat like he'd been working in a slaughterhouse.

"Ah, you're still here," he said in mock surprise. Dark flecks dotted his safety glasses. "I knew my accommodations would be irresistible."

He patted the sweatpants right over my wound. His touch renewed the ache. "You might want to get that looked at by a doctor."

Was Torquemada of the Spanish Inquisition such a ball of laughs?

Hennison turned his attention to cowboy zombie and took the

lid off the Tupperware. Hennison circled the open bowl in front of him. "Look. Brains."

Cowboy zombie's eyes snapped to the bowl. Yellow drool dribbled to his chin. "Brains." He reached for the container.

Hennison kept the Tupperware away. "Just a snack for doing such a good job in making our guest feel at home." The doctor plucked a tablespoon from a pocket on his apron. He scooped gray mush from the bowl.

Cowboy zombie dropped his arms and opened his mouth. Hennison spooned the brains like it was a helping of Gerber's baby food. Cowboy zombie smacked his lips as he chewed the brains. A dab of gray yuck stuck to his upper lip, and a black tongue licked it clean.

Hennison put the lid back on the Tupperware and closed it with a burp. "The sound of freshness." He slapped cowboy zombie on the back. "Make sure Felix sticks around." He went down the stairs.

Cracks of light leaked in from around the drapes covering the windows. The light yielded to dark as evening crept upon us.

Night was a better time to escape. Without sunscreen, daylight would burn me like a bug under a magnifying lens. I knew that pain all too well. In a previous assignment, a government assassin had chased me with a machine gun while my naked skin burned under the sunlight. I survived by jumping into the Atlantic Ocean. This time, there weren't any oceans close by.

Cowboy zombie kept his eyes locked on me. His hand remained on the switch handle.

The power rheostat indicated half maximum voltage. That's all? Damn, that hurt. What would full power do?

A feather of hope drifted into my head. An hour ago, escape

was impossible. Now it seemed possible. How? By making the zombie throw that switch.

What did this zombie want more than anything?

I whispered, "Brains."

His eyes crinkled with the teeniest of recognition.

I repeated, louder. "Brains."

His mouth sagged open and pus-yellow slime dripped over the black stubs of his teeth.

One more time. "Brains."

His free hand clawed the workbench. "Brains," he gasped.

"You want brains?" I asked. "Lots of brains?"

Cowboy zombie took a short step toward me but kept his right hand on the switch handle.

"See that knob?" I motioned to the rheostat. "If you turn it all the way to one side, it will fry me like a wienie if I try to escape. Dr. Hennison would be happy. He would reward you with more brains."

Whatever feeble juice powered his decomposing noggin, cowboy zombie labored to imagine another helping of brains. Drool trickled from his mouth and soaked his shirt.

I described brains in revenant mouthwatering detail, as if reciting recipes from a zombie Rachael Ray. Yum-O!

Cowboy zombie wiped his mouth. A thick scab fell from his hand to the floor.

"You got the idea," I said. "Now turn the knob."

Cowboy zombie leaned to one side and gripped the rheostat knob. He turned it full-on clockwise.

Drool splattered on the switch handle. His right hand slipped, and when he grabbed the handle again, the switch nudged toward the closed position.

The terror of being turned into the fried wienie made my back arch and my shoulders tense. "No, no," I said, trying to sound calm. "That's off, the other way."

Cowboy zombie's eyes remained as dull as the shells of dead beetles. His left hand turned the rheostat knob back to half.

"That's good," I commended. "Now keep going. Think brains."

He twisted the knob to the other stop.

I made the okay sign with my fingers. "Perfect."

Cowboy zombie put both hands on the switch handle.

"Bet you can't wait for me to escape?"

He answered, "Brains."

The sounds of gushing, drilling, the sparking of electric welding torches (and the burnt metallic smells), plus hammering came from the lower floor. Dr. Hennison didn't once come upstairs for a break. Although he was conducting experiments so fiendish they would make Nazis wince—and planning to roast me in the morning—I had to admire his work ethic.

My right leg was mended, but the effort fatigued me. I needed blood.

Cowboy zombie kept his insect gaze on me. Except for wiping drips of pus leaking from the sores on his face, he made no moves—no blinks, no twitches, nada—to show he was sentient.

I did a function check on my body. I flexed and relaxed my arms and legs and twisted my wrists and ankles. Quarter-inch bolts held the steel bands to the table. I should be able to tear loose. All I needed was to free one hand and my talons would rip through the table. Except for my right leg, all my limbs felt strong despite the torture and the lack of sleep and nutrition.

The rheostat knob remained on the lowest power setting. Now to escape.

I pushed my wrists against the steel bands. They held firm. I closed my eyes and put more effort into wrenching free. My muscles quaked and my hands trembled. The steel bands stretched and bit into my skin. The bolt heads groaned and rotated.

I yelled at cowboy zombie, "Hey, garbage water breath, in case you haven't figured it out, I'm trying to escape." Go ahead. Close the switch. The wooden table creaked. In another ten seconds I'd be free.

Cowboy zombie grasped the rheostat knob and spun it to full power. He slammed the switch closed and muttered, "Brains."

CHAPTER 44

I came to with my face and the front of my body burning like an attack from fire ants. I heard a sizzle.

I moved my arms and legs and more pain came from my wrists and ankles. Burns. That explained the sizzling noise. And the odor of charred meat.

My thoughts filtered though a wall of suffering. I realized that I had been flung onto the floor of the lab. I pulled my right arm up, then the left arm.

I regained my balance and slowly came to my feet. I brushed splinters and dust from my face and chest.

Everything hurt and I wanted to curl into a dark corner and rest. But there was no time for a pity party, I was free of the table and had to scram.

Smoke curled from the scorched and melted remains of the re-straining bands. Sparks trickled to the floor. The electrical surge must have had too much power and blasted me off the table.

The overhead lights flickered. The transfusion machine had stopped click-clacking.

Cowboy zombie gazed at me. His orders had been to cook me with electricity, but now that I had escaped, he didn't know what to do.

I did.

I leaped and grabbed him by the face, sinking my talons into the fissures of his skull. I threw him to the floor. I tore the table from its mount and slammed it over him. I jumped on the table, stomping hard as I heard bone crunch and flesh squish. I didn't care how much this hurt my wounded leg, I kept stomping until trails of zombie goo ran from under the table. Too bad it wasn't Dr. Hennison.

Where was Hennison? He could've been deaf and still caught on to all this commotion. What was he up to?

My priority was to escape, recuperate, and then return to raze this place. I limped across the floor to the transfusion machine. Its promise of sustenance was what kept me going. I'd guzzle the blood and break out of the lab, then head for shelter.

One of the windows shattered and the curtain billowed open. Kimberly the zombie rushed in and swung an ax.

I dodged her first blow, but on the backswing she swiped the transfusion machine. The ax blade tore through the bag and it burst in a water balloon splash of blood. The delicious aroma licked at my nose. My stomach jumped from the pangs at losing this meal. I wanted to dive on the puddle of blood and lap it from the dirty floor.

Kimberly readied for another swing. I seized the ax handle above her hands and twisted. She held tight, ignoring the tearing sound from her shoulder. I gave another twist and her right arm tore free from the socket. I grasped a handful of her hair and cocked the ax back to sever her head. Her right hand let go of the ax and the dismembered arm dropped to the floor. It twitched and flopped.

"Don't move a muscle," Hennison said.

The dismembered arm froze.

I turned.

Hennison stood at the landing of the stairway. His aura undulated with anger while his gaze raked the room. His face tightened in spasms as if counting the hours and money needed to repair the damage.

Another window smashed open and the curtain gusted the air as it fell. Papers and dust lifted from the floor. A zombie entered and he waded through the debris. He carried a long metal pipe with one end flattened to a pointed blade.

Hennison smirked. His aura blushed with pleasure.

What tickled him?

I hefted the ax and guessed the distance from me to him. I was going to bury this ax in his face.

Sonia clip-clopped into the lab on her bedroom stiletto pumps.

The zombie Reginald entered next.

Followed by Phaedra.

CHAPTER 45

Tendrils squirmed from Phaedra's aura, signaling her terror. Spots of despair bubbled through her penumbra. Her right eye quivered in anguish.

Reginald held a thin steel cable fashioned into a leash around Phaedra's neck. A pink bruise the size of a fist discolored the left side of her face. Her hair hung in stringy tangles. Her parka and jeans were dirty and torn. Both of her hands were bound together behind her back. She appeared tiny and fragile, like a porcelain figurine.

A red cloud of rage fell across my eyes. My *kundalini noir* beat against the inside of my chest. I was about to break off the ax head and throw it like a ninja star at Hennison's face. But the odds weren't good enough and I might hit Phaedra instead.

My escape had been halted as surely as if a tunnel had collapsed in front of me. I couldn't leave Phaedra here.

I threw Kimberly to the floor between us to stall for time.

Her arm dragged itself to unite with her body. I backed up to the wall.

The zombies could sneak up on me using that revenant collective consciousness. One could be ready to drop from the ceiling or bust through the walls.

My skin prickled with desperate frustration. A minute ago I was on the edge of escape. Now Hennison had me trapped once again.

Kimberly picked herself off the floor and set her arm into place.

"What do you think of my new prize, Mr. Gomez?" Hennison draped an arm across Phaedra's shoulders. "She will be Sonia's new sister."

Phaedra's eye blinked faster and she shrunk from the doctor as if he was a giant roach.

Sonia lifted one of her feet. "We both wear a size six. We can share shoes."

I yelled, "How did you get her?"

"Easy. By using my zombies." Hennison motioned to his undead subjects. "The psychotronic diviner pinpointed her as the psychic transmitter. But I did my homework first. Of the millions of people in America, why her? Does the Huntington's facilitate her psychic abilities? It's fascinating, no? I have my zombies. I have you. I have her. Soon I'll control both the physical and psychic worlds."

"You're going to make her a zombie?"

"Not just a zombie, but my *jailbait zombie.*" Hennison couldn't contain his roguish arrogance. "I feel so naughty saying it."

Sonia hugged Phaedra and patted the top of her head. "We'll wear tiaras."

"She's only a kid. Are you going to kill her and then put her into your zombie harem?"

"Mr. Gomez, you make it sound so tawdry. So Phaedra's a minor? Sixteen, for God's sake. A hundred years ago she would've been an old maid by now." He let that grin inflate into a triumphant smile. "I look forward to the opportunity. I've already told you that I can reanimate a subject—someone like her—into an almost human, rather, pre-undead condition."

A new rage pounded through me. My fingers pressed dents into the wooden ax handle.

Kimberly rummaged through a metal toolbox, oblivious to the tension between Hennison and myself. She selected a carpenter's hammer and a nail. She pushed the nail, through the shoulder of her severed arm and pinned the arm where it had been torn free. She tapped the hammer to sink the nail, then gave it a hard bash. Kimberly worked the fingers and, satisfied that her arm was functional, picked up another hammer. She stood with one in each hand.

Someone clomped up the stairs and in shuffled a zombie wearing a green polo shirt with the logo of Super Cheesy Pizza Delivery. She stepped around Reginald and Hennison. Another zombie entered, this one in a bus driver's uniform. They both carried clubs.

Kimberly, Super Cheesy, and the bus driver spread out to form a zombie encirclement. Yet more footsteps clambered from downstairs.

"Where the hell did all these zombies come from?"

"You'll be surprised how many people ride Greyhound," Hennison answered. "After you get the hang of the process, animating the dead becomes as routine as an oil change at Jiffy Lube. Even

Reginald could do it. I kick myself that I didn't think of hijacking a bus before. The riders come from the social strata no one cares about. You know the story: put the wayward children on the bus, and if the family's lucky, you'll never hear from them again."

Minute by minute, zombie by zombie, the odds tipped further to Hennison's favor.

Heavy steps tromped from below.

"That," Hennison said proudly, "is my newest experiment." He opened the cooler on the workbench and took out a Red Bull.

The steps marked the passing moments with the cadence of a macabre metronome. What new monster had this fiend Hennison created? The zombies waited, as if expecting their champion.

I sidestepped across the wall to put more distance between myself and whatever it was that emerged from below.

The weighty footfalls arrived on the landing. A tall creature, half machine, half zombie, lurched into view.

A metal breastplate covered the torso. Tubing and wires curved from the chest to a metal neck. The head was a steel dome with a human face.

Gino.

Phaedra screamed his name. Her aura boiled and shot sparks of distress and horror.

A frame of pistons, metal rods, and pins surrounded each of his legs. The frame was hinged at the knee and ankle. His right arm was a long slender box fitted with gas bottles, actuators, and a slotted cylinder.

"I don't know what's more repulsive," I yelled at Hennison, "you or this monster."

"Hey, hey," Hennison interrupted. "Monster? Don't be so biased. It's eye of the beholder, that sort of thing."

"Your creature's disgusting," I said.

"Okay, the new Gino takes getting used to," Hennison replied. "What's the point of playing God if you don't push the envelope?"

He gave Phaedra's arm a squeeze. "Don't worry, darling, this won't happen to you. Gino has one job, you'll have another."

"As his zombie sex slave," I said.

"And you'll be a real hottie," he replied. "As for Gino, looks are not important. Let me show you what he can do."

Hennison signaled with a nod. Reginald stared at the Gino zombie.

He raised his robotic arm. The end of the arm was the slender barrel of a shotgun with an aiming laser underneath.

An actuator on the arm retracted and extended, causing the shotgun to chamber a round.

Hennison took a swig from his Red Bull. "To make life more interesting for the both of us, I reloaded the shells with silver pellets and garlic powder."

Silver and garlic. I wouldn't survive those wounds.

Getting out of here would be a desperate fight. One I wasn't sure I could survive, let alone win. I had to let Hennison know the risks.

I growled at him. "No matter what happens tonight, you will die."

He dismissed me with a wave. "I've unlocked the key to immortality. Slay this"—he thumped his chest—"and as long as this"—he tapped his temple—"remains fresh, I'll be around long enough to see the sun darken to a cinder. Think of my savings. Compounded daily. I'll be a rich man."

"Not if I run your head through a meat grinder."

"Fortunately I don't have one here."

"What do you want in trade for the girl?"

"Trade? You're in no position to haggle. Besides, she's too good of a prize."

Eight zombies now faced me. More scuffed their revenant feet on the deck outside.

"Now, Mr. Gomez," Hennison said as he finished his Red Bull. "Mr. Felix Gomez. You've given me the opportunity to say something I've dreamed of saying for a long time."

I had no idea what this lunatic was getting at. "Save your breath because I don't care."

"Too bad, because I can't wait to say it. Here it comes." He raised a finger and thrust it at me, shouting, "Zombies. Attack!"

CHAPTER 46

Gino lead the zombies in a stiff-legged march. A red laser beam quivered from under his shotgun muzzle and searched for me.

My mind raced for schemes to escape. Jump through the ceiling, break into the basement. I could get away, but what about Phaedra?

Gino faced me and that enormous shotgun barrel trained on my head. The tendons connecting his arm to the shotgun tightened. The gun fired.

I ducked. The pellets chewed the wall. Plaster dust and garlic powder rained on my skin, the garlic burning.

Phaedra winced. She cried out to me.

Hennison pulled her close. "We must be strong. Remember, this is for science."

I scooted to the left and found myself in front of the big mirror.

Gino's zombie eyes locked on me, metallic and yet cruel. Tendons flexed down the length of his bionic arm. The shotgun cycled a fresh round. The spent shell spun through the air and clattered to the floor.

The glass surface of the mirror felt cool against my back.

Gino halted, like a circuit breaker had popped in his bionic head. His eyes flickered in turmoil. When I moved, they remained fixed on one spot.

It wasn't me he looked at but his reflection in the mirror.

His mouth opened and let out a long pained drawl. "*Ghaaawww.*"

His left hand groped at stitches across his face and at the metal chest plate. He fingered the tubing and wires. His hand moved as if searching for his treasured bling. He lowered the shotgun arm and advanced, left arm outstretched, and touched the mirror.

Hennison yelled, "Gino, what are you doing?"

Zombie Gino shuffled backward, still mesmerized by his reflection.

His expression become puzzled.

Then hurt.

Then angry.

Kill-everyone-in-the-room angry.

He raised the shotgun and blasted the mirror. Shattered glass sprayed the air.

His tendons flexed. A spent shell ejected from the shotgun and a fresh round was chambered. Gino swung around, his shotgun arm level.

I ducked.

Zombies dropped out of the line of fire.

The red laser beam swept through the dusty air and across Phaedra's chest.

I sprang for Gino's arm.

The shotgun went off.

CHAPTER 47

Hitting Gino's arm was like smacking a girder. It barely budged.

I tried to tackle him, but with all the metal and robotic attachments, he seemed as heavy as a forklift.

Phaedra squirmed on the floor.

I yelled her name, convinced she had taken the shot.

Hennison slumped against the workbench. His aura roiled with waves of pain. A dark blotch, big and red as a poinsettia, covered his chest.

Zombie Gino marched closer toward Hennison. Gino's face hardened into a scowl.

I wasn't a genius like Hennison but I knew Gino didn't like being a zombie. Dr. Hennison hadn't yet figured out all the angles of reanimation.

Reginald opened his lab coat and pulled out a meat cleaver. He struck Gino across the back of the neck, again and again.

Sparks and milky goo sprayed from Gino. He shuddered and jerked left to right.

Zombies swarmed over him, in a frenzy of swinging weapons and clutching hands. Other zombies ripped apart the lab, scavenging pipes and lengths of wood to use as clubs.

Reginald snagged Hennison's wrists and pulled him behind the workbench.

Phaedra lay on the floor, dazed.

I had time for one task before the zombies turned their attention from Gino to me. Either rescue Phaedra or kill Hennison.

I could return and finish him. If Phaedra died, I'd never get her back.

Phaedra's aura burned with distress.

The zombies turned from the battered remains of Gino. They came at me, two at a time. Bus Driver and Super Cheesy led the attack. They advanced with their arms stretched out, a clumsy move I realized was to distract me from the second and more dangerous wave, four other zombies armed with sharpened metal poles.

I waited for Bus Driver and Super Cheesy to close upon me. When they reached for my arms, I swung the ax across their knees, chopping cleanly through bone. Their bodies toppled like cut saplings.

The other zombies charged with their poles. I ducked left, right, and they stabbed at empty air.

I threw the ax tomahawk-fashion at a fifth zombie. The ax hit him squarely in the face, his head split in an eruption of gore, and he flopped backward. I grasped a pole from another zombie and wrenched it free. Twirling the pole like Robin Hood with a quarterstaff, I beat the remaining zombies until they huddled one behind the other. I lanced them with the pole, skewering all four into a zombie kebob that I pinned to the wall.

Bus Driver zombie pushed up onto the stumps of his legs and tottered for me like a pissed-off munchkin.

More zombies gathered at the exits from the lab, blocking the doors and the broken windows.

I pushed the shelves aside, scattering cardboard boxes and glass jars. Plastic tubes carried bubbling liquid to a row of stockpots along the wall to my left. Vapor from the cryogenic plumbing drifted from the steel bowls at the base of the stockpots—more decapitated heads à la mode.

A zombie jumped on my back, his cold hands digging into my naked shoulders. I grabbed his hair and punched him in the face. Undead goo shot from his flattened nose. I spun him though the air, holding on to his head for a hammer throw. I let go and he smashed into the other zombies, dropping them like bowling pins.

When I got close to Phaedra, I used my talons to cut the cable around her neck and sever her wrist restraints. She clutched my arms and drew herself against me.

A pipe sailed inches from my face and stuck into the wall. The zombies advanced across the laboratory in a ragged phalanx. They brandished lengths of pipe like spears.

I lifted Phaedra across my shoulder. I dashed around boxes marked biological waste—to-go food for zombies?—and sprinted out the front door and onto the deck and into the cool, fresh night air.

I sprang off the deck. My powers of levitation were weak, and with Phaedra on my shoulder, I crashed to the ground.

I got up and grasped Phaedra's hand. I began to run and dragged her behind me.

My truck was miles away. Phaedra couldn't make the run. But we had no choice.

We staggered into the gulch. My bare feet pounded the cold dirt and hard rocks. Thorns stung my heels and toes.

Up ahead, a zombie appeared on the high ground beside the gully. He carried one of those improvised spear poles.

I tightened my grip on Phaedra and yanked her along. She stumbled behind me as fast as she could. I put a good hundred feet between us and the zombie before I slowed down.

I was scraping the bottom of my reserves. Phaedra was doing worse. Her chest heaved and she sucked for breath in whooping gasps.

A faint whistling approached. I took no mind of it until I felt Phaedra shake and give a painful moan.

I smelled fresh blood.

Her blood.

The spear pole fell from her side, its sharpened point shiny and dark.

Phaedra's aura grew faint. Her legs started to bend and I hugged her tight to keep her from falling. I tore open her parka. Blood poured from a hole in her blouse along her ribs.

My *kundalini noir* slinked back in dismay and sorrow. We were so close to escaping.

I tore a strip of material from her blouse and jammed it into the hole.

Zombies silhouetted themselves against the night sky. Kimberly and more zombies followed through the gulch. They shambled in the darkness, their feet dragging across the sand so that the sound was like a giant serpent grating its belly. A second spear pole clanged across the rocks by my feet.

Phaedra's eyes rolled back into their sockets. Her face and hands became cold, almost zombie-cold.

I grasped Phaedra as if she was a sack of stolen loot. I held her around the tops of her legs. She put her arms around my neck and pressed her clammy face to my neck.

I could outrun the zombies if I knew where they were. But they had the uncanny ability to direct their numbers around me. All they had to do was slow me down enough for them to gather like army ants and overwhelm me.

I stood and adjusted my grip and took off in a run.

Fatigue took over my brain, a sensation as thick and heavy as mud. How many bad decisions had I already made? I couldn't afford to make any more or Phaedra would die.

CHAPTER 48

I took gliding strides and let my knees absorb the bounce of my steps. I tried to keep Phaedra still, but the jostling aggravated her wound. Warm blood pumped from her blouse and pooled in the crevasses where my arms gripped her legs.

The aroma from her blood was the last temptation I needed, famished as I was. A quick stop for a taste, that's all I needed. But if I did that, she'd die.

I chose a straight path over the open ground. Zigzagging cost precious moments we couldn't afford.

Up ahead, a juniper seemed to come apart. It was a zombie coming from behind the bush. The zombie loped for us, adjusting his track to intercept mine.

If I didn't have Phaedra, I could've easily sliced the zombie to bits with my claws. Hell, I could've sprinted away and not bothered fouling myself with its filthy body.

The zombie swung a chain fastened through a cinderblock

brick. He let go and the brick spun at me, the chain flailing.

Instead of aiming for my center of mass, he'd gone for my legs. I skipped and took a long bound. The brick and chain flew under my feet.

Missed me, you rat shit bastard.

I landed when a sudden painful jerk took my left leg from under me. I collapsed and rolled onto my back to keep from landing on Phaedra.

We smacked the earth and she gave a loud "Uff." Blood and bile sprayed from her mouth. Phaedra was minutes from dying.

The chain from another cinderblock missile was wrapped around my ankle. A second zombie loomed from behind a pile of rocks. He advanced in low simian crouch with a metal pipe in his hand.

I kicked the chain free and stood. Phaedra sagged in my arms. Her aura faded to a low burn.

Things were getting worse by the second.

I held Phaedra tight and took off again. I ran from the gully and crested the rise.

A Jeep charged up the other side. No lights. No aura. A zombie was at the helm.

The Jeep came straight at me. With Phaedra in my arms and dying I froze with indecision. Jump? Run? What?

I needed those wheels to escape.

I let the zombie come right at me. At the last possible instant I jumped out of the way.

The zombie swerved to hit me. In a flash of vampire speed, I snagged the steering wheel. Hard. The front tires bit into the dirt and the Jeep flipped onto its side.

I put Phaedra down and hustled to the Jeep. The zombie

lay squirming where he'd been flung against the firewall of the vehicle.

"You should've worn a safety belt." I gave him a karate chop across his neck to break his upper spine. His head lolled to one side, eyes bulging and drool gushing down his face. I grabbed him by both arms and threw him out of the Jeep.

I ran to the other side of the Jeep, hooked my hands under the front fender, and heaved it upright. The strain stabbed my back, and my right leg felt like it had gotten shot again.

I lifted Phaedra, hobbled to the Jeep, and buckled her into the passenger's front seat.

I flopped behind the steering wheel and twisted the ignition key. As soon as the engine kicked over, I stomped the gas. The rear tires threw tails of dust and pebbles as I spun the Jeep around.

The road was two hundred feet away. We bounced over the uneven ground and skidded onto the road. I straightened the track of the Jeep and raced north.

Zombies closed upon the road, moving stiff as fence posts. I zoomed beside them, seeing their pale faces gaze at us.

We had escaped. The zombies couldn't catch us now.

A quad bike rounded the bend ahead of me, a zombie at the controls. The fat rider hung on to the handlebars like they were the horns on a buffalo. A second quad bike shot through his dust trail.

Two quad bikes against this Jeep?

No contest. I aimed for the lead bike.

They came at me full speed. The zombie riders let go of their hand controls and stood on the foot pegs. They intended to ram me and fly into the Jeep.

Fools.

I kept accelerating. Drawing from the last measures of my supernatural juju, I forced my reflexes to go to vampire speed.

Milliseconds decelerated into seconds. The zombies and their bikes moved in slow motion.

They flexed their legs to leap off the pedals.

I swerved right. The Jeep fishtailed against the first bike.

We bucked to the side. The front tires of the quad bike flattened against the side of the Jeep. The struts holding the wheels ripped free and the bike somersaulted behind us. The zombie smashed against the rear panel of the Jeep.

I wrenched the steering wheel in the other direction. The Jeep nearly tipped as it careened to the left.

I bore down on the second quad bike. This zombie rider readied a large spike.

The Jeep rammed his quad bike and crushed the front end. The quad bike crumpled and dragged the zombie beneath our wheels.

Thonk. Steam and the odor of glycol sprayed over the Jeep's hood.

The zombie had punctured the radiator.

Time sprang back to normal speed.

I checked the gauges. They were still in the green. We had a few minutes before the loss of coolant destroyed the engine. My *kundalini noir* jerked spastically, twitching with anxiety because we were miles from safety.

I raced along without lights. The dust cloud trailing the Jeep glowed like a luminescent plume.

The Jeep rattled on the uneven road. The temperature gauge crept to the red line. Phaedra slumped against her lap belt. Her aura trembled like a weak flame.

I grasped Phaedra's hand. The chill surprised and frightened me.

How could I save her? I was no doctor.

Something moved to my right. The zombie from the first quad bike I'd run over was still with us. He climbed across the right rear window for the roof, nimble as an orangutan. That's because his lower torso had been ripped off.

I slammed on the brakes, hoping to catapult him loose. Instead he thumped against the roof.

I sped up. The idiot light for the coolant temperature came on. The Jeep bucked over the washboard road. The zombie bounced on the roof. Where the road smoothed, I accelerated and swerved side to side. The zombie thumped but wouldn't let go.

I braked again, then sped up. He hung on for the ride no matter what I did.

What did the zombie want?

Of course, as long as he was with me, he would use his psychic connection as a beacon for the other zombies to follow.

I reached up and felt the zombie's fingers where they hooked into the rain gutter. I braided my fingers into his and snapped the digits like breadsticks. I peeled the broken fingers from the rain gutter. "I know I shouldn't litter." I grabbed him by the wrist, jerked him loose, and pitched him like a bag of trash into the rocks.

The temp gauge was in the red zone. The engine was about to seize.

We passed the first houses where the residents rested like sleeping cows, oblivious to the plague of the undead spreading around them.

We reached the cemetery and the paved road. The engine

lights came on and the engine squealed its death cry. I stepped on the clutch and kept us rolling. The Jeep's tires hummed on the smooth asphalt. I wanted Phaedra to acknowledge that we were safe. I clasped her wrist. Her pulse was as faint as her aura.

The Jeep lost momentum near the outcropping where I'd hidden my clothes before my transmutation. I pulled off the road and let us stop as close to the rocks as I could.

"We're okay," I told her.

But she couldn't hear me. Her aura flickered, becoming fainter and fainter.

CHAPTER 49

I pulled Phaedra close. I smoothed her hair. It was moist with perspiration and cool, too cool.

"Don't die, sweetheart. Not after all that. Please."

Her aura flickered again, like a loose wire had moved into place. Her eyes struggled to open and a weak breath pulled through her nostrils.

I set her back into the seat. "Good. We're safe." I glanced south to make sure.

Her aura remained weak and her breathing shallow. What could I do to keep her from dying? I ran through the scenarios. Stop a police car and ask for help? Say, Mister Cop, I've got this underage girl here and we were attacked by zombies.

Fatigue weighed upon me. My body felt weak.

Phaedra drew a breath and it caught in her throat as if her body didn't want the air. Her aura brightened—not by much, going from dim to less dim. Limp tendrils grew from her penumbra, waving like soggy reeds in a sluggish current.

I cupped her neck and stroked her hair. "Stay with me."

The tendrils from her aura trailed into smoky wisps and disappeared.

I clenched my fists in anger and desperation. *Not her.*

A familiar panic and dread returned. I found myself spiraling down a funnel of despair. As a young boy, I couldn't help my mother in her struggles with my alcoholic father and the abuse of the in-laws who blamed her for the family troubles. *He wasn't an alcoholic before he married you.* I couldn't help her when we were evicted and lived like vagabonds on the charity of our cousins. When we studied about the homeless in school, I realized we were talking about my family.

I fooled myself into thinking that as a man I'd never again lose control of my life. Then in Iraq, despite all the might and money of the United States of America, my men and I found ourselves alone in the havoc of urban combat.

We fought in the chaos, mindful of the one misstep or the instant of hesitation that could mean going home upright and whole or on our backs in body bags. One terrible night I led my squad in an ambush and we didn't hesitate to annihilate the enemy. When the firing stopped, we had instead massacred a family of Iraqi civilians.

I went insane with despair and ran into the lair of an Iraqi vampire who, as punishment for my sins, turned me into one of the undead, a vampire.

Then as a supernatural I learned that it was my nature to fight injustice.

Now, once more, I was bound by conscience to rescue Phaedra.

The last bit of her aura danced from her head to a spot over her heart.

I had to save her. I couldn't let her go. I would do the one thing I swore not to.

My fangs sprouted and I drew close to her throat.

Phaedra wouldn't die but she wouldn't live either, not as a human.

I opened my mouth and let my fangs probe for the choicest spot to penetrate. Biting quickly, I guided my fangs through the skin and deep into her vein.

My nose sifted through the many smells: sweat, dust, and the fragrances of her blood, adrenaline, the rich cocktail of a young woman's potent estrogen, and the bitterness of her medications.

Blood gushed into my mouth. A liquid banquet of pleasure flooded across my tongue, down my throat, and to every crevasse in my body. My belly felt the heft of the blood and my limbs flushed with viscous warmth.

I pumped recuperative enzymes into Phaedra, hoping that the sudden healing of her flesh would pull her from the brink.

I pulled my mouth away. Thick drops of blood clung to my lips and teeth.

Phaedra's aura returned, the penumbra glowing cherry red.

Now to cheat death.

"Phaedra," I whispered as if we were lovers sharing a pillow. "Open your mouth."

Those young pale lips parted and her fingers hunted for my face.

Phaedra was my first human that I would turn. We were both virgins at this.

I wanted to deny the arousal but I couldn't, no more than I could deny how much I relished savoring her succulent blood.

Lust pounded through me in a drumbeat of sexual conquest. I wanted to rip Phaedra's blouse and bra apart and press my body against hers.

My hands fumbled for her belt and I had the image of me spreading her legs and thrusting into her while blood streamed from her throat, between her breasts, and over her belly.

I gripped the upholstery and my talons tore into the fabric.

No.

I would only turn Phaedra, no more.

My hands trembled from the struggle. I clasped the back of Phaedra's neck and brought my mouth to hers.

I sealed our lips together. I pushed her blood back into her mouth and licked her teeth.

A fountain of energy rose from deep inside. The fountain gathered force, as if propelled upward by an explosion.

The energy flowed from my mouth into Phaedra's. Our heads fused as one and a current of psychic force surged from me directly into her.

The current was a lightning bolt fixed between us. The energy crackled in my head.

Slowly, the crackling weakened. The lightning bolt dimmed, turned into a weak spark, and disappeared.

The force receded from me and I pulled my mouth from Phaedra.

Her aura blazed neon orange. Her eyes were open to the point of popping from their sockets, straining with horror and pain as if she'd awakened in a raging volcano.

Phaedra gasped and lurched in the Jeep. She gagged and

retched, spewing bloody vomit on her clothes and the interior.

She raised her hands, gawking with terror as if her flesh was on fire.

The scene mirrored what had happened to me in Iraq, though now I was on the other side of the experience.

The words of the ancient *ekimmu* who had turned me echoed through the years:

I've given you what you want.

Immortality.

As a vampire.

CHAPTER 50

Phaedra convulsed. She stared at me, then through me. Her face showed the astonishment of this new universe. Then the realization seemed too much, and the weight of this new world brought an overwhelming fatigue. Her convulsions eased. She closed her eyes. The undulations of her aura smoothed into an amber sheath.

I stroked her hair. It was moist with perspiration, the last time this would happen. I hope she didn't have a thing for garlic, but she was Italian.

I'd done it. Forced again into something I promised myself not to do. I've created a vampire.

Phaedra was stuck forever as sixteen. I didn't know the rules for underage bloodsuckers.

She didn't want to die and she wouldn't, at least not in human terms.

Now she was my responsibility, even more than before. Yesterday she had one kind of family, now she had another: the immortal undead.

I retrieved my backpack and hooked it over my shoulder. I took Phaedra in my arms and carried her down the hill to my Toyota.

We needed to rest. She had a new existence to start, and I had the zombies to destroy.

I drove us through town and back to the forest. I hid the Toyota in the trees and carried Phaedra and my backpack to the morada.

I emptied Phaedra's duffel bag of camping gear. I laid the sleeping bag inside one of the benches of the morada. I removed her parka and slipped her into the sleeping bag.

She shivered. Her eyeballs shrank within the sockets. Her hair was like dry grass.

My watch said 4:17 A.M. The morada gave enough protection from the morning sun, but to be sure, I zipped the sleeping bag over Phaedra's head and covered her with the bench seat, temporarily entombing her.

After washing Phaedra's blood off my arms and changing into my clothes, I chucked the sweatpants with their zombie funk into a plastic bag. I retreated to a corner opposite the door. I sat on the dirt floor, .45 pistol in hand, and arranged a coat over my head.

I didn't make the effort to stay awake. Phaedra's adolescent blood (the best, especially from virgins, but in this case, oh well) and the need to sleep hit me like a sedative.

I awoke lying on my side, my face in the dirt. I held the pistol like it was a metallic teddy bear.

A tapping noise drew me to the door.

I gripped the pistol and pulled it close to my chin as I peeked from under the coat.

The cracks in the door shone with morning light. The board covering the latch quivered and moved out of place. A small black ball poked through the opening. The ball had two beady eyes and a pointed beak.

A crow.

It cawed.

I threw the coat aside. Phaedra remained asleep inside the bench.

I waved at the crow. "You're practically inside. Come in."

The crow jerked its head from side to side as if studying what was in the room.

"What do you want?" I wondered what the Araneum needed. An update on my current assignment? A new mission?

My joints hurt and I approached the door like an old man with arthritis. The crow pulled its head back through the hole. There was a quick scratch of claws and the flutter of wings.

I eased the door open, careful to avoid any sunlight. Fortunately we remained in the morning shadow of tall Ponderosas.

The crow was gone. What did it want? Was it from the Araneum? If so, where was my message?

I scanned the forest. Phaedra and I were alone. She would awaken soon as a vampire.

I closed and latched the door. I primed a camping stove and made coffee. It's recommended that you don't cook inside an enclosed space, but we were vampires.

I inspected my right leg. The wound had healed and left me with bullet scar number . . . I'd lost count.

I sorted through Phaedra's gear to look for something of use.

I unzipped a toiletry bag. It contained jewelry and watches. One watch was a lady's Cartier, the other a Rolex Oyster. I counted six jeweled necklaces. Four diamond tennis bracelets. Strings of pearls. Gold rings.

I found a camera bag, empty except for prescription bottles stuffed with rolls of hundreds.

All this cash and jewelry made for a handy getaway kit.

Where had this stash come from? Phaedra didn't dress like she was lavished with a wardrobe budget.

She'd stolen the jewelry, I was sure. How she'd gotten the cash, I didn't want to know.

I picked up a cigar box covered in macaroni and sprayed with gold paint. Probably a crafts project from summer camp a long time ago. Sequins and costume jewels had been glued over the painted macaroni.

I opened the box, expecting childhood treasures and mementos. Inside rested a dozen razor and knife blades, all embellished with toy gemstones and dabs of gaudy fingernail polish. The blades seemed almost ceremonial in their decoration.

Under the blades I found an envelope stuffed with photographs. Some of the photos were Polaroids, others inkjet color prints. Every picture framed the same subject, a bleeding slash across flesh: an arm, a belly, the back of a leg.

The flesh belonged to Phaedra.

She was a cutter. She ritually mutilated her body out of self-hatred.

The back of the photos had short poems about the wounds. Mostly about fascination with the blood and controlling the pain.

I was too repulsed to feel pity. Even undead, I couldn't do

this to my body. This girl had huge problems and now she was one of us.

I put the photos and blades back into the box, which I pushed into the duffel bag.

The coffee boiled. I poured type B-positive to half fill a cup and topped it off with coffee.

The bench seat exploded into pieces. Splintered wood sprayed across the room.

Phaedra sat up, aura blazing. Her talons clutched at the adobe sides of the bench. Black smudges ringed her eyes and made the eye sockets appear like velvet pits. The retinas of her *tapetum lucidum* glowed crimson as if on fire. Her face had an ashen pallor and blue veins throbbed at her temples. A red tongue lapped between her new fangs.

I raised the cup to her. "Good morning. Welcome to the world of the undead."

Phaedra grimaced with pain and reached to hold her jaw as if opening her mouth was agony. She winced when she scraped her cheek with her talons. She looked at me and her eyes were incandescent with anger and resentment. "Why didn't you tell me about the pain? I feel it from my head to my feet."

"I warned you. The metamorphosis from human to vampire will pass, but it's the least of your troubles."

She collapsed and rested her head on the side of the bench. "I feel so sick."

"Take it easy on yourself. This is only the first day. Wait until you have to learn how to apply makeup without a mirror."

Phaedra squirmed and reached for her side.

"You'll find that it healed," I said.

She peeked under her blouse. "Still hurts like hell." She lay back in the bench.

I stood over her and offered my cup. "Sip?"

"No thanks. I feel like crap." She had the splotchy pallor of a fever victim. Her skin wasn't yet translucent.

"Funny thing, though I'm not a doctor, my diagnosis is that you also look like crap."

She kept her eyes lightly closed. Her throat twitched and she swallowed hard.

"Whatever you do, try not to throw up in the sleeping bag."

She rubbed her face. "When will I feel normal?"

"Human normal? Never."

"Then when will I feel better?"

"Depends. Usually, people don't want to be vampires, so they fight the turning. You wanted it, so it might be easy for you." I sat on the adobe bricks. "Here's something you have to know. It's the iron law of vampires. Human society can never know we exist. They believe we are mythical creatures. In fact, we play along with that charade."

Phaedra averted her eyes and I could see that she tuned me out.

I cupped her chin and made her look at me. "You mess this up and you die. The humans you tell will also die."

"What about me? I was a human and knew you were a vampire."

"I was ordered to kill you. I didn't because I fudged the rules. I wasn't sure what would happen, but the last thing I wanted was to turn you."

"What happens now?"

"You're one of us. You get to live."

Phaedra lay back into the sleeping bag. She closed her eyes and turned her head.

"When you get hungry, let me know."

"Just thinking about blood," she whispered, "makes me want to throw up."

I watched for a moment. She remained still and her aura cooled.

I returned to my gear. I cleaned my pistol—it wasn't dirty but I was nervous and needed something to do. I emptied the three magazines and polished the cartridges. I reloaded the magazines and put the extra loose rounds in my pocket.

We weren't that deep in the forest, but we were far away enough from the road so that the distant growl of motorcycles was obvious in the silence.

Was it zombies?

The motorcycles stopped in the vicinity where I'd parked the 4Runner. One engine cut off, followed by another. Two bikes.

I told Phaedra to keep quiet. I went outside and found a spot behind a growth of sumacs. I would hide there and observe the path to the morada.

The shiver along my arms relayed that my sixth sense had confirmed the advance of strangers. I waited for the snap of breaking twigs or the crunch of grass, but whoever approached were as stealthy as lynx.

An orange aura shimmered beyond the trees.

Vampire.

I stayed down despite the fact that my aura marked my position.

The vampire had red hair and a complexion like she'd rubbed

her face with strawberries and dotted her cheeks with cinnamon sprinkles. Her hair was gathered back and draped behind her shoulders.

Jolie.

I felt the elation of recognizing a familiar vampire, then realized that she was here for the same reason I was. As an enforcer. I also realized that the crow I'd seen earlier was a spy and that it had been sent to confirm where I was.

Jolie's aura glowed with guarded anxiety like mine would if I had to deliver bad news to a friend. She wore a black-and-red Joe Rocket motorcycle jacket and matching racing pants. The armored pads on her arms and shoulders exaggerated her muscularity. She moved like she was skating in slow motion so I knew she was using levitation to lighten her footsteps.

I had heard two motorcycles. Where was the other rider?

Jolie's eyes locked onto me. The fuzz of anxiety on her penumbra sprouted short quivering tendrils. She relented from the levitation. Her heavy motorcycle boots tromped through the grass and forest debris.

She let a backpack slide off her shoulder and held it in gloved hands.

I stepped in front of the junipers and kept my pistol in a loose grip. I didn't want to signal anything threatening. Jolie and I had a history.

If there was one vampire I never wanted to harm, it was Jolie, and here she came on a mission that might include punishing me. If I had to shoot Jolie, .45 slugs wouldn't do much good unless they were silver.

She halted a half-dozen paces from me. Her severe expression matched my mood.

I asked, "Where's the other vampire?"

"Right here." The growl came from my left.

He was a squat muscular Asian in black armored riding leathers. He passed soundlessly through the junipers.

"You got a name?"

"Nguyen Trotsky Hoang."

"You were named after a commie?"

"No. I was named after my uncle. Let's stick to business. Where's the girl?"

I gestured to the morada.

"Did you . . ." Jolie started.

The answer had to be either kill her or turn her.

"I turned her."

The tendrils from Jolie's aura shrank with relief. She zipped open the backpack and withdrew a long leather pouch. She undid the leather thong wrapped around one end.

Jolie peeled the pouch back like a foreskin and exposed an exceptionally phallic-looking wooden stake, the blunt end made of silver. I winced at the pungent odor of hawthorn resin, poisonous to vampires. She removed the blunt end and revealed a sharpened wooden point reinforced with veins of silver. A stake made of hawthorn and silver was the most effective and painful of weapons to use against a vampire.

"Who's that for?" I asked.

Nguyen said, "You."

My guts turned into pulp. I'd compromised the Great Secret and, despite the warnings, had forced a good friend into killing me or compromising herself.

Jolie cinched the thong around the stake and dropped it in

the bag. "The Araneum knows we are friends yet they also gave me this." She pulled out a short knife in a leather sheath tooled in a woven pattern. The handle of the knife was filigreed with yellow gold and platinum. Rubies decorated the pommel. The knife looked designed by the same craftsmen who made the messenger capsules.

She unsheathed the short curved blade. "I was to skin you."

Nguyen's mouth curled into a grin.

Not only was Jolie to kill me, she had orders to bring back my skin. Nguyen was to make sure it would get done. For an instant I felt that blade slice through the membrane holding my skin to my flesh, followed by the hellacious agony as the skin was ripped free. The imagined sensation scorched me to the marrow. I pictured Jolie flaying my body and folding the bloody envelope of my skin—I saw my face as a loose bag, the eyeholes, nostrils, and mouth sagging into ragged ovals.

Could she skin me?

Could I kill her?

My only escape was to murder these two, but more enforcers would be sent after me, and more after that until I was caught and my skin turned into parchment. I had forever to run and the Araneum had forever to catch me.

I could think of only one thing to say under these circumstances.

"Let's have coffee."

I led them to the morada. Since I'd been outside in the fresh air, once in the morada I became aware of stove fuel odor, coffee, and vomit.

Phaedra lay inside the bench.

Jolie and Nguyen studied a fanged bag of blood and the vomit spot on the floor.

Jolie said, "At least the girl tried to eat."

She knelt and spread the sleeping bag from Phaedra's face. "Jeez, Felix, you chicken hawk, you're picking them kinda young, aren't you?"

"She picked me." I gave my story, starting with the hallucinations.

Nguyen looked around the room. "Where is the psychotronic diviner?"

I didn't want to answer. I'd screwed up enough with Phaedra.

"Well?" The edge in Nguyen's voice said he was tired of waiting.

"The zombies have it."

"How did that . . ."

Jolie cut him off. "We'll go over that later. Right now let's see what we can do about the girl."

Tendrils betraying Nguyen's annoyance stuck out from his aura. He wanted me to think of him as the vampire in charge, but it was obvious Jolie made the decisions. He sat on his heels and picked over Phaedra's camping gear.

I explained Phaedra's diagnosis with Huntington's. My guess was that her brain disease had made her a conduit for psychic consciousness. I added that she had no chance of living past thirty, and that she wanted me to turn her into a vampire.

"And you first said no?" Jolie asked.

"I did."

Jolie stroked Phaedra's forehead in a gentle and surprisingly maternal gesture. "Yet here she is." Jolie took Phaedra's right hand

and massaged the web of flesh between thumb and forefinger. Phaedra's aura gave a tiny pulse.

I didn't need Jolie digging into the guilt I felt about Phaedra. We had enough stockpiled over Carmen.

I primed the stove and lit the burner. "How's she doing?" I measured coffee into the percolator basket, filled the pot with water, and set it on the stove. "I don't have much experience at turning."

"Doesn't take much practice. But she's doing well. Better than most." Jolie tucked Phaedra's hand back into the sleeping bag and pulled the zipper to her chin. "Vampires this young can be exceptionally powerful."

"How so?"

"The exuberance of youth. Their incredible powers of recuperation. They're more adventurous and less inhibited."

"That's Phaedra to a T, but I don't think that's a good thing."

"She'll adjust. We all do."

"I mean I don't think it's good she's a vampire."

"Don't worry. The Araneum will take care of her."

The coffee perked. I offered Jolie and Nguyen their choice from the bags of blood. She fanged open an O-negative.

"I only have two cups."

"You and I can share." The comment was directed at me but meant for Nguyen.

We split the bag between two cups that I filled with coffee. He took the second cup and flipped a resentful gaze at her.

Jolie placed her backpack on the floor and sat on the adobe bricks of the bench. She got close and examined my face.

"You look like you've been on the wrong end of an ass kicking."

I told them about Dr. Hennison and the zombies. They listened pensively, their auras contracting and expanding like bellows. I emphasized a warning about the zombie collective consciousness.

"What's the next step?" Nguyen asked.

"We destroy them as soon as possible," I said. "Dr. Hennison's got bad wounds. His priority is survival. The zombies are good at chasing, they're not so good at being chased. Now that I know the layout of their lair and their capabilities, we should have no problem wiping them out."

"Who's minding the girl?" Jolie asked.

"Figured you were," Nguyen said.

Jolie shook her head. "Guess again, hot stuff. You stay here."

"Bullshit to that. I'm no babysitter."

"Do what I tell you."

Nguyen stood and glared.

Jolie remained on the bench. "Either sit back down or I'll kick your ass from here to Denver."

Nguyen shot a puzzled, embarrassed look like I was going to come to his rescue. Why did he bother? If a boulder fell on him this instant, I'd cheer for the rock.

Nguyen didn't sit. He flicked his hand in a rude wave and turned his back to us. Mr. Bad Ass bloodsucker in his black leathers stood by the door and pouted.

Jolie asked, "What's next?"

"We'll need weapons. A machine gun. A flamethrower."

A tendril lashed from the top of Jolie's aura. "No problem. I'll go to the nearest Home Depot and get a dozen of each. Seriously, where do you plan to get them?"

I pulled my cell phone from a coat pocket. "Not from where, but from who."

"From who, then?"

"From the last guy who wants to hear from me."

"That's a long list," Jolie replied. "Be more specific."

"Sal Cavagnolo."

CHAPTER 51

I gave Jolie the rundown on Cavagnolo. He'd supply me with guns.

"Even a flamethrower?" Jolie asked.

"If he has one, I'll take it. Otherwise, I'll improvise something."

"Let's go." On her way out the door, she slapped Nguyen on the arm. "Don't lose the kid."

We trotted down the slope to my Toyota. Two big adventure-touring motorcycles stood beside my 4Runner. Jolie explained that the BMW was hers, the Buell Ulysses was Nguyen's. She put on a full-face helmet.

I drove to Cavagnolo's house. Jolie followed on her bike.

On the way to Cavagnolo's I thought about the plan to get Hennison. I was glad Jolie was with me. There wasn't a better brawler anywhere. Plus, her loyalties were on my side.

Nguyen? If he had to fight, would he back off at a critical time and let the zombies do his dirty work?

And providing we did return safely, what about Phaedra?

I paused at the gravel turnoff to Cavagnolo's property. Jolie halted. In my rearview mirror all I could see was her riderless BMW motorcycle proceeding upright like an invisible ghost was at the controls.

Cavagnolo's house was an older ranch style covered in plain beige stucco. The original structure was a simple rectangle and over the years additions had been grafted to the sides so that the house sprawled across the width of his lot. Lush rosebushes bordered a small, yellowed lawn.

I followed the gravel road to a driveway on the east side of his home. A white Porsche Cayenne was parked in front of a garage at the end of the driveway.

Jolie rode her BMW off the road and halted beside a thick stand of shrubs. She dismounted and disappeared into the shadows.

I hadn't thought about Cavagnolo's reception. Jolie was wise in anticipating trouble.

Two unseen dogs barked.

A woman appeared in the screen door of the main entrance. As I drove close, the woman opened the door and stepped into a pair of lime green gardening clogs by the front mat.

She looked mid to late thirties and wore jeans and a loose blouse—typical country working attire. She shared Cavagnolo's Mediterranean complexion and I couldn't decide if she was his wife or a sister.

She came straight to me, her face hostile. "Who are you?"

"I'm a friend of Sal."

"What friend? What do you want here?"

Cavagnolo came out the front door. "How do you know where I live?"

"Phaedra showed me."

"Where is she?"

Cavagnolo's wife complicated the situation. With her around, I couldn't ask him about guns, so I pretended my visit was only about Phaedra.

If I told Cavagnolo she was with me, then he'd make a fuss about bringing her here, which I wasn't going to do. Instead I said, "I don't know."

"Oh, no." His eyes softened in worry. "Is she in trouble?"

"Hope not." I wanted to reassure Cavagnolo but couldn't without giving away about what I knew Phaedra. "I'm not sure where she is. Might help if you tell me more about her."

"She's a squirrelly girl."

"Squirrelly? She's fucking bananas," the woman said. "A crazy, manipulative little witch."

"This is my lovely wife, Lorena."

Her expression was nowhere near "how do you do," more like "fuck you and drop dead."

"Phaedra's been missing since last night," Cavagnolo said.

Lorena blurted, "That's three times this month and now you're worried about the little tramp? You wanna find her? Try the goddamn jail."

"Lay off," Cavagnolo snapped. His tone implied there was much he was keeping from his wife. Like Gino's and Cleto's disappearances and the other murders.

I needed time alone with Cavagnolo to ask him about the

guns I needed. "Could we go in Phaedra's room? Maybe we'll find something that'll tell us where she's gone."

Cavagnolo led us around the side of the house. A pair of hounds snarled and barked from behind a chain-link fence surrounding the backyard. He put his hand on the latch of a gate through the fence. He asked Lorena to hold the dogs, but the glance she tossed at us said that she'd rather watch them tear me apart.

We walked on a brick path through the dried lawn to a cottage at the back of the yard. The place looked homey despite its apparent origins as a toolshed or stable.

While Lorena held the dogs, Cavagnolo took me to the cottage's front door. He turned the knob.

"Was the door locked?" I asked.

"No. Out here, nobody locks their doors."

They better start.

The room wasn't much larger than a walk-in closet. The only window was to the left, above a desk with a computer monitor, a wooden chair, and shelves. To our front: bunk beds, a credenza, and more shelves. The furniture was mismatched hand-me-downs. At the right, another door opened to a tiny bathroom.

Other than the computer, I didn't see much of a preoccupation with schoolwork. A few books and cups with pens but most of the shelves held stuffed animals and glittery toys. Girly stuff.

Cavagnolo made room for me to pass.

A comforter was draped over the top mattress of the bunk bed. A black cloth hung like a curtain from the edge of the top bed to obscure the space above the bottom mattress.

"What's in there?"

"A place for storage. As you can see, there's no closet. Phaedra used to be a real slob. Clothes everywhere. The damn dust was so thick you could've planted onions. I'm surprised the county didn't condemn her toilet."

Outside, the dogs barked like they'd seen a she-bear.

Cavagnolo ran a finger over a shelf. He held up a clean fingertip for me to inspect. "Then three months ago, click, like a bulb had gone off in her head." Cavagnolo made a pulling motion beside his ear. "She went into a cleaning fit. At first I was worried it was one of those presuicide rituals, you know where someone tidies up their lives before offing themselves. But it wasn't, fortunately."

"Wasn't what?" Jolie said.

Cavagnolo turned, startled by the sudden appearance of the muscular redhead in motorcycle leathers. Her slicked-back hair and sunglasses added to her mysterious and intimidating posture. The dogs barked and snarled behind her, Lorena barely managing to keep them under control.

"She's my partner," I explained.

"Can I take a look?" Jolie motioned to the black curtain.

Cavagnolo remained astonished. "Y . . . yeah, go ahead."

"Will Phaedra mind?"

"I'm sure she will but serves her right for taking off on us."

Jolie parted the curtain and peeked inside. "What do you think of this?" She pushed open the curtains.

Clothes on hangers dangled from a cord tied under the top bunk. Under the clothes lay charcoal drawings like the ones Phaedra had in her hideout.

The drawings were of the little Iraqi girl, self-portraits of Phaedra, and one of me.

That drawing was a three-quarter view with my eyes staring

at the viewer. I didn't remember taking a photo of myself this way but the likeness was unmistakable, especially the tips of my fangs poking from under my upper lip.

I stared, unsettled and uncertain.

"How did she manage this?" Cavagnolo asked, surprised as I was. "I never saw her draw and she got your face on the money." He pointed to the fangs. "Except for these. What's with that?"

"I dunno."

Jolie flipped the drawings and lingered on one depicting a box receding to an infinite distance. There was a figure of a girl in the foreground with her back to the viewer. Smaller rectangles were arranged inside the box. Stars filled the background. After a moment, I realized that the figure was Phaedra and she was looking into the void, what she had called the astral plane. The rectangles represented doors or passages to the void.

"She was keeping a lot to herself," Cavagnolo said. "I figured she was on the computer, not making these."

"Can we keep them?"

He took the drawings and slipped them behind the curtain. "No. They belong to Phaedra. If she finds out we've been going through them, she'll throw one of her tantrums." He shepherded Jolie and me from the bed.

"I don't know if this is related"—I closed the door—"but I've got a handle on those who took Gino and Cleto."

Cavagnolo straightened. "Who?"

"I can't say."

His voice got an edge. "Can't or won't?"

"Some of both. I have to take care of them but I'll need some special hardware."

"Like what?"

"You got a machine gun?" I asked.

"You crazy? The feds hear a whisper about any kind of automatic weapon and the ATF will swim up my butt faster than piranhas."

"You didn't answer my question. Let me sweeten the pot. I'll take care of this problem and your nose stays clean." In case he didn't understand, I added, "Of the government."

Cavagnolo turned introspective. He nodded to himself. "All right." He looked at me. "What kind you want?"

"A Browning. An M249. I'll even take an M60."

"It's possible."

"Any dynamite?" I asked.

"For what?"

"Clearing stumps."

"None of that stuff is here. I have to make a few calls."

"Then do it," I said. "Arrange for a place to meet. Tell them you got a buyer. Keep in short. Keep it simple."

Cavagnolo used his cell phone and mentioned something about horses. We left Phaedra's room. As soon as we cleared the gate, Lorena let go of the hounds and they threw themselves against the fence, snarling and snapping.

I took Cavagnolo in my 4Runner. Phaedra followed on her BMW. He gave directions to a county road north of the highway and east of Morada. We pulled onto a long straight private drive to a farmhouse and barn surrounded by mowed fields with square bales of hay. Cavagnolo made another call and said it was us arriving.

Jolie rode up to the door of my Toyota. I halted and rolled down the window.

She leaned from her bike and shouted. "Can you take care of this yourself?"

"Why?"

"I'm going to stay behind and watch your back. And another thing. Pick me up an accessory."

"Any size or style?"

"Something ladylike."

CHAPTER 52

I laughed, said okay, and continued. Jolie turned around and went the other way.

A man and a woman left the house through a side door and stood beside the barn. They both wore plaid flannel shirts, and jeans over work boots. As we approached, the man went to the front door of the barn and pulled it open. The woman passed through and disappeared. The man waved that we follow.

I halted the Toyota and warned Cavagnolo. "Make it easy on yourself and cooperate. If there's a double cross, you won't live to brag about it. My friend is out there, waiting."

"Felix, you've made your goddamn point. All this guy wants is money."

"Which comes out of your pocket."

"That wasn't part of any deal."

"It is now."

I drove into the barn and the man walked alongside us. The

air became humid with the smells of fertilizer, hay, and horse-shit. The woman led a horse from the last stable in a row along the far wall.

The man thumped my fender. "Yo, hold it here."

I halted. Cavagnolo and I got out.

"Eric," Cavagnolo said. They shook hands.

I was introduced but kept my distance.

We followed Eric into the stall the woman had taken the horse from. He pulled at a plank along the side wall, reached inside, and tripped a latch. The bottom half of the wall swung open and scraped aside the matted hay and fresh horse dumplings. The opening revealed a stairway inside the wall.

Eric made a follow-me nod and crouched to enter the opening. Cavagnolo went next. The woman returned and shut the door behind me. I heard her rake along the door, probably to hide the entryway.

The basement smelled of horse piss and moldy hay.

We passed through a curtain. Eric yanked on the cord of a pull switch. A line of overhead bulbs flashed on. We were on a concrete floor of a cramped hallway that turned left. Good planning. I wouldn't advise building a basement under horse stables.

The hall opened into a room of about twenty by thirty feet. The air had the greasy odor of Cosmoline. Shelves crammed with crates and boxes lined three of the walls. Battered metal cabinets stood against the other wall. Guns lay in pieces on a workbench in the center of the room.

"What do you have in a .45?"

Eric ran his hand along aluminum suitcases on a shelf. He selected one suitcase and set it on the workbench. He opened the suitcase to display an assortment of pistols.

I picked a Dan Wesson Bobtail, extra magazines, and a box of cartridges.

Eric looked pleased by my choice.

"Plus explosives." I said. "Hand grenades. Dynamite."

Eric's expression lost its enthusiasm. "What exactly are you planning?"

"I've got a big score to settle."

"I'll bet." Eric turned to Cavagnolo. "This is more than a big favor. Your friend blabs, I'll stick a machine gun up your ass and fire until the barrel glows red."

"He's not my friend. And don't threaten me. We're in this business together."

Eric opened one of the cabinets and brought out a cardboard box filled with spare gun parts, loose cartridges of various calibers, electric fuses, and blasting caps. "I once had a whole carton of M67 hand grenades but the state patrol bought them all. They used them in a sting operation to get some white supremacists."

"Why buy the grenades from you?"

"Less paperwork."

"What happened to the grenades?"

Eric shrugged. "This is a cash-and-carry operation. What the customer does with the merchandise after the fact is none of my concern."

"The cops don't mind?"

"You kidding? Course they mind, but we got this agreement. I pretend I don't have them, and the state patrol keeps the ATF out of the loop. The deal is I keep this stuff from the hands of unstable elements." Eric squinted. "You unstable?"

"Not today." I gave him a three-fingered salute. "Scout's honor."

"What about the sunglasses? You doing drugs?"

"Naw, nothing like that. I got an eye condition, that's all."

"In both eyes?"

"Yeah, and it's contagious." I stepped toward Eric.

He put his hands up for me to keep away.

Cavagnolo said, "The fucker thinks he's a vampire."

They both chuckled.

"That true?" Eric asked. "You a vampire?"

"What do you think? Want to see my union card?" I took electric fuses and blasting caps and put them in my pocket. "Get me two sticks of dynamite."

Eric looked from me to Cavagnolo and back again. "Who's got the bucks?"

I pointed to Cavagnolo. "Put it on his tab."

He gave me the stink eye but shouldn't have been surprised.

I picked up a rumpled garment from the workbench. It was a bird hunting jacket made of oilskin, now cracked and ripped. "How much?"

"For that rag? Take it."

I opened my scout knife and cut off the jacket's sleeves; all I needed was a vest with lots of pockets.

"What about a machine gun?"

Eric went to the bottom shelf on the northern wall and grasped a rope handle on one end of a long wooden crate.

Eric talked as he eased the crate to floor. "These are worth plenty on the black market but they're hell to get rid of. I gotta be real careful who I sell to. Goddamn gangbangers would get a hard-on this big"—Eric spread his hands a foot apart—"for any of these. But they can barely handle pistols, so these would be like giving chainsaws to monkeys."

The crate was longer than my leg and eighteen inches deep. The stenciled lettering on the top read: Water Pump Bearing Rod. Eric undid the four brass latches on the long sides and removed the top.

A machine gun lay inside the wooden support cutouts. The gun had a long perforated jacket over the barrel. It looked like the weapons the Imperial Stormtroopers carried in Star Wars.

"It's surplus from the former Yugoslavia. The weapon is the modern version of the German MG42." Eric gushed with the enthusiasm of a collector who finally had an audience. He mentioned something about the best machine gun ever made, the American army almost adopted it but fucked up the design, yada, yada.

"Thanks for the trivia," I interrupted. "You ought to get a job with the History Channel. What I need to know, does this work?"

Eric chuffed as if I had offended him. "No point if it doesn't. That's like dating a girl who won't give head."

I lifted the machine gun from the crate. The finish was oily and cool. I cradled it under my left arm and wrapped my right hand around the pistol grip. I appreciated the familiar weight and potential for mass carnage.

Its heft and smell took me far away, to my service in the Third Infantry Division. The last time I held a machine gun, it was the day I became a vampire. Second by second, the gun grew heavier until its weight threatened to pull me to the floor. Remaining upright took great effort. The room dissolved into the dust of war-torn Iraq. The cacophony of battle filled my ears: explosions; the zippered bursts of automatic fire; the chaos of radio chatter; confused shouts; the cries and sobbing of the Iraqis.

Something cracked inside my headset and I realized it was the snapping of fingers. Eric stood before me, his thumb snapping against his index finger. "You okay?"

The machine gun practically fell from my arms, but once I set the butt on the floor, the gun's weight returned to normal. The noise of war faded like a dying radio signal.

"Sorry, I was getting a little wistful for my days working for Uncle Sugar."

"The rate of fire is 1,100 rounds a minute," Eric said proudly. "When this bitch talks, people listen."

I did quick arithmetic in my head. "That's about eighteen rounds a second. Burns quite a lot of ammo."

Eric waved to the crates and olive green metal cans on the opposite wall. "No problem. I can sell it to you by the ton."

I went through the logistics. Machine-gun ammo comes in belts of fifty. Four belts in a standard ammo can. That's two hundred rounds. Weighed around sixteen pounds, if I remember. It's not the weight but the convenience. How would I carry that much ammo and feed it through the machine gun? For all that trouble I'd only get about twelve seconds of shooting time. Plus, I'd be spraying bullets all over the hills.

I set the machine gun back in its box. "Too complicated. Do you have anything simpler? More basic? Yet a little exotic?"

Time was passing, and I wanted to be ready by nightfall.

Eric turned from me, frowning and disappointed at losing this sale. He tapped along boxes and bundles on a shelf beside us.

"Simple. Basic. Exotic."

He yanked a bundle in a grimy cloth. He unwrapped a stubby antique double-barreled gun. "It's a Pedersoli Kodiak elephant gun I bought at a police auction. In mint condition, it'll be worth eleven grand. As you can see, the previous owners—crack dealers—weren't interested in the gun's pedigree."

Eric ran his hand over the cut-down stock, the wood gouged and scratched. The metal work was pitted and rusted from the twin triggers to the truncated barrels. The twin muzzles still had hacksaw scratches.

Eric broke open the stock and showed the enormous chambers. "Ten-gauge."

A 10-gauge elephant gun? "Got ammo?"

"Of course."

Perfect. "I'll take it."

CHAPTER 53

I left Eric's place. Cavagnolo had to get his own ride home.

Jolie appeared behind me on her big BMW. We stopped in a little clearing along the river to discuss our plans to attack the zombies.

I handed her the Dan Wesson pistol. She accepted it with only a simple thanks. While I studied the topographical map, she played with the gun, disassembling it into a pile of shiny pieces, then in a blur of fingers had it back together again. She loaded the magazines and after slapping one into the Dan Wesson, dropped the extras into a leather fanny pack.

She said, "In case you wondered how the zombies snatched Phaedra from her uncle's place, I found a bunch of footprints behind the little cottage."

"How'd they get past Cavagnolo's dogs?"

Jolie pulled a plastic ground beef wrapper and a prescription bottle of Ambien. "It's a miracle the little poochies didn't get poisoned."

"Told you the zombies were clever."

I sketched the layout of the zombie lair and we drew up our plan.

We'd get into position on her BMW, which could cover all but the worst terrain in a hurry. I'd dismount and she would draw the zombies away from me.

"Don't try any stunts like running them down," I said. "The zombies catch on quick and they'll sacrifice one of their own to set you up. Don't be shy about using the pistol."

"I'm not shy about anything," Jolie replied.

We spent the rest of the afternoon going through our shopping list. Afterward, we returned to the clearing and got ready as we waited for night to fall.

I tested the number of a cheapie cell phone I'd bought in a convenience store. It worked. I opened the phone case, removed the vibrating mechanism, and in its place attached an electronic fuse. I called the number and a red LED on the fuse illuminated. I turned the phone off—hell of a time to get a wrong number— and inserted the blasting cap into the fuse. I extended a talon and poked a deep hole into a stick of dynamite. I inserted the blasting cap into the hole and wrapped the cell phone tight against the dynamite with electrical tape. I taped the second stick of dynamite to the first.

After loading all the guns, I tucked my pistol into its holster and slipped spare magazines into the pockets of my cargo pants. I dropped a flare gun, flares, and the cell phone bomb into one pocket of the vest and dumped the 10-gauge cartridges into the other pockets.

The sun sank below the western hills and the long fingers of night reached across the valley. I sat cross-legged while Jolie stretched out and propped herself on her elbows.

I said, "Assuming the raid goes off okay . . ."

"There's no assuming, Felix. Not after what you and I have been through." She meant Carmen. "We get in and destroy."

"I was getting at your partner, Nguyen. When we get done, what about him? I think he's going to make a stink about not coming along."

"Notice that he didn't protest too hard about me bracing him."

"I thought you were pulling rank."

"I got no rank on him. He reports directly for the Araneum." Jolie cocked a thumb to the sky. "The very top."

"As?"

"As a snitch. Plus he's a fake."

"Fake?" I asked.

"Yeah. A real poser. He likes wearing the leathers and talking smack but he can't ride a motorcycle worth a shit."

"He looks tough."

"In a vampire way but he doesn't have what it takes to be an enforcer. Few will stick their necks out like you have to, to be one of us."

"Would you have done it?" I was referring to the stake and the skinning knife.

"I don't know."

"You mean it depends?"

"No. It means I don't want to talk about it." Jolie plucked a stalk of grass and stuck it between her teeth. "I didn't like getting tapped for this job, Felix."

"I wouldn't of, either."

"There's a lot the Araneum didn't tell you."

"About what?"

Jolie's aura shrank to a simmer of worry.

"Wanna talk about it?"

"I can't," she said.

"Is it about the zombies?"

"No. The Araneum is in the dark about them."

"So it's about Phaedra?"

Jolie didn't say anything, which meant yes.

We kept quiet for a long time. Jolie took off her jacket and began a series of katas, her legs and arms becoming a whirlwind of kicking and punching.

I made coffee over a Sterno stove, enough for Jolie and myself. I added blood. I didn't need the caffeine or the nourishment—I was plenty jacked up on adrenaline—but the snack grounded me and softened my too-sharp senses so that I relaxed and became more aware.

At 1:00 A.M. Phaedra put her jacket back on and clicked the fanny pack around her waist. I did a final check of my equipment. She put on her helmet and started the BMW. I climbed on the rear seat and we rode two up from the clearing.

The Jeep remained on San Diego Avenue where I had abandoned it. Dust and scratches covered the windows and the dented body. The zombie I'd thrown aside was gone. When Jolie and I passed the cemetery, I asked her to turn off the motorcycle's lights.

A half mile from Ghoul Mountain, we veered off the main road to approach Deadman's Gulch from the northeast. The BMW crossed the gullies as nimble as a mountain lion.

We paused on a rise that overlooked Hennison's house. Light

glowed from the cracks around plywood sheets nailed over the broken windows. The gasoline tank—a military surplus water buffalo—was on a metal stand next to the garage on the eastern side of the house.

"Step one," she said. We were here.

I got off the bike. Jolie turned the fanny pack to the front to get better access at her pistol and magazines.

Now for step two. Jolie would distract the zombies while I planted the bomb to topple the gas tank into the house.

Step three. Get into the house. Find Dr. Hennison. He was in poor shape the last I'd seen him. He might have used some of his black science to keep alive. This time I'd make sure he's dead.

Step four. Detonate the bomb, drop the gas tank, and burn the house to ash.

Step five. Destroy any remaining zombies.

Step six. Maybe the hardest part of the plan. Escape and confront the Araneum about Phaedra.

Jolie adjusted her helmet and slugged my arm for good luck. She crept down the rise on the BMW, the engine rumbling in the darkness. Unless the zombies had gone deaf, they knew we were here.

I searched for zombies but until they moved, they remained inconspicuous against the texture of the night. I walked down the hill with the elephant gun loaded and ready.

A hundred feet away, a human shape walked from beside a juniper bush. Another shape moved. Then another. Within a minute, I had six zombies advancing, two carrying lumber studs fashioned into clubs.

I leveled the elephant gun. They sensed the threat and kept their distance.

Instead of approaching, I hustled from them. The zombies followed and bunched up one behind the other. I lowered the elephant gun and fired both barrels.

The gun roared, the muzzle blasts brilliant as lightning, the recoil like a kick against my shoulder.

The large slugs plowed through all of them in an explosion of slime. They collapsed in a heap of black mush.

I made for the gas tank. I broke open the elephant gun. The ejected spent cartridges tumbled free with a whoop and loops of smoke. I reloaded and snapped the gun closed.

Sheets of plywood fell from the windows along the back of the house. Zombies lunged through the openings toward me, Kimberly leading the charge.

I scrambled for my target, the gas tank.

My senses pinged. Something was wrong. Their attack was too obvious.

A shape darkened the stars over the roof. Then another. A sharpened pole shaved alongside me and ripped my vest. The two zombies got ready to spring from the roof.

I fired the elephant gun. Once. Twice. The blasts engulfed the zombies and they plopped into the ground, their guts streaming behind them.

I ran and reloaded the elephant gun. A first wave of zombies tromped over their fallen comrades.

Jolie BMW's roared through the darkness. She zoomed alongside the zombies, close enough that they turned toward her. She stood on the motorcycle pegs, leveled her pistol in her left hand, and blasted away.

Zombie heads exploded like rotten cantaloupes.

She fishtailed through the dirt, leaving the surviving zombies a disorganized mob, not certain whether to go after her or me.

I fired the elephant gun, reloaded at vampire speed, fired again, and again and again.

I had fired so fast that the spent cartridges were still looping smoke in the air when I stopped. The blasts echoed in my ears.

Jolie circled for another strafing attack, and in the wake of her high-speed pass, she left zombies in squirming piles.

I proceeded to the gas tank and fastened the bomb to the bottom of a leg closest to the garage. The bomb would sever the leg and the weight of the gas tank should drop the tank through the garage and into the bottom floor.

I turned on the cell phone. The screen flashed.

I went to the porch. Jolie waited, having ditched her motorcycle and helmet.

Guns at the ready, we entered the lab. Shelves and equipment littered the floor. Discarded heads and empty canisters lay in puddles of oily liquid. The heads rested on their cheeks, the lifeless eyes clouded and empty, the skin gray and gummy.

Jolie kept her .45 pointed at the heads. "Where is everybody else?"

"I don't know." I put my hand on the floor and kept still. I felt the tremble of bodies moving below. Hennison?

We went through the top floor room by room but no zombies or the doc. Jolie stood with me on the landing to the bottom floor.

Below us, a coil of tubing and cable unraveled down the stairs. The tubes and cable went through crude holes punched in the walls. A light shone from a wide door in the middle of the hall.

"Seems too quiet down there," Jolie said. "It's a trap. One wrong move and we're zombie chow."

"Who goes first?" I asked.

"I'll do it." Jolie tensed her legs to leap.

"Hold on. If it's a trap, how about neither of us goes first?" I rolled a cart from the lab and pushed it down the stairs. The cart clattered a few steps, spilling surgical tools and bottles, then tumbled end over end. When it crashed against the bottom, a curtain of mist sprayed across the threshold.

The odor burned my nose like acid. My eyes watered.

Garlic oil.

Clever, that trap would harm no one but a vampire.

Five zombies leaped from around the corner and surrounded the cart. They banged on the metal cabinet like enraged baboons before realizing their mistake.

I got two with the elephant gun. Jolie finished the rest with her pistol. I whisked a tarp from the floor, covered my head and arms, and bounded down the stairs.

CHAPTER 54

I landed on top of the zombies, not levitating so I hit them with all my weight.

They collapsed beneath me and I sprang away. The fine mist of the lingering garlic oil stung my nose and eyes. I reached clean air before shedding the tarp. I searched my pocket for another couple of cartridges for the elephant gun. The pocket was empty. No problem, I had plenty of ammo. I searched another pocket. My fingers poked through. The pocket had been sliced open. I tapped the other pockets, anxiously searching for more ammo.

We were getting deeper into the lair and losing our advantages by the second. Jolie landed beside me.

I asked, "How are you fixed for bullets?"

"Down to half. Sure are a lot of these fuckers."

I threw away the elephant gun, drew my .45, and went through the door in the hall.

Banks of lights clamped to the ceiling illuminated with a

brightness and heat as intense as a summer sun. The dirty humid air smelled like a polluted swamp.

Rows of aquariums sat on metal shelves, containing human parts instead of tropical fish. At the bottom of one aquarium, bubbles spewed from a plastic clam, a tiny frogman trapped inside its pearly jaws. The bubbles frothed around livers, spleens, and kidneys.

Pairs of eyes bobbed in Mason jars. As we walked in, the eyes followed us as if they had nothing better to look at.

A naked and legless human torso lay pinned with cabinet-maker's clamps against a picnic table perched at a slant with a car jack. Stitches held the arms to the shoulders. An assortment of feet sat alongside on a workbench as if they were shoes to try on for size.

The top of the head was open, the cap of skull hanging off to one side. Wires and small colored cables were strung from the empty skull to a battery of cheap-looking electrical gizmos as if this were a kit from *Popular Science*.

As a vampire I'm an expert in corpses, dining regularly on the blood of the innocent and guilty, ripping the flesh off the bones of my enemies, etc. And having seen an alien hoodlum pull a prosthetic robotic eyeball from his head, in short, I've witnessed plenty of freaky ass, capital A-S-S, shit in my short undead existence.

But this house outside Morada, Colorado, took the cake. And the icing. And the creamy filling.

Jolie noted the bloody handprints smeared across the walls. "Hennison?"

"I hope so. If he's lost this much blood, he's close to biting the big one."

Where were Reginald and Sonia? Maybe this was yet another trap?

Zombies dragged their feet on the floor above. Three, maybe four zombies gathered for another attack.

Jolie and I followed the streaks of blood to a second lab.

Another naked body lay on the table, feet and crotch toward us. It was a man, obviously. Tubes and wires draped from incisions in the arms, the legs, and the torso. Three ragged holes marred his chest, one by the sternum, the others closer to the left shoulder. Gunshot wounds.

The needles on the gauges of the adjacent pumps and electrical console twitched. A row of laptops presented black screens, and blinking power lights indicated sleep mode. This had to be the main reanimation lab, where Hennison created his zombies.

I kept my pistol ready and I advanced, my senses at maximum gain.

I stepped around the table to examine the face. As I got close to see over the chest, I discovered there was no head. The neck had been neatly sliced from the shoulders.

I started to ask myself who this man was when my foot dragged through a pile of clothes on the floor. Heavy shoes, black trousers, a white shirt and lab coat soaked with blood. Hennison's clothes.

This corpse belonged to Hennison.

What happened to his head?

I tripped on something.

Something hairy and decayed.

Cleto's head. Hennison had abandoned it to take parts from the canister.

He had mentioned refining the reanimation process so that

even Reginald could do it. Rather than die, Hennison had himself decapitated to preserve his living brain and escaped. He would get another body later.

Where had he gone?

There was another door at the back of the lab. Dirty footprints led across this threshold.

I took one side of the door, Jolie the other. I signaled that she kick the door open and I'd rush inside first. With fingers poised over triggers and our fangs at combat length, we did the silent count head bob. On three, she kicked the door off its hinges and I rushed inside.

CHAPTER 55

Reginald was hunched over a small cart. Sonia shoved clothes into a Pullman suitcase. The two psychotronic diviners sat on a table next to the suitcase.

Reginald's lab coat was still bloody and stained from yesterday's fight. Sonia wore a gold leather jacket over leopard-print leggings and gold stiletto-heeled pumps. The jacket was unzipped midway and her enormous breasts seemed ready to launch themselves like weapons.

Tools, instruments, and dozens of jars and bottles were crammed into a metal shipping container.

Seems these two were ready to escape. And Hennison?

At this angle I couldn't see much of Reginald's face. With him being a zombie, I really couldn't tell what he was feeling, but he acted annoyed.

Sonia gave an exasperated groan like Jolie and I were a sudden nuisance.

The cart emitted a whirring noise, various clicks, and a rhythmic sucking, like the action of bellows.

"Step aside, Reginald," I ordered. "Is that Hennison?"

Reginald stood. By his feet sat Hennison's head on the cart. His complexion resembled the skin of a frozen, uncooked chicken. His neck was clamped inside a ring suspended over the cart. Lights blinked along the neck ring. Servos, tubes, and wires ran into his neck stump. Blue reanimation fluid bubbled from a gallon-size glass bottle by his right ear. By his left ear, a piston slid back and forth inside a clear plastic cylinder in time to the sucking noise. The servos under his neck clicked to animate his face.

He stared from dark, bruised sockets. His eyes searched for me and I could tell his head strained to face me. The wheels under the cart rotated and it pivoted so that Hennison could look at me straight on.

"This is . . . not a good . . . time . . . for me," he said, his voice halting and mechanical. "Could you . . . come back . . . later?"

"No can do," I replied. "I've got a schedule to keep."

Hennison sighed and his face wrinkled like a deflating balloon. "I'm not . . . in a very . . . good . . . position . . . to negotiate . . . am I?" The cart inched crab-like so he could face Jolie.

She said, "No."

A plastic drinking straw angled from the front of the cart to his mouth. His lips reached for the straw and drew the tip close. He sucked on the straw and a gurgling sound came from three cans of Red Bull connected to a plastic manifold.

For a decapitated head sitting before his executioners, Hennison certainly seemed calm.

Son of a bitch was up to something.

Sonia held up a sweater. "You think you have problems? Look at what Mr. Mad Scientist expects me to wear. Do you know what this is?" She shook the sweater in one hand and whined, "An irregular."

Reginald sprang for me, whirling about with a meat cleaver. I gave him three quick shots in the chest. A fourth in his head at near point-blank range flung his brain matter against the wall like a bowl of black pudding. His body flopped against the table and dropped to the floor.

Sonia raised a revolver from behind the sweater.

Jolie capped her with two well-placed shots in the chest. Silicone gel sprayed from Sonia's jacket. She dropped the sweater, grabbed what was left of her boobs, and shrieked.

Jolie aimed at her face.

Sonia let go of her left boob and covered her nose. "Leave this alone. It finally looks perfect."

"Too bad." Jolie fired.

Sonia toppled backward and slumped to the floor, a mass of bleached hair covering what was left of her face.

Hennison darted forward on the cart. He rammed Jolie's shins and she jumped away, more surprised than injured.

The cart raced through the door and into the other lab.

An electrical cord spooled out the back of the cart. Midway into the outer lab, the cord went taut and the pronged end popped from an electrical socket next to Reginald. The cart slowed. Hennison rocked his head in a futile attempt to keep up the momentum. The cart wheezed to a halt.

I grabbed the electrical cord and pulled it hand over hand. As I reeled him toward me, Hennison kept repeating, "We . . . can . . . talk."

I knelt beside him and spun the cart to face Jolie and me.

"One shot," she said.

"Lacks irony," I replied. I studied the mechanisms keeping him alive.

"You . . . don't have . . . to do this. I have . . . money."

"I don't need money. I need revenge." I disconnected the tube supplying the reanimation fluid from a central fitting under his neck. I unhooked the tube pumping the Red Bull and attached it to the central fitting. Red Bull gurgled through the manifold and the neck tube. Hennison's servos clicked like berserk crickets. His face contorted in spasms.

He gasped and coughed. He chattered uncontrollably as undiluted caffeine went straight into his tissues. The lights on the neck ring flashed faster and faster and one by one went out. His skin turned puke green. His eyes bugged out. With a final zombie *"ghaw,"* his tongue, black as a tire, extended between eggplant-purple lips.

Dr. Hennison was dead.

"Better make sure," Jolie said and ventilated his skull with her pistol.

She asked, "What about the psychotronic diviners?"

"Leave 'em. The bomb will destroy them."

Now to escape.

While Jolie and I had taken care of Hennison, zombies swarmed into the outer lab. Their lusterless eyes gazed at us. Pus and blood oozed from their sores and out of the corners of their mouths.

I shouted, "Give it up. Your boss Hennison is dead."

There was no reaction from the zombies. They pushed into the room and bumped against one another.

The zombies separated into three files to advance along the walls and down the middle of the room. They moved slowly and deliberately as if they had all of eternity. Which they did. So did I, but I didn't want to spend it here.

Their bodies filled the room and blocked the exit. We couldn't afford to waste ammunition by fighting our way through the lab. I'd make a shortcut to the hallway.

"Keep me covered. I'm gonna punch through the wall."

Jolie fired as I pounded a hole in the drywall and slipped through.

Out in the hall, still more zombies continued to stumble down the stairs. We weren't much closer to an escape.

Jolie scrambled through the hole and stood next to me. Smoke curled from her pistol.

The wall buckled. Dozens of grimy zombie hands broke through.

We fired careful head shots to conserve ammo. One zombie per round. Eyeballs, gore, and bone splattered through the air.

With every spent bullet, a sense of desperation and futility rose within me. I felt like the floor beneath was a plank that kept getting shorter and narrower.

Jolie shoved the pistol into her fanny pack. "I'm out."

Zombies stepped over the bodies of their comrades. Those on the floor wiggled toward us.

I reached into a pocket. Also empty. I had the flare gun and a couple of shells and that was it.

The zombies plugged the exit with their bodies.

I shoved the pistol in its holster. Jolie and I backed up until we hit the end of the hallway.

Now it was undead versus undead at its most primitive level.

Our talons extended to maximum length.

The stupid thing would be to charge into them. Of course, the more stupid thing was that we had come down here in the first place.

I reached for my cell phone.

When the bomb exploded, it would drop the gas tank right—I glanced to the ceiling—on top of us.

There had to be another way, but I couldn't see it. What I had, to paraphrase Albert Einstein, was a failure of imagination.

Jolie shielded me with her body. "Do it, Felix. Do it."

I worked the phone's keypad.

No time for good-byes.

The zombies advanced relentlessly in one colossal mass.

I pressed SEND.

CHAPTER 56

Time hovered like the big clock of the universe had stopped working. The zombies, their blank eyes expressing only the cold-blooded determination to destroy us, showed nothing of their—our—impending obliteration.

My mind's eye could see the screen on the cell phone outside light up; the calling number displayed. The electrons would whir through the circuits. The signal would trip the logic switch: Ring or Vibrate?

Vibrate.

The electrons would pulse through the electric fuse, which in turn would spark the detonator. The resulting compression wave would initiate the combustion of the dynamite and blast apart the metal strut holding up the gas tank. We'd be drenched in hundreds of gallons of gasoline.

I could feel the nanoseconds pass by, as tangible as the air flowing around me.

A lot could have gone wrong. Maybe the cell phone didn't receive the call. Maybe the fuse had worked loose. Maybe the battery had gone dead.

Maybe, if and when the bomb went off, the gas tower fell the other way . . . or the tower dropped in place.

A mighty concussion slapped through the hall. Plaster dust shot from the ceiling. Jolie stumbled against the wall.

I blanked out all fear and watched the event unfold as if it were the end of someone else.

Wood splintered and creaked. The ceiling broke open and the cylindrical tank of the gas tower crashed through the joists and ceiling plaster. The tank came to rest upside down. Gasoline splashed from around the lid and saturated the air with its vapor.

A wave of surprise broke across the zombies. Their eyes understood their doom just as the tank broke through the ceiling, flattening them like a gigantic hammer.

Pieces of the floor above funneled into the large hole made by the falling tower. Debris skittered through the hole and pinged off the metal tank. The smashed bodies of zombies writhed under the tank, broken plaster, and shattered wood.

Jolie lunged off the floor. "This way."

She jumped on the tank and up through the hole. I scrambled after her and climbed onto the splintered floor of the main level.

Zombies lumbered toward the stairway, still on autopilot to destroy us and ignorant of the disaster that awaited.

Jolie and I sprinted for the front door.

A zombie lurched across the threshold from the porch. Jolie clawed him with her talons, sinking them into his shoulder and snagging bone. I punched him in the head and leaped clear of the house.

Jolie and I tumbled off the porch and rolled across the sand and dirt. I came to my knees and waited for the house to explode. The twisted legs of the gas tower stuck out from the torn roof. Embers and sparks whirled against the legs.

"Where's the boom?" Jolie yelled.

"Right here." I pulled the flare pistol from my pocket and cocked the hammer. I aimed through the open front door and fired. The flare shot into the house, a red streak leaving a smoky tail.

The flare thumped as it ricocheted inside. A yellow flame flickered.

Fire whooshed through the windows and doors. A gigantic flame twirled out the torn roof. Explosions loud as artillery boomed from within. The fire licked under the eaves, and within seconds, flames rolled up the siding and gnawed along the outside walls. Debris fell across the windows and doors.

Zombies crawled from the exits. They emitted ugly gasps, like air venting from rotting tires. Tentacles of fire spiraled around them. The zombies sputtered and crackled and I took the same ghoulish delight as I had in the army when we plucked lice and fried them on a hot tent stove.

The main floor gave way and the house collapsed upon itself in a roaring cloud of embers and billowing smoke. The smoke cleared and left the burning roof trusses looking like a rib cage inside a roasting pit.

Zombies staggered out of the gloom toward the burning house. They must've been summoned by that collective consciousness, from their immolated undead comrades crying out for help. They halted on the edge of the inferno, confused by what to do next.

Jolie shot from the darkness on the BMW. She herded the zombies toward me.

I found one of the steel poles and used it to jab the zombies over the edge of the foundation and into the pit.

It was burn, baby, burn. I hummed "Disco Inferno."

Zombies tumbled in, only realizing their fiery destruction at the last second.

Jolie and I patrolled the area for evidence of zombies and our fight. We tossed zombie parts and spent ammo shells into the pit. We destroyed all the clues we could find, including parts of the cell phone I'd used to trigger the bomb.

The fire burned hot as a crematorium. Flesh and wood would be reduced to ash, and metal—especially the psychotronic diviners—into one pool of slag.

Jolie asked, "What are the authorities going to say about this? Was it mass murder, suicide, an accident, or all the above?"

"Who cares?" I answered. "Anything as long as it's not about zombies and could be traced to us."

Satisfied that we'd destroyed all trace of zombies, I climbed on the BMW and we rode around Ghoul Mountain.

The fire bathed the facing hills with a yellow light. A glow illuminated the quilt of smoke hovering over the house.

Daybreak was another two hours away. Dogs barked at the rumble of the fire and the smell of smoke. Porch lights came on. People silhouetted themselves against windows and doorways.

The first of the red and blue emergency lights flashed up the road from Morada. Sirens yowled in the night and the dogs barked harder.

Two police cruisers zoomed by on the dirt road, the second car enveloped in the dust from the first. A minute later, fire trucks trundled by at high speed.

We joined the confused parade of vehicles barreling up and down the road between the fire and Morada.

Cops in reflective vests guided those of us coming down the hill to side streets away from the convoys of fire trucks and ambulances.

Abundance Boulevard was a carnival of red and blue lights and emergency vehicles going east, west, and in circles.

Minute by minute, we drew farther away and I relaxed. Jolie dropped me off at my Toyota.

Her aura bubbled in pleasure. "That was fucking amazing. Who knew killing zombies could be so much fun."

"We were almost killed."

"Adds to the spice. We get major bragging points for this fight." Jolie gunned the BMW, popped a wheelie, and circled my Toyota.

We drove west and onto the forest road toward Phaedra's hideout. Nguyen's Buell motorcycle was still parked where he'd left it.

We hiked up the slope to the morada.

"Seems quiet," I said.

"I'll bet Nguyen's sleeping," Jolie replied. "It's about what he can handle."

My skin tingled, not from picking up clues but from the lack of them. "We should hear something." A conversation. The rustle of clothing.

The air smelled of pine, nothing unexpected.

Too bad I was out of ammo. A full magazine in the pistol would've comforted me.

My talons and fangs sprang out. I put my senses on hypersensitivity. Still nothing.

I levitated to hide my footfalls in the grass. Jolie followed my lead.

We halted outside the morada door. Nothing.

I reached to open the latch and the door swung free.

I looked in.

The sleeping bag remained inside the bench. Phaedra's camping gear and belongings lay across the floor. Empty bags of blood were scattered like candy bar wrappers. Phaedra wouldn't know about vampire housekeeping—leaving evidence like this of our feeding was bad practice—but Nguyen should've told her.

Where were he and Phaedra? Did they leave in a hurry?

Where to? How? His motorcycle was still close by.

I called Phaedra's number. Her voice mail picked up and I left a message.

I felt a sinking despair. If Nguyen and Phaedra were in trouble, I had no idea where they were or how to help.

Sunrise approached. Jolie and I couldn't do anything but hide.

CHAPTER 57

Were Nguyen and Phaedra safe? I knew he would take care of her. Provided he could.

I shut the door of the morada and retreated to the darkest corner for protection against the sunrise.

Jolie scooped up the bags of blood in case there was any left. They all had neat punctures and had been sucked dry. "Phaedra must've found her appetite."

Morning light trickled through the cracks in the door.

Jolie cursed. "I hate feeling so goddamn vulnerable. A one-legged midget could bust through that door and we'd be helpless because of the morning light."

She curled next to me and we tucked close to each other under the sleeping bag.

At a quarter of eight, long after the sunrise, we got up and tidied the morada. I found the hawthorn stake discarded in the dirt of one corner. I couldn't believe Nguyen had been so careless or that he'd been so rushed to leave that he had left the stake behind.

Carefully, so I wouldn't touch the silver veins, I picked up the stake.

"Has it been used?" Jolie asked.

"I can't tell." Vampire blood would've turned to dust and become lost in the dirt smudging the wood and silver.

The leather pouch was inside the sleeping bag. I tucked the stake into the pouch and dropped it in my backpack.

"Seen the knife?"

"I'm still looking." Jolie pointed to gold bits of macaroni and costume jewels around a smashed cigar box. "You know what this is about?"

"Phaedra's way of saying good riddance to a lot of bad memories."

Inside the sleeping bag I discovered bottles of Phaedra's medications, full of pills and capsules. She wouldn't need these anymore.

I asked, "Where's the toiletry bag?"

"What for?"

"Phaedra stashed jewelry and money. Stuff that's easy to pawn for quick cash."

Jolie asked, "She's been planning her getaway?"

"Seems that way."

"And Nguyen went with her? Not a brownnoser like him. Doesn't make sense."

We went back down the mountain. I hoped to see Nguyen and Phaedra and give myself a laugh for all the grief I'd suffered for nothing.

But no Phaedra. No Nguyen.

His motorcycle remained where it had been. The panniers were unlocked and empty save for a few small parts and loose pennies. I'm sure he traveled with some belongings, bags of blood and makeup at least.

Boot prints had been tracked around the Buell. I recognized mine, Jolie's, Phaedra's, and a fourth set, which had to be Nguyen's. So the two of them had come back to the motorcycle, retrieved his things, and then what?

Jolie went down the road.

I lost Phaedra's and Nguyen's prints in the rocks and hard dirt. I tried the scout trick of spiraling out from the motorcycle to pick up their trail. The only tracks I found were their prints going from the morada to the motorcycle.

Jolie returned. Her aura burned in anxious confusion. "Nothing. Either they grew wings or hiked out a different way."

I tried Phaedra's number again. Voice mail.

The paranoia felt like a cold rain. Wisps of fog snaked through the trees. The silence of the forest sucked hope from me.

CHAPTER 58

Jolie zipped the front and the sleeves of her motorcycle jacket. "The cops are going to swarm all over town. We better get." She stood next to her motorcycle and put on her helmet. "Besides, I'm sick of this place."

"What about Nguyen's motorcycle?" I asked.

"He's the Araneum's boy. They can take care of it."

She mounted her BMW. I got into my Toyota and followed her down the road to the highway.

Back in Denver, we spent the next several days tracking Nguyen's whereabouts. There wasn't much to go on. His last address was in Sacramento, California, and none of the vampires in that *nidus* had recently heard from him. Phaedra was another snipe hunt.

Another week passed, and about ten one morning, I got an unexpected phone call.

Sal Cavagnolo asked, "You heard from Phaedra?"

"Unfortunately, no."

"I see." He sounded disappointed. "I'm in town. Let's meet and chat."

"I don't have much to say."

"That's all right," he replied. "Maybe I want to talk and need somebody to listen. Do it as a favor to me."

Cavagnolo's voice reminded me too much of all the trouble I had in Morada. "Sorry, I'm all out of favors."

"Remember, I bought you all those fucking guns. You owe me."

True. "Okay. Where? When?"

We met at Gaetano's. Mid-afternoon. I figured Cavagnolo chose the place out of nostalgia because back when, the bistro was Denver's mob central.

I watched from across the street. Cavagnolo arrived alone. The last of the lunchtime clientele wandered out. No one's aura betrayed any signs of trouble.

I let him wait for ten minutes, replaced my contacts, and went in.

Cavagnolo sat at a back table. He didn't smile when he saw me, nor did he offer to shake my hand. Fine, I didn't want to shake his, either.

After I sat, he turned a copy of the *Pueblo Chieftain* for me to read.

The headline for an article below the fold was: "Investigation into Gruesome Murder Site Continues." Here in Denver, the story no longer ranked the front page.

The situation at Dr. Hennison's played out like this: he was a disgraced physician who ran a meth lab and surrounded himself with a cult of drug peddlers. There was a turf war with other meth dealers and a confrontation erupted with disastrous consequences. The fire so consumed the remains that medical examiners had identified only sixteen people.

Thirty-two others remained missing, including some locals, and the passengers and driver of a Greyhound bus found abandoned outside of Morada. The police said most of the passengers had criminal records. Rumor was that they were part of the meth ring and had hijacked the bus.

County records showed the property was deeded to Dr. Hennison. DNA testing identified some of the partial remains as belonging to him.

"Unfortunately," remarked the chief investigator, "the response by firefighters had so contaminated the crime scene that most of our conclusions may remain speculative."

Complete destruction. Gruesome remains. A macabre mystery. For me, good news.

Cavagnolo asked, "What was that shit with the mutilations?"

I told him what he expected to hear. "Intimidation. Maybe voodoo. Santeria. Some of these druggies get pretty paranoid and start believing in the occult to protect them."

He replied, "I thought so."

I pushed the newspaper back to him.

His droopy eyes and expression begged at me.

"What's the problem?" I asked.

He put a finger on the newspaper. "Gino?" As in, was he there?

"Yeah."

If Cavagnolo's expression fell any lower, his face would be on the table.

"I couldn't do anything for him," I said. "He was dead." Actually undead but why quibble?

"Phaedra?"

"She wasn't there."

"You sure?"

"I saw her the day after all this happened."

"Where?" Cavagnolo withdrew his finger from the newspaper and his voice rang with hope.

"In the mountain park. Close to town. She had a hideaway."

"Yeah. That place." Apparently he knew more about Phaedra than she suspected. "The sheriff didn't find much there."

I waited for Cavagnolo to mention Nguyen's motorcycle, and when he didn't, I was sure the Araneum had scrubbed the area of vampiric presence.

The waitress brought a basket of bread, a saucer of olive oil, and a small bowl with marinara sauce. Cavagnolo ordered a Diet Coke and the veal parmesan special. I asked for a cup of coffee.

"That's it?" Cavagnolo asked. "The food here is delicious."

I knew that. But the only meals I've gotten from Gaetano's were takeout, which I ordered without garlic and once home, drowned in blood.

"Coffee is fine. I didn't know you had lunch in mind. I've already eaten."

Cavagnolo pleaded with his hands as if to refuse was to hurt him. "What's an extra bite?"

I slapped my belly. "Gotta watch the weight. I prefer to get my bites somewhere else."

"At least try the bread. The garlic seasoning is incredible."

"No thanks," I insisted. "Allergies."

"You mean one of those gluten aversion things?"

"No, it's the garlic."

"Allergic to garlic?" He tore a chunk of bread and chomped on it. "Might as well give up breathing."

That too, but not because of allergies.

I didn't want Cavagnolo to think because we both worried about Phaedra that we were now on the road to becoming big chums. I decided to push him off balance.

"How does this affect . . . the thing?"

"What thing?"

"The deal you got with your buddies." I pointed to an American flag over the bar. The feds.

"Oh." Cavagnolo kept quiet. Nothing like the possibility of blackmail to drive a wedge between us.

He surprised me with a smile. "Can you believe it? The cops asked me about this Hennison creep. For once my hands were cleaner than a virgin's panties." The smile turned shrewd. "What's come out of this deal is that I've gotten a bigger blank check to do what I've always been doing."

"Playing the system?"

"Like a fucking piano."

The waitress brought the Diet Coke and my coffee. Cavagnolo sipped the soda and his eyes focused on the faraway. My coffee was cold. I thought about asking for another, but no, I wasn't staying.

He gave a long sigh, like he'd dropped a great weight off his shoulders. "Much as I've tried to help, that girl has always been trouble. Wouldn't surprise me if all this shit spooked her and she took off."

"Run away? Where to?"

"Who the fuck knows? It's not the first time. Phaedra acted like she was hearing voices from another planet. I think everyone's accepted the inevitable."

"What are you getting at?"

He put the soda down. The droopiness was gone from his eyes and they looked hard. Stoic. "Why the concern? You don't have a thing for her, do you?"

"No, I don't have a thing for her. She's a kid in trouble, that's all."

"What makes you think you're so special to her?"

I turned her into a vampire.

"No matter what you've done," Cavagnolo continued, "I'll tell you how she'll show her gratitude. The same as she's done with everyone else. By leaving you on a goddamn limb. I know her. She used the excuse of the Huntington's to break all the rules. Drugs. Sex. She stole from her school. Her aunt. From me. I'm saying this out of love. Her problems aren't just here." Cavagnolo tapped his brow. "But here as well." He thumped his chest over the heart.

Not anymore.

His voice trailed to a mumble. "She ran off on her own, no?"

She was last seen with Nguyen, but I didn't need to mention this. "As far as I know."

"Then forget it. A girl her age, she wants to run away, you

couldn't keep her home by chaining her legs to the goddamn plumbing. I told you before. She is nothing but fucking trouble."

Cavagnolo grabbed a hunk of bread and ran it through the marinara. The sauce dripped off the crust like blood. "Trust me, the next time you see Phaedra, you'll regret it."

CHAPTER 59

I was back in my office in the Oriental Theater. Three weeks had passed since my return from Morada. I should've been concerned with getting new cases: schmoozing my contacts and hanging out at the lawyer watering holes. So far all the work I'd accomplished was to open and sort my mail into two piles. Stuff I'd ignore today. Stuff I'd ignore tomorrow.

Jolie lay next to me. Our naked bodies pressed against each other.

The disappearance of Phaedra and Nguyen rekindled the anguish we'd felt after losing Carmen. We'd fallen back on each other. Sex was a way to feel safe and familiar. In the familiar we could feel our individual sorrow.

I spooned against Jolie as best I could on the narrow chaise longue. Our feet dangled off one end.

I slipped my arm under hers. "You seem distracted. What's going on?"

"Besides losing Phaedra and Nguyen?" She clasped my hand and stared at the far wall.

I waited for her to complete an answer but she didn't.

Jolie rubbed her head along my shoulder. "How much longer are we going to keep screwing?"

Sex wasn't what troubled her. "You mean today?"

"No." She let go of my hand. "I mean until we move on."

I cupped her breast and dragged my fangs across the back of her neck. "Might take a while."

She slapped my thigh and sat. "Then take care of business on your own. I gotta go."

Jolie shimmied into her panties, a tank top, and leather motor-cycle pants. The black cuffs made her naked feet look pink and raw. I slipped on jeans and an aloha shirt that I didn't bother to button. The rest of our clothes remained on the floor.

Someone knocked. My ears and fingertips buzzed in alarm.

Jolie's aura flashed with surprise.

Her eyes asked: Who could this be?

I responded with a shake of my head. The other three tenants on this floor had never bothered me. As far as I knew, I was alone in the building today. No one could come up without getting buzzed through the entrance.

Another knock.

My fangs and talons grew to fighting length.

A dog barked.

Dog?

Jolie put her back to the wall beside the door, her talons and fangs extended.

I approached the door. My contacts were out, so I'd zap first and ask questions later. My reflexes tensed to respond at vampire speed.

The dog gave another bark. I opened the door.

Orange glows surrounded two female vampires. Both wore sunglasses. The dark-skinned one was Phyllis. She held the leash to her weird retriever/blue heeler mutt.

The other vampire was a blonde wearing wraparound shades and a black trench coat. Her nose and cheekbones looked sharp enough to cut salami. Her hair was as shiny and perfect as a sheet of polished gold. The haughty attitude told me she must also be from the Araneum.

Jolie stepped into view.

Phyllis removed her sunglasses. She gave a wan, fangless smile that said: I'm here with bad news, let's make the best of it.

I stood aside. "Phyllis, I can't say it's good to see you"—I motioned to the other vampire—"or your friend."

The blonde took off her sunglasses and folded them into a pocket.

Jolie surprised me by making the introduction. "This is Nathacha De Brancovan."

Nathacha glanced at our naked feet, my open shirt, and the clothes scattered by the chaise longue. Jolie had lingering fang marks on her shoulders and neck. I'm sure I had plenty of my own.

Nathacha's undead eyes smoldered with disdain, first at Jolie, then at me. "Am I interrupting?" she asked in a dismissive French accent, more a statement than a question.

The last conversation I wanted to have was with someone from the Araneum. I already had enough grief; I didn't need to parade my troubles in front of an audience to feel worse. "Would it make a difference if I said yes?"

"Of course not," Nathacha answered.

The dog strained to get in. Phyllis held the leash tighter. Nathacha entered first. No question about the pecking order here.

Nathacha swooped toward the chaise longue and gave the discarded clothing another once-over. She didn't step close, like she was afraid of contracting sex cooties. She circled behind my desk and pushed my executive chair adjacent to an ottoman.

Phyllis took another chair from in front of my desk and turned it around, careful not to scoot close to Nathacha. These two may be from the Araneum, but they sent out a vibe like a pair of magnets repelling each other.

Phyllis sat and clipped the dog's leash to the chair's chrome tubing.

After unbuttoning her coat, Nathacha relaxed into her chair as if we were here for a long meeting. With her shiny pewter blouse, black flared pants, and black slides with stiletto heels and long points, she might have been mistaken for the senior editor of a fashion magazine. She crossed her ankles across the top of the ottoman, claiming her presence as the alpha bitch.

Phyllis said to me. "Close the blinds."

I didn't like the mystery or taking orders. "Any reason?"

"Just close them," Nathacha said.

I wanted to tell her to get off her Frenchie ass and do it herself, but if this was bad news, I better keep my mouth shut and not make it worse. I went to the windows and shut the blinds. The room became twilight dark.

Phyllis pulled a filigreed cylinder from the pocket of her windbreaker. She held the cylinder in her hand like a baton. The cylinder resembled the message capsules the crow brought but was the size of a rolling pin.

My previous messages were tiny swatches of parchment. What tome did Phyllis carry in that cylinder? I'm sure we needed the darkness to keep the vampire parchment inside from bursting into flames.

Phyllis shook the cylinder, implying that I should take it. I'd rather hold a live grenade.

I grasped the cylinder. It weighed about a pound, same as a live grenade.

Nathacha said, "Open it."

This was a moment when I wanted to push the fast-forward button. I only wanted to deal with the aftermath and skip the thorny details along the way.

The faceted rubies on the cap of the cylinder made for an easy grip. The cap twisted off. The horrendous odor of rotted meat belched out. I let the air clear before peering inside the cylinder. It held a rolled sheet of parchment.

I gave the cap to Phyllis. I tapped on the end of the cylinder like it was a bottle of ketchup. The edge of the parchment slid out. I pulled it free. A rubber band kept the parchment in a roll. I clipped the rubber band with a talon. The parchment uncurled with a snap and released another gust of funky smell.

Jolie tugged at my shirt. I sat beside her on the chaise longue. She took the cylinder from me.

I read the parchment. The writing was in calligraphy. The top two lines read:

Mémorandum

Des mesures disciplinaires pour Felix Gomez

Great, the damn thing was in French. Disciplinary measures? If this was punishment, the Araneum should've at least had the balls to give it to me in a way I could understand. The writing started neatly enough but a third of the way down the page, the lines became sloppy as if the author had gotten rushed. Spots and smears of brown ink—or blood?—marred the copy.

This parchment was thicker than the onionskin messages the crow brought. There was a watermark along one long edge. I held the parchment to the overhead light. The watermark was a faded tattoo of the Virgin of Guadalupe, something a barrio gangster would wear on his back. Despite what he might have done, I pitied the guy the parchment had come from. Vampires don't willingly donate their skin.

"What's this about?" I asked.

"Felix, this is the second time that you've failed the Araneum," Nathacha replied.

Failed. The word hit me like a gob of spit.

She added, "Because of you, we lost Carmen Arellano."

My face heated with anger. "I've owned up to that. Her loss means more to me than it does to you."

Jolie put her hand on my thigh.

"I don't doubt it." Nathacha's words dripped with a patronizing tone. "At least one consequence of this fiasco is that we don't have to worry about Dr. Hennison or zombies."

"I wouldn't be too smug," I replied. "The fire destroyed his lab, but on the other hand, we lost clues on how to track a future reanimator. What chemicals and equipment should we be watching for? What about his psychotronic diviner? Dr. Hennison managed to make one. How much longer before another reanimator starts poking into the astral plane?"

Nathacha kept her tombstone expression on me. "Like I said, a fiasco."

My *kundalini noir* jolted from the insult. "How was that my fault?"

Jolie's hand groped for mine.

"Because your investigation was, as you say"—Nathacha snapped her fingers—"*une absolue* fuckup."

Jolie let go of my hand. She jumped to her feet. "That's enough."

Phyllis, Nathacha, and I seemed to lurch forward as if we'd all collided together. Even the dog noticed the outburst and tucked its head behind Phyllis's legs.

"The Araneum set Felix up."

My mind whipped from anger to confusion, then whipped back to someplace in between. I started to rise but Jolie kept me down by pushing her talons into my shoulder.

She said, "The Araneum knew all along about Phaedra's powers but they didn't warn Felix."

Phyllis frowned and her eyebrows clenched. Her eyes swiveled from Jolie to Nathacha and back. "How do you know?"

Jolie pointed the cylinder at Nathacha. "Because she told me. The Araneum learned that Phaedra's powers were the strongest they'd seen. They knew about her unstable personality and decided she was too dangerous. It was her idea"—Jolie jabbed the cylinder at Nathacha—"to confirm the Araneum's suspicions. She had them send Felix and not warn him."

My anger curdled into disgust. "Why?"

Nathacha answered, "Because if Phaedra could read your mind, she'd get all your secrets. If you didn't know, she wouldn't know. It was a tactical decision. For the greater good."

Phyllis kept her aura smooth, but it glowed hot like the flame from a blowtorch. "What part of this greater good said not to tell me about this? Felix reports to me."

Phyllis, Jolie, and I kept Nathacha in the cross fire of our gazes. She'd come here to lash me to a burning stake, and instead the fire licked her feet. But if she regarded this change in situation as more than an inconvenience, she didn't show it.

Jolie kept her back straight and defiant. "Felix, just so you know, I wouldn't have done *it*." She meant killing and skinning me. "Please forgive me for keeping what Nathacha told me from you."

At least Jolie was having an attack of conscience. "Nothing happened. What's to forgive?"

Nathacha remained with her feet propped on the ottoman, unruffled by our drama. She gestured for the parchment. Of course, I had to walk to her so she didn't have to budge from her chair. She held up a finger and shushed us to stay quiet while she read.

Nathacha pushed the ottoman out of the way. She sat up, handed the parchment back to me, and nodded to the window. "I regret any misunderstandings."

Misunderstandings? She had almost gotten me killed. Her apology meant little; she might as well have written the words in yellow snow.

My aura must have been a banner of indignation. Phyllis made a palms-down calming motion and I tried to Zen out as best I could.

I forced the window open and threw the parchment outside. The parchment tumbled through the sunlight and exploded into flames. A cloud of gray smoke brought the odor of charred meat.

I shut the window.

"We still have other business," Phyllis said. "Where are Phaedra and Nguyen?"

Nathacha pointed her icicle-dagger eyes at me like that problem was my fault.

"Why are you looking at me?" I asked. "Send a crow to find them."

"We've tried," she said. "None have come back."

Phyllis stood. She took the cylinder from Jolie and screwed the cap back on. She dropped the cylinder into her windbreaker pocket and unclipped her dog from the chair. "Felix, we'll get back to you."

Nathacha came to her feet. She and Phyllis locked eyes. They shot words back and forth in French like broadsides from frigates. They abruptly came to a mutual cease-fire and let their animosity fade behind calm faces.

Phyllis opened the door. She took my hand and squeezed it. "Take care of yourself." She gave a parting nod to Jolie and followed her dog into the hall.

Nathacha buttoned her coat and put on her sunglasses, her imperial demeanor unscathed.

Jolie said, "Nathacha, I know what you need."

"What's that?"

"A good fuck. Might do wonders for your attitude."

She smiled grudgingly. "You would know. *Au revoir.*"

CHAPTER 60

I returned to my apartment. I needed a drink. I made a manhattan and sipped from it as I wandered through my place.

Everything around me felt small. I didn't feel bigger, I think it was that I was aware how my world had shrunk around me. I was boxed in.

I examined the hawthorn stake. The phallic design was someone's idea of a black joke. Final words to a vampire: Screw you.

This stake was the one souvenir I never wanted but was the only item I had to remind me of Phaedra. I put the stake on the table next to my coffin.

I darkened my apartment and prepared to go to sleep. Usually, I like a snack—half a bag of blood—before I lie down.

I didn't feel like eating; I only wanted to close my eyes and let time soften the sharp edges of what happened today.

I thought about all the occasions, as a human and as a vampire, that I tried my best and came up short. If it was only me who bore the consequences, then I could make peace with myself. But I had caused others to suffer and I would always be to blame.

I rested against the satin lining of my coffin. I needed to relax, but my mind wandered back to the meeting with Phyllis and Nathacha. It felt like a cue ball cracking hard during a break. My thoughts ricocheted and scattered across my mind.

I've given my best to the Araneum and yet they were willing to sacrifice me.

What did it mean to be loyal?

The question burned heavy and hot where my heart used to be.

My *kundalini noir* tensed, like it expected another blow.

My mind grasped at the one remaining lifeline, a blind faith that all would work out.

Give it time. You have an eternity.

I lay in the dark stillness, a serene quiet like the calm surf after a storm.

I heard my name and the familiar echo.

Phaedra was alive.

I sat up.

The echo became siren loud.

My *kundalini noir* twisted upon itself, the siren shriek stabbing with needlelike pain.

The shrieking filled my head. I put my hands over my ears though I knew the noise came from inside my brain.

My psychic column trembled like a jet of water pulsing through a narrow hose. The straight lines and right angles in the room twisted and bent. I tried climbing out of the coffin, lost my balance, and collapsed to the floor.

Up, down, left, right, the directions tumbled in dizzying randomness while the shrieking bounced against the inside of my skull.

Nausea crawled up my throat.

I backed against the table where my coffin laid.

I put my hands flat on the floor and tried to regain my bearings. A table leg pressed against my back and I faced the front door of my apartment.

The cascade of noise fed the nausea and I convulsed with dry heaves.

The door shook and it flung open, splintered wood flying where the dead bolt broke through the jamb.

Phaedra stood in the threshold, backlit by the streetlamps.

Her aura blazed like the exhaust fire from a rocket engine. A burr of malevolent thorns quivered across her penumbra.

Her eyes shone bright as electric arcs. Long fangs glistened from a mouth bent into a cruel smile.

She wore a long black dress covered in black lace. A black sash wound across her thin waist. A necklace of small black shapes swung over her bodice. Each velvety shape had a shiny spot—an eye—and a black point. A beak.

It was a necklace of crow heads.

In her left hand she carried a leather bag weighed down with an object the size of a bowling ball.

Phaedra kept her fierce gaze locked on me. She swaggered in. Flip-flops slapped her feet. She grabbed my wrist with her free hand and dragged me from the table.

I lay powerless, limp with nausea.

Phaedra kicked off her flip-flops and put a bare foot on my throat. She raked her talons across my scalp to grasp a handful of hair. Blood trickled from my skin.

She shook my head. The motion made me want to retch. I closed my eyes to keep from vomiting.

"Look at me." She yanked my hair.

I opened my eyes. Phaedra appeared huge and menacing, grotesque, like a giant's reflection in a funhouse mirror.

Bile filled my throat. I pleaded, "Make it stop."

Slowly the shriek faded to a hum, then silence. The nausea passed and the bile receded down my throat.

She let go of my hair and cupped my chin with her knife-like talons. Her eyes probed mine and I could feel her thoughts slither into my brain and slither back out.

Phaedra's eyes glistened with an amused twinkle. "So the Araneum knows about me? Good." Her face regained its youthful appearance.

The lines in my room became straight and my sense of balance returned.

Phaedra released my chin and pulled her hand away with a slap. "I've come to thank you, Felix."

"Much obliged." Blood oozed from the stinging wound on my cheek. "You didn't have to trouble yourself. A phone call would've been sufficient."

"Always with the jokes."

"I'm not laughing," I said.

"Then laugh at this. I chose you because of your weakness. Your guilt. That weakness would let me pry into your head and bring you to me. You were the vampire hero and I beat you."

I felt raw and exposed, more than I would if naked. I felt used. Violated.

Shame washed over me.

I couldn't live with the disgrace. But I could live with vengeance.

Phaedra would die.

My mind clearer, I thought about what weapons I had close by. My aura could signal my intentions, and if I sprang at Phaedra, by the time my feet were off the ground, she'd cripple me with another psychic mind blast. When I attacked, it would have to be sudden and thorough.

My pistol was in the next room. But it wasn't loaded with silver bullets.

What happened to the hawthorn stake? Was it still on the table? Or had it fallen? I moved my arm and felt the stake slide across the T-shirt under my right shoulder. Now to wait for the chance to strike.

"I brought you a present." Phaedra undid the knot cinching the leather bag in her hand. She upended the bag.

A head with spiky black hair thumped against the floor. Phaedra toed the head until it faced me.

Nguyen's vacant eyes gazed from the puckered recesses of the sockets.

The dread, the horror, made my neck and shoulders lock up.

Nguyen's lips were black as ink against his purple skin. He'd probably been dead for days, though with some vampires it's difficult to tell.

"He never liked me," Phaedra said, "so I killed him."

I stared at the head. "Why?"

"Because he said no. I offered him the chance to join me."

"In what?"

I moved and rolled the stake close to my right hip.

"My destiny. I've known it since the time I first became aware of myself. The world pitied me. 'Poor Phaedra, what a raw deal from life.' But I knew if I could escape that sentence, if I could cheat God out of what he'd given me, then the world would be mine."

"How?"

"Because vampires, humans, everyone would belong to me."

My expression must have said, *you're insane.*

Phaedra responded, "Why? Because I'm young? Alexander the Great was only sixteen when he set out to conquer the world."

"The Araneum will stop you."

Phaedra clasped the necklace of crow heads. "This is what I think of the Araneum. I will destroy the Araneum." She kicked Nguyen's head. "Just like I did him."

I saw my chance. When she went out through the door, I could leap after her and tackle her. If I hit her hard enough, the advantage would be mine. I'd run her through with the stake.

She narrowed her eyes. A smile wormed across on her lips and her eyes opened wide in theatrical sarcasm. "Oh no, the stake." She jammed a foot under my ribs. She jerked her foot and the stake clattered across the floor.

"You shouldn't worry about the stake when I have this." Phaedra pulled the skinning knife from her waist sash. "It cuts well. Ask Nguyen."

She sheathed the knife and tossed the leather bag onto my chest. "Go show the Araneum what I've done." She slipped on her flip-flops and stepped back to the door.

"Where are you going?"

"To learn. There's so much I don't know and yet look at what I've done to you."

Phaedra stopped at the threshold. "When you report to the Araneum, tell them I will have more of this."

Her aura flashed like the blast from a cannon. Her eyes burned with megawatt intensity.

The noise started in my head, rising to a pounding like I was at the bottom of a waterfall. My psychic column shook like it wanted to tear free of my body. Spots erupted before my eyes, jittering as the walls and floor pitched.

The nausea overwhelmed me. My vision narrowed to a tiny point. My knees buckled and I crumbled to the floor.

The shrieking stopped. The nausea vanished. I became aware of gravity and felt the refreshing coolness of the wooden floor against my cheek.

The echo shrank to nothing. The silence left a void in my head and my thoughts trickled in like sand.

I sat up and stared about the room. Things seemed so normal I could imagine that I had hallucinated everything. But Nguyen's severed head and the splintered wood from my broken door put me front and center before reality.

I balled the leather bag in my hand and got to my feet. I wiped a trace of sour spit from my lips.

I knelt and scooped Nguyen's head with the bag. I juggled the bag until his head rested on the bottom.

I found the hawthorn plunged upright through the lining in my coffin.

I felt nothing. No anger. No shame.

I made myself another manhattan and let the ice melt to mellow the bourbon.

The emotion that first came back was the desire to see things as they were.

Phaedra was gone.

I was still here.

I sipped the manhattan. It tasted good.